DON'T SWIPE RIGHT

'Utterly compelling and laugh-out-loud funny'

Katy Brent, author of *How To Kill Men and Get Away With It*

'You'll come for the addictive murder mystery, and stay for the brilliant satire of modern dating at its worst'

Hayley Quinn, author of *The Last First Date*

'A remarkably assured debut: well-written, neatly plotted, pacy, unguessable and hugely enjoyable. Humour doesn't always sit well with crime but Chilton has found the sweet spot'

Sussex Life

'Rarely is murder so much fun! I raced through *Don't Swipe Right*, the pages practically turned themselves'

Rachael Blok, author of *The Fall*

'A brilliant book, crying out to be made for TV'

Bella

'As if Bridget Jones found herself in a Scream film. Murderously clever!'

Rupert Holmes, author of *Murder Your Employer*

'So cleverly plotted. I felt like I was on some kind of terrifying ride and I just had to let it all happen'

Laura Pearson, author of *The Last List of Mabel Beaumont*

'A dark comedy that'll make you think twice about using Hinge, we laughed our way through this brilliant book'

Closer

'*Don't Swipe Right* kept me guessing right to the end... felt fresh and original while being funny and quirky to boot'

Nicole Kennedy, author of *After Paris*

'Offers the reader suspect after suspect as the narrative gallops on'

Literary Review

'A funny and outspoken comedy of manners... a proper whodunnit with a well-chosen list of suspects'

The Morning Star

'A dark and gripping comedy, we laughed our way through this brilliant book'

That's Life!

'Hilariously dark'

Platinum

DON'T SWIPE RIGHT

L.M. CHILTON

HEAD of ZEUS

An Aries Book

First published in the UK in 2023 by Head of Zeus
This paperback edition first published in 2024 by Head of Zeus,
part of Bloomsbury Publishing Plc

9 7 5 3 1 2 4 6 8

A catalogue record for this book is available from
the British Library.

ISBN (PB): 9781837930265
ISBN (E): 9781837930227

Typeset by Divaddict Publishing Solutions Ltd.

Printed and bound in Great Britain by
CPI Group (UK) Ltd, Croydon CR0 4YY

MIX
Paper | Supporting
responsible forestry
FSC® C171272

Head of Zeus
5–8 Hardwick Street
London EC1R 4RG

WWW.HEADOFZEUS.COM

For all my red herrings.

ONE

I've done some bad things.

I don't mean your everyday, run-of-the-mill misdemeanours. Listen, I'll freely admit I've got at least two more credit cards than I need, a mild crisp addiction and I really, really need to work on my core. No, I'm talking about the *truly* awful things, the ones you'd like to bury so deep that you can pretend they never actually happened.

Rough estimate, I'd say I'd done, maybe fourteen things, total, that Mary Berry would raise a concerned eyebrow at. But out of all of them, I'd say the *second* worst thing I'd ever done was currently unfolding right in front of me: my best friend's hen do, a.k.a. the hen do from hell (I say hell, but I was pretty sure even the devil had never been forced to drink Bellinis out of penis-shaped straws at 8.30 p.m. in Cameo's on a Thursday evening).

And, plot twist, as maid of honour, it was totally my own fault. My excellent plans for karaoke and Chinese food had been deemed 'untraditional' by Sarah's old school-mates, as if dressing in T-shirts emblazoned with the badly photoshopped face of the groom was what Henry VIII had envisioned when he invented hen dos (I'm assuming he had something to do with it along the line). So, this was what I'd come up with instead, and it was currently dying on its arse.

'Everyone! Time for Mr and Mrs!' shouted Amy (I was pretty sure her name was Amy, but it could equally well have been Helen or Anne. Or Daisy).

The six of us were sitting awkwardly around an overly shiny table in one of the U-shaped booths that surrounded Cameo's (currently very empty) light-up dance floor. It was too early to be busy, and we pretty much had the place to ourselves, save for a couple of businessmen at the bar, who looked about two vodka and Red Bulls away from wrapping their ties around their heads and attempting the haka.

'So… question one, what is Richard's shoe size?' Amy/Helen/Anne/Daisy asked.

I closed my eyes and sank into the faux-leather, hoping it would envelop me.

'Fuck knows,' Sarah slurred as she fiddled with the Bride-to-be sash that hung around her shoulders, her face turning a ripe shade of beetroot. 'Ask me something dirtier!'

'Okay, umm…' Amy (probably) said, frantically looking down the list of questions for something suitably risqué before giving up. 'Err, what's his favourite position in bed?'

I couldn't take any more of this. As the group groaned in unison into their Bellinis, I pulled myself out of my seat and took slow steps backwards into the clouds of dry ice that billowed up from the dance floor. Guided by the neon lights that spelled out 'Create your own adventure' across the wall, I made my way to the sanctuary of the bathrooms, praying someone had dug an escape tunnel behind the condom machine.

Once there, I found an empty stall, nudged the toilet seat

closed with my foot and sat down. As the thumping bass of the generic house music faded to a dull thud, I pulled my phone out and opened Connector, the dating app *du jour* that was either: a) thwarting any chance I had of a sensible post-break-up recovery, or b) providing a useful distraction from my increasingly dubious life choices, depending on who you listened to.

After a good ten minutes of swiping through the endless stream of almost identical men looking far too fresh after climbing Machu Picchu, I was interrupted by the sound of the bathroom door swinging open. Seconds later, I heard Sarah's voice echoing off the tiles.

'Gwen! Are you hiding in here? You're going to miss Pin the Cock on the Groom!'

'Shit,' I mouthed, quickly stuffing the phone back in my bag and poking my head out from the stall to see Sarah standing in the middle of the bathroom holding two plastic champagne flutes.

'Ah, there you are,' she said, handing one to me. 'Please tell me you've not been sat in there playing on dating apps again?'

'No, just reading the graffiti,' I lied.

Sarah looked at me the same way people look at a really cute puppy that's peed on the floor.

'I know what this is about,' she said, shaking her head and smiling sadly. 'I was worried all this might be a bit much for you. It's only been a couple of months since, well, you know. You don't have to stay if you don't want to…'

'What, and miss sticking a cardboard penis on a picture of your naked fiancé? No way! I mean, I'd only be doing the exact same thing at home anyway.'

'Gwen,' Sarah sighed. 'You can drop the act with me. It's okay to be upset about Noah, you don't have to—'

'I keep telling you, it's fine, I'm fine, really, everything is *fine*,' I said.

Usually, I found that if I repeated the word fine often enough, I could at least convince myself that everything would be, well, you know, fine.

'Okay, well, good, I guess,' she said. 'Come on then, I need you out there, I'm getting totally mullered at Mr and Mrs.'

'I'm not surprised,' I said, hopping up onto the bank of sinks so I was at her eye level. Sarah was a good three inches taller than me, even without the block heels. 'Sar, are you really sure about all this?'

'The hen night?' Sarah said. 'No, not really, it's awful, but you said Flares wouldn't let us in again after you—'

'No, no, not the hen. I mean, are you sure about *this*.' I pointed to her neon-pink bride-to-be sash. 'The wedding, Richard…'

'Oh for God's sake, not this again.' She rolled her eyes. 'I know you and Richard aren't exactly BFFs, but you don't know him that well yet—'

'Do you?' I interrupted.

After some bad experiences with dodgy boyfriends at uni, Sarah had mastered the art of spotting red flags, immediately jettisoning any man who showed even the slightest indication of being a tosspot. That's why I'd been surprised when she fell for Richard so quickly. While there was nothing intrinsically wrong with him, beyond his obvious good looks and trust fund, there was nothing very right with him either. I guessed that's what she liked about him – he was completely average. Their romance had snowballed since meeting (in real life, just like our grandparents used to!) at a work conference last summer. Shortly afterwards, Richard had surprised her during a hike up some random hill with a ring secreted in one of the many, many pockets boasted by his favourite cagoule.

And now, six months later, Sarah was about to move out of our shared flat, leaving me to face the horrors of singledom without her. And that was absolutely fine. I was totally, totally okay with it and anyone who suggested otherwise didn't know me very well *at all*.

'We may not have been together long, but I do know he's one of the good ones,' Sarah said. 'And God knows there's not many of those around. So I would love it if you two at least tried to get along.'

I looked down at my scruffy Converse. As I opened my mouth to say something, a telltale beep rang out from the depths of my bag, cutting me off. Sarah's eyes swivelled towards it like a trained sniper.

'I knew it!' she cried as I reached for my phone. 'You *have* been swiping! Can you leave that thing alone for just one evening? This is supposed to be the best night of my life!'

'Um, isn't that the wedding night?'

'No, that's the second best. The best night,' she said slowly, taking my wrist and pulling it gently from my bag, 'is dancing 'til two a.m. with your closest friend in Eastbourne's second worst club and getting pissed on champagne.'

'Hun, this is not champagne,' I said, waving my plastic flute at her.

'Whatever.' Sarah released my wrist. 'It's the end of an era, right? Sar and Gwen, one last night on the town before I move out. That's just as important to me as the big day.'

'Well then, you really should straighten your tiara, mate, it's all wonky.'

As Sarah turned back towards the bathroom mirror to fix her tiara, I stole the chance to reach into my bag again. That familiar beep only meant one thing: I had a new Connector message, and I was insanely curious to see who it was. But just as my fingers curled around my phone, I heard Sarah exhale loudly, like the air being let out of a tyre.

'For Christ's sake, Gwen, have you forgotten how mirrors work? I can see you!' she snapped. 'Give me that thing!'

'Fine!' I sighed, holding the phone out for her between my thumb and forefinger. 'It's your wedding photos that will look asymmetrical if I don't find a plus-one before next week.'

The wedding was, predictably, on Valentine's Day.

'If it's going to be a dickhead off this thing,' she said, putting down her glass and plucking the phone from my hand, 'I'd rather you didn't bring anyone.'

'Hey, come on, they're not all bad,' I cried.

'Really? What about that guy last week who used hand sanitiser instead of deodorant?'

'Well, at least he was resourceful,' I offered. 'And at least I'm trying to get back out there. It's not easy, you know. We can't all magically bump into the love of our lives in a conference centre in Milton Keynes.'

'The problem isn't *you*,' Sarah said. 'The problem is, this app is chock-full of absolute bellends.'

As if to prove it, she began poking at the screen with her index finger, like a grandmother trying to choose a chocolate biscuit from a selection box.

'See what I mean? They all look like serial killers,' she said.

'Woah, woah, slow down!' I cried as she abstractly swiped

left and right through about twenty profiles. 'You're missing some real potential there!'

Suddenly the phone beeped again.

'Oh look, it says you got a match.' Sarah sighed.

'Gimme that!' I squealed, snatching the phone from her.

I scanned the app frantically, terrified to see who she'd accidentally matched me with. But the image on the screen was surprisingly pleasant. Dirty blond with dark eyebrows, 'Parker, 34, Data Analyst from Eastbourne' had an almost feminine face that made him quite striking.

'Likes going out and staying in, travelling, movies and roasts on a Sunday,' I read out loud.

'And, oh, works in fucking IT, obviously,' Sarah said, looking over my shoulder.

'Well, nobody's perfect.' I shrugged. 'Look, it says here he has a good sense of humour, doesn't take himself too seriously and, as you can see from the excellent selection of photos, he really enjoys laughing in various pubs with two to three different mates.'

'Is there an "unmatch" option?' Sarah said, miming sticking a finger down her throat.

'Well, I could block him, but...'

'Good, and when that's done, turn that thing off and come back to the table.'

When she saw me wavering, her face softened for a second, and she placed her hand on my shoulder.

'You promised to lay off the dating, remember, at least 'til after the wedding. All these silly boys won't replace Noah, you know?'

I bristled. My ex was the last person I wanted to think about right now. I sighed and put my phone face down on the sink.

'Oh, and listen, don't hate me, but Richard's on his way,' Sarah added matter-of-factly.

I flung my head back and groaned dramatically. If there was one thing that could make this night even lamer than it already was, it was Richard.

'Are you fricking kidding me, Sar?' I whined. 'Is that even allowed? What happened to this being a traditional hen night?'

'Oh come on, Gwen, I think it stopped being traditional the second Daisy inhaled the willy-shaped helium balloon.'

'Dammit, I knew her name was Daisy!' I hissed to myself.

'Don't stress, he won't cramp our style,' Sarah continued. 'He can just sit quietly in the corner until we finish the games.'

'Great, can it be the other corner?'

'Gwen! Be nice. It's the twenty-first century, everyone is having a "Sten Do" now. And it's a good chance for him to meet the girls before the wedding. Please try, just for me, okay?'

I folded my arms sulkily. 'Fine. Just gimme a minute to freshen up, will you?'

'You're not going to message that Parker guy, are you?' Sarah said, looking at me suspiciously.

'Definitely 100 per cent not,' I said.

'Smart,' she said, checking her tiara one more time before turning to leave.

'Hey, Sar, wait a sec,' I called out.

'Yeah?' she said, looking back over her shoulder.

'Twelve,' I said.

'What?'

'Richard's shoe size,' I said. 'It's twelve.'

'Shit, of course,' Sarah said. 'Thanks! How do you even know that?'

'Cos I wrote the quiz, you idiot,' I told her. 'Now get out of here.'

And with that, she blew me a kiss and walked out, leaving me sitting on the bank of sinks staring at my distorted reflection in the stainless-steel tap. I might have been stranded in singledom, but I desperately wanted Sarah to have the wedding of her dreams and never, ever have to navigate her way through the minefield of flotsam on a dumb dating app to find a halfway decent human being to share her life with. Deep down though, something about this particular 'happily ever after' didn't feel so, well, *happy*.

I hopped down from the sinks in an attempt to shake the feeling off. As I went to stuff my phone back in my bag, I caught a glimpse of Parker's profile, still open on the screen. I paused, my finger hovering over his face. With my other hand, I grabbed my glass and downed the last of the warm prosecco.

'Fuck it,' I thought, as I typed out a message.

Gwen: wyd? currently stuck at the hen do from hell, fancy giving me an excuse to get out of here?

TWO

I wandered back to the booth to see Sarah, blindfolded with her bridal sash, waving a crudely constructed cardboard phallus in the air. The hens were trying in vain to direct her to the correct location on a drawing of a ludicrously muscular man, whose head had been replaced by a photo of Richard's face.

I sat back down and, safe in the knowledge Sarah couldn't see me, flicked through the rest of Parker's Connector photos. He'd ticked off all the classics, like posing next to two (not quite as good looking) mates, clutching a cheap-looking trophy at a work do, a moody black-and-white shot and one dressed as a zombie for Halloween, but in a way that made sure you could still tell he was very attractive.

Now, I'll admit, it's not like my own profile was a groundbreaking Proto-Renaissance work of art. Yes, I'd spent an entire afternoon I'd never get back attempting to craft a sexy, hilarious, unswipe-left-able dating profile, but in the end I'd given up and plucked a few old photos from the depths of my camera roll. I'd settled on five that ranged from 'cute and I know it' to 'casually sexy without even realising it', and suddenly, there I was: Gwen, 29, barista, Eastbourne, officially on the market. And despite how revolting being 'on the market' sounded, so far, it had been fun. Well, I say fun – actually, most of the men I'd matched with were either a) complete weirdos or b) absolute grade-A fuckboys. So probably a more accurate description of my love life would be 'interesting'.

'Am I close?' Sarah shouted, almost knocking over a tray of fresh Bellinis onto my lap.

'Close to soaking me,' I yelled. 'When's Richard getting here?'

'Um, I dunno, I'm kind of busy right now, Gwen,' Sarah said, turning towards the sound of my voice. 'Any minute now, I guess.'

'Right,' I said, and Sarah suddenly swung back round to her right, this time connecting with the drinks on the table.

The hens shrieked in unison as they dodged splashes of prosecco. Sarah pulled her blindfold down and surveyed the debris, then shook her head at me disapprovingly.

The hilarious bespoke Love Heart sweets I'd ordered – bearing such witticisms as 'U CAN DIE 1st', 'OK 4 UR AGE' and '2NITE U PICK NETFLIX' – were scattered over the table, slowly disintegrating as they soaked up the spilt cocktails.

'You said "right"!' she yelled.

'No, I meant— never mind,' I said, wiping soggy slices of fruit off my jeans. 'My bad. I'll go get some more.'

I made my way across the dance floor, refreshing Connector as I weaved through the handful of people swaying out of time to Ed Sheeran. Before I reached the bar, a message had popped up.

Parker: Hen do from hell? Sounds fun. Can I get in on that?

Grabbing a stool, I ordered a round of drinks, plus an extra shot of tequila for me, and tapped a message back.

'No, you cannot!' I wrote. 'But I could meet you at The Brown Derby by the pavilion?'

With any luck, I could be out of here before Richard arrived. As I went to pay, I heard a voice from the other end of the bar, and I looked up to see a guy in a crumpled shirt, waving a Mastercard in my direction.

'Allow me,' he grinned.

Although he looked like he'd come straight from an important board meeting at Middle-Aged Office Guy PLC, the half-finished pint in front of him was clearly not his first drink of the evening. His suit jacket was draped over the bar and even as he spoke, the sweat patches under his arms seemed to spread across his no-longer-white shirt.

'No thanks, I'm with them,' I said, motioning to the booth.

I immediately buried my head in my phone, in case any part of that sentence indicated that it was, in fact, my greatest dream to be seduced by an increasingly damp man under bad lighting. And even if it had been, the strains of 'Tragedy' by Steps were just loud enough to turn any attempt at conversation beyond small talk into a lip-reading exercise. I tapped out another message to Parker.

Gwen: Hey, I'm being hit on by the regional manager of Sainsbury's here. I need rescuing! What do you say, The Derby in 10?

The barman placed five Bellinis on a tray and slid the shot

of tequila over to me. I scanned the club, there was no sign of Richard yet, but the hens had moved onto the dance floor.

'Come on, *come on*,' I whispered to my phone, willing Parker to say yes so I could sneak out before Richard got here.

I could feel the guy at the bar's eyes burning into me, and sure enough, when I looked up, he was swirling his finger around his now-empty glass and smiling at me.

'Stood up?' he shouted in my direction. 'Well I'm still here, sweetheart, have a drink with me.'

'No thanks,' I said firmly.

'Heh, don't talk to strangers, isn't that what they used to say?' the man said. 'I thought that was all girls like you did these days? Talk to strangers on your phones?'

Ignoring him, I downed the tequila and grabbed the tray of drinks. Even if I could think of a pithy response to that, I decided I'd rather save my energy for something more useful, like getting away from him as soon as possible.

'Wrong kinda stranger huh?' he called out as I walked away, balancing the tray in one hand while I refreshed Connector with the other. There was still no reply from Parker, so I stuck it in the back pocket of my jeans.

As I reached the middle of the dance floor, I looked up to see Richard, wrapped in a waterproof jacket and flushed from the freezing cold weather outside, making his way through the crowd towards the hens. I looked over my shoulder, wondering whether to retreat to the bar, only to see the office guy watching me, his tongue practically hanging out of his mouth.

I stopped in my tracks, stranded. Just then, my phone finally buzzed. Holding the tray with one hand, I pulled it out and swiped my thumb across the screen to open it.

Parker: Sorry, gonna have to reschedule. It's not safe out there for guys like me.

Underneath, he'd pasted a link to a local news story with the headline: 'Police advise caution after man found dead by joggers'.

I clicked on it, a flutter running through my stomach as the page loaded, revealing a photo. The softly handsome, strawberry-blond guy smiling at his graduation ceremony looked familiar, a lot like someone I used to know.

'Robert Hamilton's body was found at 6.30 a.m. by two runners in Sovereign Park,' the first sentence read.

Rob Hamilton.

At that moment, my arms turned to jelly, and the tray of drinks fell from my hand, sending orange liquid flying across the light-up floor. The hens looked up in surprise, as the few dancers jumped back to avoid splashes.

Rob didn't just look like someone I used to know. He *was* someone I used to know.

I'd been on a date with him a week ago.

THREE

I stood on the dance floor, damp and dumbfounded, as the club seemed to spin around me. Hands shaking, I tapped out a reply to Parker.

Gwen: wtf?

What I really wanted to type was 'What the fuck are you doing, sending me links about suspicious bodies found in parks?' but my hands were wobbling too much.

I read the news story over again. It was scant on details, but it certainly didn't sound like Rob's death was an accident. The police were looking for anyone with information, it said, and part of me felt like I should call. But what the hell would I say? That I went on a crappy date with him weeks ago?

'Gwen!' Sarah's voice rang out, breaking the spell. 'What are you doing? You're standing in the middle of a pool of prosecco, texting!'

'Uh, I need to talk to you, now,' I mumbled. 'It's an emergency.'

Suddenly, Richard came up behind her. He gave me an

awkward smile as he snaked his arm around his fiancée's waist.

'Oh, uh, hi Dickie,' I said, leaning past Sarah and giving him a wave. 'Didn't see you there.'

'What's the emergency? This outfit?' Richard said, gesturing in my direction.

I made a face at Sarah, who got the message.

'Richard, be a babe and go get us some new drinks, will you?' she said, patting him on the back with the cardboard penis she was still holding.

'Is that my…' he said, with a look of revulsion on his face.

'Yep, actual size,' I said, giving him a sarcastic smile. 'I'll have a tequila, thanks.'

As he strode off towards the bar, I pulled Sarah into the corner where all the coats were piled up.

'Listen, you remember that guy, Rob, I went to the wine bar with?' I hissed.

'No, which one was that?' Sarah asked.

'You know, the handsy guy who wasn't over his ex?'

'Oh yeah, the one who spent the night crying into his pinot noir and then tried to cop a feel, I remember!'

'Well, he's dead,' I said.

'What?'

'No shit,' I said, showing her the news story on my phone.

'Fuck.' She grabbed the phone to hold it steady as her eyes scanned the headline.

'Yeah, I know,' I replied. 'Poor guy.'

Richard interrupted us, holding a fresh tray of drinks and looking bemused.

'Who's dead?' he said. 'What did you do now, Gwen?'

'Nothing!' I cried. 'I didn't do anything!'

Sarah leant over to show him the news story on my phone screen.

'One of Gwen's exes,' she said.

'He's not an ex!' I cried. 'It was one date!'

'Ouch,' Richard said, his eyes narrowing as he studied the article. 'What was he like? Bad sort?'

I took a shot glass of tequila off the tray, downed it and sank back into the coats. It felt weird to think about Rob again, now that he was, you know, dead. I closed my eyes and tried to block out my surroundings, but the beat of the music vibrated through the dance floor and into my bones.

'I dunno, he was alright, I guess,' I said, a wave of sadness washing over me.

'She's being charitable,' Sarah told Richard. 'He was a massive loser, like all of Gwen's dates.'

She turned back to me.

'And didn't you say he went all weird at the end?'

'Uh, yeah, well I guess he was a *little* odd,' I said.

'What did he do?' Richard asked.

I looked past him and made a face at Sarah.

'Come on, just tell me!' Richard asked again.

So I did.

FOUR

Rob's profile photo shows off a stylish beard and a neat haircut, both completely unobjectionable. Immediately, he tells me he's an investment banker from Bexhill with a great sense of humour, two facts that seem to wilfully contradict each other. But we persevere, messaging back and forth for a few days before he invites me to a wine-tasting event on the Grand Parade.

It sounds super pretentious, but I say yes because he has a nice smile and I like wine. Besides, I figure that it's time to actually stop hiding behind the safety of my phone and get back out there. It's been weeks since I broke up with Noah, when my life collapsed in on itself, and years since I went on what people used to call a 'blind date'. But it was time to dust myself down and move on.

Unfortunately, the minute I downloaded Connector, I was so relentlessly bombarded with messages from those aforementioned complete weirdos and absolute fuckboys that I'd turned off all notifications on the app. For the first couple of weeks, I only checked it in times of extreme boredom, or at 2 a.m., half-cut and feeling amorous. And, okay, fair cop, that was how I'd matched with 'The Banker'.

We agree to meet at 6.30 p.m. outside Hudson's Wine Bar. Of course, I texted Sarah beforehand, pinging her the location, just in case he turns out to be an axe murderer. But when I arrive, he's waiting outside for me, looking handsome in his work suit, with no bloody weapon in sight.

'Gwen?' he asks, and I smile back in recognition.

'Hi,' I say, kissing him on the cheek. He smells of expensive cologne mixed with that crisp, fresh-air smell that someone only has when they've been standing outside for a while.

'Shall we go in?' I ask. I'm wearing a short leather jacket over a cropped brown jumper and skinny jeans with semi-heeled boots, so I'm desperate to get in the warm.

Inside, the bar is full of people fresh from the office, standing around individual tables. As we find our spot, a smartly dressed woman announces they'll be bringing round five different wines to try, but first they will teach us how to taste with our nose. I try to listen, because so far in life I had only managed to master the art of tasting wine with my mouth, but Rob was keen to chat.

'You look nice,' he says in my ear. 'How was your day?'

'Yeah good!' I whisper back. 'Yours?'

'Stressful. But this should help.'

He nods at the two half-filled wine glasses heading our way. The waiter places one next to each of us, and we dutifully stick our noses in.

'What notes are you getting?' the woman asks. 'Don't be shy, there are no wrong answers.'

'Sandalwood,' I say. I have no idea what sandalwood smells like, but at these sorts of things the answer was always sandalwood.

'Good!' she trills. 'Anyone else?'

'Oh you're a natural,' Rob whispers to me.

As the evening goes on, the waiter regularly swaps our empty glasses for full ones. After four rounds, Rob seems a little woozy.

'Black cherry!' he shouts at random, and sniggers.

When the final glass comes out, he downs it.

'What do I win?' he grins at our host.

'I'm not sure it's a competition,' I say. 'Come on, maybe we should go to the bar.'

Half an hour later, and Rob is on his sixth glass of wine and shovelling sea salt crisps into his mouth, in between telling me how much his last quarterly bonus was.

'How long have you been in banking?' I ask him.

'Too long!' he says, and laughs much too loud.

I begin to feel my fate is as inevitable as those sea salt crisps, plunging to their inescapable doom.

'Sorry,' he coughs. 'I've not been asking you enough questions. I know that's what I'm supposed to do, isn't it? Be curious about your life? You're a barista, right?'

'Well, sort of. The only barista in the world who hates coffee. But I like to think I'm more like, I don't know, an entrepreneur? I used to be a social media manager for the snacks company Delicioso, do you know them? The guys who make Snacky Nuts and Munchie Crunch? But last year I bought an old ice cream van and converted it into a mobile cafe. The plan is to take it round festivals in the summer,' I say. 'But yeah, I serve coffee too.'

It felt weird to say 'I'. The truth is, Noah and I had bought the van together. It had been Noah's dream: save up enough money to quit our boring nine-to-fives and tour the country in our little coffee-mobile. Sadly, we'd only managed to get as far as the 'quitting our jobs and buying the van' bit. But Rob doesn't need those kinds of specifics. At least not on Date One.

'Cool, cool,' he says. 'How's it going? Making you rich yet? Not many tourists around at this time of year, I suppose?'

'It's great,' I lie. 'Everyone else in the world loves coffee, right? It's almost like it's addictive.'

'Ah, well, I don't know if you know, but actually caffeine does boost your dopamine levels, so yes, one could become dependent on it,' he explains.

'Right, thanks, good to know,' I say, nodding.

'Well, I take it easy on the old demon bean front. I'm more of a Frappuccino man myself,' he grins.

'And a wine man, I see.'

'Black cherry!' he shouts triumphantly, again, before stuffing his nose too hard into his glass and almost spilling it over himself.

'Careful,' I say, looking around to see if anyone was staring at us.

'Graham, make sure you edit that bit out!' he yells over at an empty corner of the bar.

'What?' I scan the room again. 'Who's Graham?'

'Oh, ha ha, like, I was pretending we're on a reality TV show, and the cameras are hidden over there!'

My face remains completely unimpressed.

'Ha,' he says, his laughter slowly petering out like a dying engine.

Luckily, everyone else from the wine tasting event has wandered off and the bar's pretty empty. I look back at Rob to see him pouring the crisp crumbs from the packet into his wide-open mouth.

'Sorry, did you want some?' he asks, wiping his mouth with his sleeve and refocusing his eyes on mine.

'Bit late now,' I smile.

'You're so nice, I bet you'd make someone a really great girlfriend,' he says when the river of crumbs finally runs dry.

'Uh, thanks,' I say. 'To be honest, I've not been single for long so right now I'm happy just seeing what's out there.'

'Uh oh, am I being rejected already?' he laughs.

'Hah, no,' I say. 'I'm just keeping my options open.'

'Well, I'm very open to being an option,' he slurs.

I can't work out if that was clever wordplay or he was talking drunken nonsense, so I do my best ambiguous smile and nod.

'I really struggled to match with people on Connector *at first,' he continues. 'But then, well then I found out that...'*

He stops and puts his hand to his mouth, like an overexcited mime artist.

'Oops sorry! You know, I shouldn't really tell you that...'

'Tell me what?' I ask.

He taps his nose conspiratorially. 'Sorry, trade secret.'

'No, come on, tell me what you mean?'

Rob starts to say something but suddenly stops again mid-sentence, and his eyes widen as if he'd just remembered he'd left the iron on. His face goes grey, and he puts his glass down for the first time that evening.

'Excuse me,' he mumbles, before getting up and walking very fast in the direction of the bathroom.

Nearly ten minutes later, he reappears, looking paler but steadier.

'You okay?' I ask.

'Yes,' he says, sitting down delicately. 'Sorry. Look, to be

honest, this is the first date I've been on since I broke up with my girlfriend. I guess I was a bit nervous, so I drank too much.'

'I thought you were hitting it a little hard,' I smile. 'It's okay. We've all been there.'

'No, it's really not on, is it?' he says, looking ruefully at his half-full glass. 'I've rather fouled this one up, haven't I?'

I take a deep breath and push my hair back behind my ears. 'How long has it been?' I ask.

For the next hour, Rob tells me about his ex, how he'd proposed with his grandmother's ring on her birthday, after asking her father for permission. Three months later, he'd sunk half her savings into bad investments, and she'd left him to travel around South America, building goat huts. By the time we leave the bar, he's drunk again, but, to be fair, so am I.

'Shall I walk you home?' he asks.

'I'm going to bus it,' I tell him. 'It's only twenty minutes.'

'Okay cool, I'll walk with you to the stop then,' he says, stumbling over the kerb on the pavement.

Halfway to the bus stop, Rob's phone dings and he pulls it out, the light of the screen illuminating his face. I see his eyes widen and he staggers back slightly. Steadying himself against a nearby lamp post, he jabs angrily at the screen. In his drunkenness, he can't seem to hit the right place to open the message.

'Something wrong?'

'I just wish this bastard would leave me alone,' he says, his voice wavering.

'What do they want?'

'Money, always more money,' he mumbles.

'HMRC? Tell me about it, I'll do it on January 31st at 11.45 p.m. and not a second before,' I say.

'No, worse than them,' he says.

I look at him and his face stiffens like he's about to throw up again. 'Forget it, I'm drunk. Talking rubbish.'

We walk the rest of the way in silence. When we eventually reach my bus stop, I look glumly at the electronic display that informs me I face an agonising six-minute wait.

We stand there awkwardly, watching spots of rain pepper the Perspex of the bus stop.

'You can go!' I say eventually, putting on my best friendly smile. 'I can wait on my own, and it's freezing out here! Forecast says it might actually snow, and you don't even have a coat!'

'Oh, it's no problem, I don't feel the cold,' he says.

'Yeah, that's the benefit of drinking three bottles of red,' I laugh.

'And the two pints I had before we met,' he says. 'Bit of Dutch courage never hurts, does it?'

Just when I think I'm stuck in some hellish time loop where I'm forced to discuss the merits of pre-game drinking with Rob until the end of eternity, I see the bus approaching in the distance.

I lean in to kiss him on the cheek goodbye, and his hand slips around my waist and slowly, but very surely, down to my bottom. I immediately break away.

'Whoa, slow down cowboy,' I say, placing my hand on his chest and gently pushing him back.

'But I thought...' he says, looking crestfallen.

'Sorry,' I say, then curse myself inwardly. Why the hell am I apologising?

'I think you need to get over your ex before dating anyone else, Rob.'

But I notice he's not looking at me, but over my shoulder. I turn around to see a busload of people staring at us.

Even through the cold, I feel my face burn.

'Gotta go,' I say, patting him on the shoulder and jumping on board before he has a chance to protest.

I quickly squeeze my way to the back of the bus, avoiding the judgemental looks of my fellow passengers.

'Stopping here for a minute to regulate the service,' an announcement bellows over the tannoy.

God, not now, I cry inwardly. Anytime but now.

Once I'm ensconced in the back seat, I stick my earpods in and turn the volume up. I turn to see if Rob's still waiting. It's started to rain, and he's looking blankly at the bus, slowly getting wetter and wetter, but seemingly still not feeling the cold. Then he gets out his phone and starts waving it in the air, shouting. I flip out one earpod to try and hear what he's saying.

'...don't need her. Got loads of matches! Loads!'

Rob holds the phone up to the bus window, and through the splashes of rain on the glass, I can make out his Connector app, proudly displaying a new match.

'See?' he yells to his captive audience. 'Twice as fit as her.'

He points at me, and I stare into my lap, unable to hide as the whole bus compares me to the image on Rob's mobile screen.

Come on, move already, I telepathically beg the driver.

I hear the engine start and praise the bus gods. We pull off, leaving Rob waving his phone desperately at the taillights as the rain turns to snowflakes.

For the rest of the journey, I sit with my head leant against the window, the sheen of singledom scraped off me in a single date. I'm back in the trenches, and war is hell.

FIVE

'And now he's dead?' Richard said. 'Wow, that's awful.'

'Yeah, date with Gwen, then found dead in a park. Not sure which is worse,' said Sarah.

I shot her a look. 'Don't,' I said. 'He seemed really shaken up by that text message. I wonder who it was?'

'Maybe he owed the wrong sort of person money...?' Richard started.

'And then when he never paid up, they...' I tailed off.

'Or, maybe his ex lured him into the woods and took her revenge?' Sarah cackled.

'No, she's in the middle of Peru, saving goats or something,' I said.

'Or is she?' Sarah said dramatically, grabbing my phone and poring over the article. 'Look, it says here he was found in the bushes in Sovereign Park, isn't that near the wine bar?'

I shivered.

'Um, somewhere round there, I think.'

'Ooh, maybe that's where he takes all his dates!' Sarah said. 'And when he tried it on with one of them, she let him have it!'

Sarah shook her fist up and down, miming the *Psycho* stabbing motion.

'Sarah!' I scolded. The thought of someone doing that to Rob made me feel sick. He was a bit of a melt, but he didn't deserve that. No one did.

'What?' she said in mock indignation. 'Come on, Gwen, he was a right soft lad.'

'Hey, he was alright, just a bit heartbroken,' I said. 'Anyway, it doesn't say anything about murder here, maybe it was an accident.'

'It does say they're looking for witnesses though,' Richard said, pointing to the appeal at the end of the piece.

'You think I should call?' I asked, suddenly feeling guilty. I wanted to help, of course, but I didn't really know anything about Rob. Nothing that was of any use to the police, anyway. I silently cursed myself for not paying more attention on the date.

'No, you're not a witness, the date was ages ago,' Sarah said. 'This arsehole probably just felt up the wrong person. Sounds like he had it coming.'

'He seemed nice enough on the app,' I sighed.

'So what? Guys like that can go from super nice to super intimidating in a millisecond. I told you this app is a cesspit, and this proves it. You can't even get through a hen do for your best friend without swiping on that thing. Why don't you just delete it?'

'Because the chances of meeting someone decent in real life are about the same as Richard telling a vaguely amusing anecdote. It's never going to happen. I think you're the last person in twenty years to achieve it.'

'You met Noah in real life,' Sarah countered.

I felt my cheeks redden. That stung.

'Yeah, and look how that worked out,' I said.

A horribly familiar tingle ran through me, the same little electric shock that pricked my skin every time I thought about that night, just a few months ago, when everything fell apart. Seeing me shudder, Sarah put her hand on my shoulder.

'When are you going to tell me what really happened with you two?' she asked.

I bristled at the question.

'I've told you a hundred times, nothing "happened". We just grew apart,' I said. 'That's it.'

Richard and Sarah looked at each other conspiratorially.

'Why, has he said something to you?' I asked, suddenly sitting up straight.

'Haven't heard from him in weeks actually,' Richard said.

'Neither of us have,' Sarah said.

I flicked my eyes between the two of them before relaxing back into the coats again. I had a pretty good bullshit detector. Well, usually. It did tend to falter when I'd downed three shots of tequila in quick succession.

'Why are you so desperate to meet someone anyway?' Sarah asked. 'Can't you just enjoy being single for a bit?'

'I'm moving on,' I said. 'That's what you're meant to do after a break-up, right?'

'Moving on doesn't mean throwing yourself at every moron with a pulse in Eastbourne, Gwen. It's been, like, two minutes since you broke up with Noah. You're not a shark. If you stop moving, you won't sink and die.'

'That's actually an urban myth,' Richard started. 'Sharks can pump water through their gills and—'

Sarah threw him a glance and he went back to sipping his pint quietly.

'Listen. You need to stop distracting yourself with stupid boys for a second and sort your life out. The van, the break-up, everything,' she went on. 'I bet you haven't even started looking for a new flatmate, have you? I move out in a week, you know.'

I could feel every muscle in my body tensing up as she rifled through my Rolodex of mistakes and bad choices. I took a deep breath and put on my best maid of honour smile.

'What is this, an intervention? We're supposed to be on a hen do, right? Shouldn't we be doing karaoke or something?'

I looked over at the dance floor, where the other hens were currently trying to replicate the 'Thriller' dance. At least, I hoped that's what they were doing.

'You know what?' Sarah said, ignoring me. 'You're not a shark. You're an ostrich. An ostrich with your head firmly wedged in the sand.'

'Now that I take exception to,' I said, holding up a finger. 'For one, sharks are waaay cooler than ostriches—'

'Stop joking for a second, Gwen. We're worried about you,' Sarah interrupted. 'You quit your job, broke up with Noah out of the blue, all just as I'm moving out. You know I'm always here if you need.'

Sarah and I had played netball all through university. She was brilliant at it, and I was absolutely rubbish. She'd always shout 'here if you need' when I had the ball – because more often than not, I *did* need, being utterly unable to shoot straight – and the phrase had kind of stuck. But right now, I didn't 'need' anything. I could easily forget about unsold lattes and dead dates for a little while longer. All I had to do was create some good memories for Future Gwen to wipe over the old, bad ones. But for that, I was going to need alcohol, and a lot of it.

'Okay, one,' I said. 'I am in the process of finding an amazing new boyfriend as we speak, and two, the van is super successful. I'm selling chemically addictive hot drinks, it can't fail. Now, come on, let's salvage the rest of this hen do with some hard liquor and karaoke at The Brown Derby.'

'There's no karaoke machine at The Derby,' Richard said.

'Who says we need a machine?' I replied.

SIX

And so, God knows how many tequilas later, I was standing on a pool table serenading the hens with 'I'd Do Anything for Love (But I Won't Do That)', while Sarah joined me on backing vocals. Or maybe she was just shouting at me to stop, I really can't recall. All I knew was that, when I woke up the next morning, I was willing to sell my left kidney for a glass of water and an ibuprofen.

Squinting through the blur of notifications on my phone, I was appalled to see it wasn't even 6 a.m. yet. I immediately rolled over and went back to sleep. When I opened my eyes again two and a half hours later, I didn't feel any better. I turned my face into the pillow and stared into the blackness, trying desperately to convince my brain it was still night-time. On the plus side, I did seem to have drunk enough alcohol to blot out approximately 95 per cent of the hen do, and Parker's weird Connector message.

When I remembered Sarah had gone back to Richard's, my heart sank. There would be no one to bring me toast in bed and pick over the bones of last night with (not that I could remember much of it). When I was a teenager, Dad would bring me a bacon sandwich and a steaming hot mug of sweet tea whenever I'd overdone it the night before. Funny, it was always these little rituals that you missed most when someone you loved left. But I guessed I'd have to get used to being on my own for a while.

As I lay there, headfirst in goose down, wondering if McDonald's would consider delivering chicken nuggets to me via my bedroom window, my phone flashed.

Sarah: Still alive?

Gwen: Just. I didn't do anything completely stupid last night, did I?

Sarah: Define stupid.

Gwen: Anything worse than Flares on my 25th birthday?

Sarah: Well, you didn't puke in my Marc Jacobs on the way home this time.

Gwen: That saved us a £100 Uber cleaning fee, babes. You should be thanking me. And please stop talking about vomit. I think I'm going to be sick.

Sarah: Eat something. There's fresh orange juice in the fridge, and I left bagels on the kitchen table.

Gwen: I fricking love you.

Sarah: Now get up and go to work. Here if you need.

Suddenly, there was a sharp knocking on the front door. This was always a bad sign – the doorbell had been broken since we moved in, so if anyone was knocking, it meant they'd already been pushing the bell for at least two minutes, and, with no success, had moved on to more aggressive methods of getting my attention.

I closed my eyes and tried really hard to close my ears, but each knock had an increasingly persuasive quality to it, and by the twelfth one I was eventually won over.

Pulling on last night's jeans and my dressing gown, I sloped downstairs. I opened the door, expecting a nonplussed Amazon delivery guy to shove a neighbour's parcel into my reluctant arms. Instead, I found myself face to face with two men, one stocky, with a chunky moustache, and a younger guy neatly dressed in a shirt and navy blue blazer, holding up an ID badge.

Through the haze of my hangover, I could just about make out what it said.

'Police.'

SEVEN

It's odd, you know, to see a police officer up close. Sure, I'd seen them on TV, or while rubbernecking across the street, but seeing one just a metre from your face at 8.45 a.m. was kinda weird. I had the immediate sense I was in trouble, even though I'd done nothing wrong. Well, unless flawlessly performing the hits of Meat Loaf using a pool cue as an air guitar was illegal.

'Gwendolyn Turner?' the older guy grunted.

'Yes,' I declared defensively, as if he was accusing me of being me. And while I was 100 per cent guilty of that, I was pretty sure it wasn't a criminal offence either.

'Can we come in?' the younger man asked.

I stepped aside from the doorway and let them past. In situations like this, where I was completely blindsided, I always thought it was best to say as little as possible. Plus, I was sort of worried that the vast amount of tequila still lolling about in my stomach could make a break for it any second. So I kept my mouth shut and watched as the older officer walked past me into the lounge and sat on the sofa without asking. I followed the younger one in. I didn't offer him a seat, so he stood awkwardly in the middle of the room while I went and sat on a stool in the kitchen.

Our lounge and kitchen were open plan, which was perfect for eating cereal on the breakfast bar whilst simultaneously watching the TV, and, turns out, keeping your distance from shady-looking cops in your living room.

Just as I was wondering how long it would be before I could order a Double Sausage and Egg McMuffin and go back to bed, Moustache Guy cleared his throat.

'I'm Detective Chief Inspector Forrester,' he announced. 'And this is Detective Lyons. We wanted to speak to you about a recent homicide case.'

I don't know quite what I'd been expecting, but when he said that, a jab of fear sliced through my hangover like someone had taken a meat cleaver to my throbbing, jelly-like brain. Still, I remained silent, which probably made him think I was either a murderer or a complete weirdo. Or both.

'I mean, surely most murderers are weirdos, right?'

'Excuse me?' DCI Forrester muttered, raising one of his chunky reddish eyebrows.

I suddenly realised I'd said that out loud.

'Sorry, nothing,' I mumbled. 'So, um, what has this got to do with me?'

The low rumbling of paranoia I felt in the pit of my stomach was now accompanied by the sensation that somebody was very forcefully playing the bongos on my forehead. It was like a really shit conductor had decided to orchestrate my current predicament, and it was totally not helping.

'Did you know Robert Hamilton?' Detective Lyons asked, in a calm but deliberate tone. His bright blue eyes took the edge off the puffiness around them that betrayed a lack of sleep.

'Rob? Yes. I mean, I read about it – him, I mean. I read what happened. I didn't know him well. Not really. We went on a date.'

'When?' Forrester asked. The detached, almost bored, tone of his delivery made me think he'd had this sort of conversation many times before.

'Um, about a week ago, I think,' I said.

'So you weren't close?'

'Er, no,' I said. 'It was only one date.'

'It didn't go well?' Forrester raised a bushy eyebrow.

'Um, I guess not,' I said, now beginning to wonder where this line of questioning was going. 'He seemed like a nice guy, he just wasn't… he wasn't The One? You know. Do you know? Maybe you don't know. Sorry.'

Detective Lyons nodded like he really *didn't know* and wrote something down on his pad. As the initial shock of having two police officers in my lounge asking questions about dead people began to settle, I noticed he couldn't have been much older than me. In fact, the more I looked at him, the more something about him looked very familiar. I wondered if I'd swiped past him on Connector or something. He had cropped dark brown hair and, despite some flecks of white in his stubble, boyish good looks that seemed at odds with his practical demeanour. Forrester, on the other hand, was short and broad, like a ginger Super Mario.

'We found messages from you in his phone, on the Connector app,' Lyons said. 'And when we spoke to his flatmates, they told us he'd been a little upset about your date.'

'What do you mean, upset?' I asked, my mouth suddenly feeling very dry.

'Bad date, they said,' DCI Forrester mumbled, not looking at me. 'Apparently he came home almost in tears.'

'What?' I cried. 'If anything, I should've been the one crying! It might not have been the best date in the world ever, but there was nothing for *him* to cry about. Maybe he was upset about his ex? He seemed pretty cut up about that.'

'His flatmates told us you ran off and left him to walk home in the rain on his own,' he continued.

'Oh for God's sake,' I cried. 'That's not what happened! He tried to grope me, my bus turned up and I got on it! It's not my responsibility to make sure he gets home okay.'

'It's okay, Gwen,' Detective Lyons said. 'We're just trying to verify his last movements.'

'What do you mean "last movements"? Our date was a week ago.'

'As you read, he was found dead yesterday in Sovereign Park,' DCI Forrester said, still with zero emotion in his voice. 'But the body had been there for significantly longer. It wasn't discovered earlier because it had been covered by the snow.'

Usually in Eastbourne, a sleet shower was the best we could hope for. That or a deep frost that turned the grass crispy and the air bitter. And that was fine. Snow never lasted, and unless you got up before the rush hour, by the time you saw it, it had been trampled into brown and black clumps, shoved off the roads and into the gutters. But this year, real, chubby snowflakes had dusted everything in sight with a soft powder of white.

'Oh,' I said, suddenly aware I was a potential suspect in

a murder case and wearing a pink dressing gown and fluffy slippers that didn't even match.

'Which puts his date of death as February 1st,' the detective continued in the same flat tone. 'The night after your date.'

I felt my legs wobble. I couldn't tell if it was shock or my hangover, but I suddenly had the desperate urge to throw up.

'So, I need to ask you, Ms Turner, where were you that night between six and eight thirty p.m.?'

'Can I... am I allowed to look at my phone?' I asked, fishing in the pocket of my dressing gown.

'Go ahead,' Detective Lyons nodded, and I scrolled through my calendar.

Date Freddie 7.30 it said on February 1st.

'Okay yes, look,' I said, with genuine relief, holding the screen up to show them. 'I went to meet this guy, Freddie. We went to Toppo's on South Street. 7.30 p.m.'

The two detectives looked at each other.

'That's really useful, thank you Gwen,' Detective Lyons said. 'And what time did you leave?'

'We had a couple of drinks and then called it a night,' I said, bolstered by this apparent proof of my innocence. 'So maybe nine-ish? I got the bus home so I would've been back before ten. Just go and ask Freddie, he'll tell you.'

I folded my arms and waited for my full pardon. No one said anything for a minute.

'Okay, well, if that's everything, officers, I really need to get on with my day,' I said.

Lyons looked at me doubtfully as I stood up and pulled my dressing gown cord tightly around my waist.

'Actually, there is something else, Ms Turner,' DCI Forrester said, flicking through his notebook. 'You read about Mr

Hamilton, but what hasn't been reported yet is that another body was found yesterday.'

I stopped in my tracks and stared at him.

'The victim's name was Freddie Scott,' Forrester said, and lifted his head to look me in the eye, watching for a reaction.

He got one. I vomited on the kitchen floor.

EIGHT

'You recognise the name?' Detective Lyons asked, as if the vomit on the floor had somehow failed to confirm that, yes, obviously, I did recognise the fucking name.

'Give me a second, let me clean this up,' I croaked, wiping my mouth with the sleeve of my dressing gown.

'I'll get you some water,' he said, stepping over the sick and past me to the sink.

I knelt on the floor, listening to the tap running, and wondered what the hell I was going to say, while DCI Forrester watched me with a mixture of disgust and suspicion from the sofa. I gave him a weak smile. Seconds later, Detective Lyons handed me a glass and I sipped quietly, waiting to see if he would repeat his question. He didn't.

'I went for one drink with him,' I said eventually, 'I haven't seen him before or since.'

'It does mean, of course,' DCI Forrester said, 'that we'll need to verify your whereabouts on the 1st. We obviously can't check with Mr Scott.'

'I, I, just went home to bed…' I stuttered. 'You can check with my flatmate, Sarah.'

'You understand, Gwen, that we're not accusing you of anything,' Lyons interrupted, not unkindly. 'It's very likely just a coincidence that you knew both victims. We're just following up any leads we have at the moment.'

'Right,' I said, gently manoeuvring myself back onto the stool.

'When we found Connector messages from you on both phones, it made sense to eliminate you from any enquiries,' Detective Lyons went on. 'Don't worry, we read through all the chats on the app. They don't give us any reason to think you have anything to do with this.'

I don't know what was more mortifying: that I was being suspected of murder or that this guy had read through my painful attempts at flirting. I downed the rest of the water.

'From the messages, it does seem Freddie was rather perturbed at the end of the evening though,' DCI Forrester said. 'Another bad date?'

I looked up from my empty glass.

'I had a great time,' I deadpanned.

'I think you better tell us exactly what happened, Ms Turner,' DCI Forrester said, his moustache wobbling slightly as he spoke.

'Fine,' I said, taking a deep breath. 'I'll tell you everything.'

NINE

I almost don't recognise him at first. I don't know if it's Facetune or if he has a better-looking younger brother, but IRL Freddie is a little more… mature than his photos. His hair is receding and speckled with grey, rather than the glorious auburn bouffant displayed on his Connector profile. He also seems to have applied a shade of fake tan that's bordering on the problematic.

'Hello, you!' he calls over to me from the table. He's already sitting down, a crisp white napkin tucked into his plaid shirt.

I've broken my golden rule of 'no sit-down meals on the first date' partly because 1) I was hung-over and 2) I was hungry and 3) Freddie had been funny and charming when we'd chatted on the app. And it was for that reason that I decided to accept his invitation to Toppo's, a passable Italian on South Street.

'Would you like me to order for you?' he asks, standing up to pull out the chair so I can sit down. 'I come here all the time, so I know what's good.'

'Nah, that's okay,' I tell him. 'I've got weird tastes.'

'Ooh, kinky!' he laughs.

'Ha, sorry, nothing like that!' I say. 'I just have a penchant for anchovies.'

He screws up his face at me. 'Hmm, not sure about that. Tell you what, I'll suggest a few things, and we'll go from there.'

Ten minutes later, a waiter brings me a porcini mushroom salad, and a fillet steak and fries for him.

'You look a bit different in real life,' I tell him as he inspects his meat gingerly with his knife.

'Ah well, I should probably tell you, I'm actually forty-two,' he says. 'I don't know why Connector thinks I'm thirty-seven, but the stupid thing won't let me change it!'

'Oh right, I think you can just go into the settings and adjust your date of birth—'

'Still, I certainly don't feel forty-two!' Freddie interrupts.

He pauses, waiting for me to say he doesn't look it either. But instead I stick a mushroom in my mouth and chew slowly.

'The food here is great, isn't it?' he says eventually.

'Uh, yeah, it's nice,' I say, ogling his chips as I poke around a leaf on my plate. 'So, if you could only eat one meal for the rest of your life, what would you choose?'

'Ooh, that's a good one,' he says, popping a chunk of pinkish steak into his mouth. 'Well, I was going to say a good old-fashioned chicken bhuna and double naan. But if I'm honest, these days I'm about twenty-five per cent vegetarian. So let's make it a butternut one, eh? What about you?'

He takes a huge bite of meat and fixes me with an intense gaze as he swallows, like an anaconda devouring a boiled egg.

'I always think I'd choose pizza. At least I could have a different topping every day, you know?'

'No, I don't think that's in the rules,' he says seriously. 'Besides, you don't look like you eat a lot of pizza.'

He looks me up and down in the same way he just eyed up his eight-ounce steak a second ago. I say nothing and chew on another mushroom.

Freddie goes on to tell me all about the two-bedroom flat in Pevensey that he's just put an offer in on, and recounts the plot of a TV show I've already seen in great detail. Meanwhile, I try to smile and look impressed at the right moments. When the waiter brings over the dessert menu, he waves him away and asks for the bill. Despite his protests, we end up splitting it.

'Let's get a drink,' he says.

In truth, my headache has faded to a dull pulse, and after nursing just one glass of wine all evening, I feel like something stronger.

'Okay cool, just one though, I have work in the morning,' I tell him, which is technically true because 11.45 a.m. is officially the morning, and no one can prove otherwise.

When he stands up, I notice he's more than a little shy of the six foot one he'd claimed on his Connector profile (which he'd followed with the immortal line: 'as apparently that's important?'). Not that I really cared (Noah was a tidy five ten), but I started to wonder if the Freddie I saw before me bore any relation to his profile at all.

Freddie pulls on a very bright orange body warmer and steers us to a swanky-looking cocktail bar nearby. Inside it's all low lights, soft jazz and even softer furnishings. He orders two Negronis before I have a chance to offer a preference.

While we're waiting, I go to the bathroom and text Sarah.

Gwen: Moved on to a cocktail bar on Neil Street.

Sarah: Sounds promising?

Gwen: I dunno. I think he just wants an obedient young housewife for his new love nest.

Sarah: Typical. Tell him about the Shakira dance routine you did in school assembly. Or better still, give him a demonstration. That'll scare him off.

Gwen: It's been ten years, I'm not sure I remember all the moves.

Sarah: A few more shots and it'll all come back to you.

Gwen: A few more bottles more like.

Sarah: Okay, bad idea, forget I mentioned it.

Gwen: Too late, going back in, love you x.

As I walk back to the table, Freddie wipes his hand across his forehead in a mock 'phew' gesture.

'You were gone so long I didn't think you were coming back!' he laughs.

'Oh don't worry, I never walk out on a drink,' I say, picking up my Negroni and taking a sip. 'I was just texting my friend.'

'Oh, letting her know I'm not a complete nutter, eh?

'Actually, I was telling her the address of the bar in case I need rescuing.'

'That's what friends are for,' he says.

When he says that, I think about Sarah and stare into the crimson depths of my drink. The strong lights above the bar reflect red streaks across my face.

'Let's talk about something else,' I say.

'Okay, so tell me, Gwen, why is a gorgeous woman like you single?' he asks, resting his head on his hand like that meme of Willy Wonka.

'Um, maybe I'm just picky?' I say. 'I'm not sure what I'm looking for at the moment. To be honest, I'm just enjoying meeting different people right now.'

'Oh right,' he mumbles, looking a little crestfallen.

'I just broke up with someone,' I explain. 'Long story, I won't bore you. What about you? Are you enjoying Connector?'

'It's been an absolute godsend, to be honest,' he says. 'I really struggled to meet girls who could match my, um, exuberance for life, shall we say? Women my age can't keep up with me! But once I figured out all the little tips and tricks to get my Connector profile perfect, I started getting loads more matches.'

'Wait, what do you mean, tricks?' I ask.

He looks down into his cocktail.

'Oh, nothing,' he says, his face reddening now. 'Just picking the right photos I guess. Anyway, even though I get lots of matches now, I still never seem to get past the first date…'

'Well, it's always best to be honest on your profile,' I say. 'The truth always comes out in the end.'

'Everyone tells a few fibs!' he says. 'Besides, if I hadn't, would we have matched? Women are pretty shallow on these apps. Are you telling me you never told a white lie in your whole life?'

I open my mouth to answer, to tell him no, that I'm a book without a cover, but I stop. Because that would be a white lie in itself.

'Maybe it's the hair!' he says, before I have the chance to formulate a better response. 'You young ladies can't stand a baldy!'

He rubs his hand on the back of his head, where there's a noticeably thinning patch, and makes a jokey sad face.

'Aw, it's not that bad,' I say, trying to reassure him. 'It could be worse, you could have had one of those awful hair transplants in Turkey.'

'I have been tempted, actually, but they're about three grand,' he says. 'And with my new mortgage and everything, plus I'm absolutely balls deep in crypto right now…'

Eventually the droning of the music, the mortgage chat and the mix of Negroni and wine and fricking mushrooms in my stomach starts to weigh me down, like a heavy blanket. So this time when he insists on paying for the drinks, I don't argue. Suddenly all I want is fresh air. Outside the bar, the cold breeze hits me like a slap in the face, and I perk up a little bit.

'I think winter is here,' I say, meaninglessly.

'Here, wear this,' Freddie says, and whips off his gigantic body warmer before I have a chance to reply.

'Uh, I'm fine, thank you,' I smile.

'Gwen, don't be silly.' He's now dangling the thing above my shoulders, like a matador taunting a bull with his cape.

'No thanks.'

'Put on the gilet,' he commands.

'Freddie,' I say. 'I'm not cold.'

'But you just said—'

'I didn't,' I say, sharply this time. 'I said I'm fine.'

Freddie puts his jacket back on and we walk on in silence for a few minutes. Once the novelty of being outside and the warmth of the Negroni wears off, I begin to feel the cold. I do my best not to noticeably shiver.

'Okay, this is me,' I say, when we reach the bus stop. I step back deliberately, putting a good foot of distance between us as we say our goodbyes.

'Three,' he suddenly says out of nowhere.

'What?' I reply.

'Two,' he goes on.

I look at him in confusion.

'One...'

As he says 'one', Freddie leans in and kisses me unexpectedly on the lips.

'Oh!' I cry, taken a little aback.

'Sorry, wanted to give you plenty of notice, just in case you weren't up for it. Don't want any "hashtag me too" accusations, now do we?' he laughs, making air quotes with his fingers.

He clocks my stony expression and runs a hand through his thinning hair.

'I had a really good time tonight. Could we do it again sometime?'

'Uh, maybe,' I reply.

'Maybe... next week?' Freddie lifts one eyebrow in a suggestive manner.

I look at my shoes and wish I had a mushroom to chew on. 'Next week's a nightmare actually,' I say. 'Why don't you text me and we'll see when we're both free.'

'I'll definitely do that,' he says, his face beaming.

'Bye then.' I smile and turn around.

'Let me know when you get home safe.'

'Sure,' I say, managing another smile, only more weakly this time. 'You too.'

On the bus, slightly fuzzy from the cocktail, I jam in my earpods, sink back into the faded blue fabric and scowl at my reflection in the window. Closing my eyes, I turn up the true crime podcast I was currently addicted to, Danger Land. *The softly spoken Canadian narrator informs me that new evidence that could potentially blow the case wide open has been found after languishing for years in a backwater Calgary coroner's office. So apparently the chap they all thought did it might not be so guilty after all. Well no shit, Sherlock, it's never the guy you think it is.*

I regret the invitation to Freddie to text me, because it opens the floodgates to a deluge of pleading messages before I even reach my doorstep, each one somehow managing to make me fancy him less.

After a simple 'I really enjoyed your company tonight', his patter quickly degenerates into a campaign for a second date as soon as possible. When I admit that I don't think we're compatible, his attempts to convince me otherwise include the classics: 'look, you can't deny we got on', 'you have nothing to lose and everything to gain', 'is it because of my hair?' and finally 'can I call you?'

When these pleas are met with increasing indifference, he moves his attention to my social media, 'deep liking' twenty-five of my old Instagram photos and following me on Twitter (where I have not been since 2016 when I tweeted 'it's a con, all pasta shapes taste exactly the same' to a grand total of three likes). When I wake up the next day, there's a single message from Freddie on my phone.

Freddie: Please reply, Gwen. It's a matter of life or death.

I take a deep breath and block him.

TEN

I drained the final sip of water out of my glass and looked at the detectives.

'And you weren't alarmed by that last message?' DCI Forrester asked.

'No,' I replied. 'Guys send that sort of crap all the time, they're usually just trying to guilt you into a response.'

Forrester ran his finger and thumb through his moustache and sniffed loudly.

'Did Freddie and Rob know each other?' Detective Lyons asked. 'Either ever mention the other one?'

'No. I mean, for all I know, they could've been best mates, but…' I said, my voice faltering. 'Are you saying Rob and Freddie were murdered? You don't think, you don't think I'm in danger, do you?'

'No,' Detective Lyons said. 'But we may invite you to the station to give a full statement. Call us if you remember anything else that might be helpful.'

He handed me a pristine business card. When I reached to take it, I noticed him looking at my shaking hands. He fixed me with a questioning stare.

'Sorry, I'm just a bit, you know, in shock right now,' I mumbled.

'I can see that,' DCI Forrester said, looking at the rapidly congealing mess on the kitchen floor.

'Do you have anyone you can talk to?' Detective Lyons asked.

'Yeah,' I said. 'My flatmate. She's at her boyfriend's. Fiancé's, I mean. I'll be okay, she'll be back later. Like I said, I didn't really know those men. We only met that one time. It's just, well, it's just…'

'Weird?' he said.

I looked at him, and he looked back at me blankly.

'I'd better clean this up,' I said.

'One more question,' DCI Forrester said. 'Have you been on a date with anyone else recently?'

'What?' I said. 'Why?'

'It's just a question,' Forrester said.

'Right,' I said, pushing my hair behind my ears. 'Well, yeah, a couple of other people, nothing serious. Is this important?'

Lyons threw a glance at Forrester. 'It's not,' he said.

'Right, well, I need to get to work, so…'

'Of course,' Lyons coughed. 'Thank you for your time, Ms Turner.'

'We'll let ourselves out,' Forrester said, stepping towards the front door.

Lyons hesitated a moment before turning to leave. 'Save my number in your phone and call me if there's anything you need, Gwen,' he said.

There was something about the way he kept using my first name I didn't like. I thought police officers were meant to be deferential, especially when they thought any connection between you and two dead people was purely coincidental. Well, *probably* coincidental – that's what he said, wasn't it?

'Do I know you?' I asked.

'Uh, yes,' he replied. 'Well, sort of. I know *you*. I was four years above you at school. My sister, Grace, was in your year. You guys used to hang out.'

'No way!' I gasped. 'Dandy Lyons? I don't believe it. All my mates had a crush on you! You were in that terrible band that played at our prom. Wow, it really is you, isn't it? How's Grace? I haven't seen her in years.'

'She's good, thanks, but maybe let's drop the nickname in front of my superior here,' he said, glancing back towards Forrester. 'No one really calls me that any more.'

'Oh, sorry, old habits,' I said. 'So you're a police officer now? That's cool.'

'Uh, yeah, well, sometimes,' he said. 'What about you?'

'Mobile cafe down on the seafront,' I said. 'Which is nuts, because I actually can't stand coffee, but—'

I was interrupted by a loud cough from DCI Forrester's direction.

'Sorry, Gwen, I really have to go,' Lyons said, looking back at his superior, who was waiting for him on the front step. 'Stay safe.'

I heard the door click shut and went to the sink to get a sponge and a bottle of Flash. As I scrubbed at the floor tiles, I tried to think if there was any other link between Rob and Freddie. For all I knew, they could've been cousins, co-workers, anything. Eastbourne was a small town.

I left the wet sponge on the floor, grabbed my phone and googled 'Rob Hamilton + Freddie Scott'. Nothing. Lyons was right, Freddie's death was yet to be reported, but news about Rob's death had started to pop up everywhere.

I opened the fridge, pulled the orange juice out and sat at the breakfast bar, shoving mouthfuls of toasted bagel into my flushed face. As I sucked every remaining morsel of butter off the knife, I found a pretty lurid account of what had happened to Rob on the *Mail Online*. There was a lot more detail than on the local news story, and I scanned it for any connection he might have had to Freddie. Lyons clearly thought there was one, but I couldn't find anything that suggested they even lived near each other, or worked in the same industry, or anything. The only connection seemed to be they'd both been on one date with me. But that could be true of a hundred other girls in Eastbourne. The dating pool here wasn't that big to begin with, and thanks to Connector, it was shrinking by the day.

As much as I racked my hung-over brain, I couldn't remember Rob mentioning much about his personal life, except for his ex. As for Freddie, he hadn't stopped talking, but it was mostly about his mortgage repayments. I caught myself. I shouldn't think ill of the dead. *Dead*. The word swung through my head like a bell clapper. I couldn't believe it.

I looked Rob up on Instagram, but his account was private, and the only thing I could see was his profile picture, the same one he'd used on Connector. A little thinner in the face and a little more tanned than he'd been in real life, but with the same flirtatious smile that had drawn me to him in the first place. The same smile that had disappeared in an instant when I said I didn't want to go home with him. I felt a pang of... what? Sadness? Grief? Fear? I wasn't sure. I'd known the guy for less than three hours, total. How was I supposed to feel?

The rest of Rob's social media had been shut down or

deleted, probably to stop journalists from contacting the family or grabbing photos. But there was a tribute page set up for him on his old college website. I glanced through the messages from school friends and cousins. One caught my eye.

'*He was so kind, always looking out for people. Even when he really drove me crazy, he could flash me his little sheepish smile and inside, I would instantly give in. I wish I could tell him that I forgive him, for everything. Love, Rachel,*' it read.

Must be his ex, I thought. I couldn't help but wonder what Noah would write on *my* tribute page if I managed to run myself over with the van one afternoon.

I put down my phone and slid it across the breakfast bar. The flat now smelled faintly of sick and detergent, I was already late for work and there was little point in sitting there waiting for the heating to come back on (Sarah had set it to switch off at 8 a.m., and I had never figured out how to change it). I wished she was here now, instead of curled up like a croissant in bed with Richard. Not just to fix the damn heating but also to tell me to stop sulking, get in the shower and go to work.

Without Sarah to give me a lift, I was going to have to retrieve my under-used bike from the shed round the back of the flat, so I pulled on a hoodie and went out to investigate. When I pinched the tyres, they felt disconcertingly squidgy, but even if I did have a clue where the hell the pump was, I had no inclination to fix them. I hadn't ridden much since the summer the year before, when me and Noah had taken a long ride to the Seven Sisters on a drowsy, hot afternoon. We'd got the train back that time, and my legs had thanked me for it ever since with a dull but relieved ache. But, hey, I did a spin class most Wednesday lunchtimes, so I was confident I still had the legs for a quick cycle across town to work. (Side note: okay fine, *some* Wednesdays.)

I cycled aimlessly, with no real desire to reach my destination, through what remained of Old Town. Away from the main high street, the only shops left open were faceless bookies and grim-looking fried chicken shops. The windows of the other stores were whited out, with 'For Lease' signs stickered over the doors. The trickle of tourists descending on Eastbourne had slowly come to a stop, and the cheap flights to Marbella had lured away the last of the sunseekers, leaving us with the pensioners and locals. It was only the oncoming flood of displaced Londoners, keen to escape the smog and empty skyscrapers that they no longer needed, that kept a little hope alive for local businesses (and kept the Eastbourne dating pool topped up with fresh blood).

Eventually, some sort of subconscious GPS kicked in and I found myself outside Noah's place. Leaning my bike up against the parking meter, I looked up at his bedroom window. The curtains were closed, even though it was past 9 a.m. His studio flat there had been the scene of a million unremarkable but unforgettable moments, and an equal amount of stupid fights. My memories of him were so meshed with that place that whenever I happened to pass it, my thoughts were involuntarily wrenched back to that time, like an unruly dog on a short chain.

Of course, I'd unfollowed him on everything since we broke up. Well, okay, only after a very thorough last trawl through his social media. But there was nothing. Well, nothing that revealed anything interesting. No sign of another woman, no airport selfie as he fled the country, no emotional coming-out video. *Nothing*. To be fair, the most he'd ever posted when we were together was a photo of the ice cream van on the day we bought it – #lazysundaes #justchillin' (Noah had unfairly vetoed my suggestion, #teamcream).

Muscle memory almost took me up the steps to the battered blue front door, where I'd jabbed at his bell so many times before and waited to hear his steps coming down the stairs. It would be so easy to press that button now, and have him appear at that door, like magic, to save me once again.

But I resisted, and got back on my bike, pedalling on in a sort of daze, not really thinking about anything for longer than thirty seconds, until the cold began to work its way into my bones, and I turned back around and dragged myself to work.

ELEVEN

When I arrived at the seafront, I found Charlie, my one and only employee, leaning on the back of the van, a vape pen hanging out of his mouth.

'Bit early for that, isn't it?' I said.

'CBD oil, boss, great hangover cure,' he said, taking it from his lips and offering it to me. 'Looks like you need it.'

It was so cold I couldn't tell where the smoke ended and the condensation of my breath began. The smell of hemp turned my stomach.

'Ugh, no thanks,' I said. 'I've already been sick once this morning.'

'Getting too old for partying, huh?' he laughed.

I kicked his shin and unlocked the van shutters.

'I'll open up then, shall I?' I said.

'I was just about to!' Charlie said, sticking the vape in the top of his jeans.

'Just building up to it, huh?' I said.

'Come on, boss, it's not like we're fighting off customers right now,' he said, gesturing to the vast swathes of empty beach around us.

'Well, that doesn't mean we shouldn't make an effort,' I said, as I pulled on an apron emblazoned with the cafe logo (a cartoon Al Pacino, in his famous wild-eyed *Scarface* pose, but holding a steaming cup of coffee instead of a grenade launcher).

If you liked coffee, a good-not-great selection of pastries and intermittent Wi-Fi, then Cuppacino was the place for you. We catered for all your twenty-first-century coffee needs, from short ristrettos to long macchiatos, like every other coffee shop in Eastbourne. But we did have something they didn't: while I'd given the old ice-cream van a super cool makeover, I had insisted on keeping the Mr Whippy machine. Me and Noah had painted over the garish, twisted fake Mickey Mouses and Pikachus that had adorned the sides of the van with duck-egg blue, and peeled off the stickers of day-glo ice lollies from the windows. Our pitch down by the seafront had three white circular tables, decorated with little white flower pots and surrounded by white wooden ladder-back chairs.

After the break-up, I became de facto manager, mostly because a) I was the only member of staff left, and b) I look great in an apron. I was free to run the place as I chose, and I chose to run it in a super fun but generally haphazard way, turning up at nine (ish) and leaving at 6 p.m. on. the. dot. Not because I didn't care about my job, I just cared more about eating my dinner on time and getting drunk with my friends.

I had made *one* excellent managerial decision, which was to employ someone to do three very important tasks:

1. Handle all the boring jobs e.g., mopping
2. Workshop hilarious nicknames for the customers with me
3. Listen to all my amazing-slash-tragic-slash-amazingly-tragic dating stories

Charlie had started shortly after New Year. A protégé of Richard's, he had just quit his job at the mind-numbingly dull IT firm they both worked for. When I'd met him at The Brown Derby, he'd told me he wanted a stress-free job so he could 'get back in touch with himself' or some such nonsense, and I had the feeling he was probably secretly writing a self-help manual or studying transcendental meditation or something. He'd started work a couple of weeks after Noah left, and so we were instantly bonded by a mutual confusion over how to work the till and having no one else to go to lunch with.

And no, I couldn't really afford to hire someone, especially in these winter months, but to be honest, I couldn't stand another day, by myself, staring out the van window into the rain. Some days, just for a laugh, I threatened to march him up and down the beach wearing a sandwich board, but mostly I just got him to sweep the pitch and replenish the packs of Splenda.

So that was it: me, Charlie and Cuppacino's mascot, Rocco the French Bulldog, who was normally found nestled under the van, only looking out if someone ordered a cheese toastie. Rocco belonged to our one and only regular customer, Jamal, a sharply dressed Gen Z-er who had the unique ability to make a grande cappuccino last approximately one thousand years. I got the impression he was more interested in my free Wi-Fi than my excellent range of crisps and sparkling customer service.

'Come on then, what's the goss from last night?' Charlie asked. 'You look awful, so I'm assuming the hen went well?'

'Uh, just start setting up, will you? I'm still processing,' I said, climbing inside the van.

To be fair, I always spilled the tea to Charlie after a big night or a bad date, but this morning, I had no idea where to begin. So while he set the tables out on the promenade, I curled up on the driver's seat, rested my head against the cool glass of the window and idly scrolled through Connector. Normally, I'd be putting in a good solid hour of swiping right about now, but after everything, the thought of that made me feel sick.

I pulled up Parker's profile and flicked through his photos again. I'd forgotten all about his message last night, and now that I thought about it, I wanted to know why he'd sent me the link about Rob. Did he know I'd been on a date with him, or was it just a coincidence? And how many coincidences need to happen before they're not really coincidences any more?

It was far more likely Parker was just being a dick, I told myself. And normally that sort of behaviour would have earned him an instant block and report, but there was something about him that made me hesitate. Maybe I should just ask him outright? I tapped out a message.

Gwen: what was that link all about?

As I pressed send, I was interrupted by the end of a broom tapping on the window. I looked up to see Charlie with a big dumb grin pasted on his face. I wound down the window and he peered inside. With tight brown curls that seemed to sprout out of the baseball cap that was forever jammed on his head and eyes that were too big for his face, he almost looked like a caricature of himself, like the ones of out-of-date movie stars that street artists drew for day trippers on the seafront.

'Ooo, who's that? One of your hot dates?' he asked, the slight northern lilt in his voice betraying his childhood in Manchester.

'I'm doing the accounts,' I said, returning to my phone. 'Someone around here has to do some work.'

'If that's your accountant, he suddenly got a lot better looking,' he said, motioning to my phone screen with the end of his broom. 'Come on, boss, you can tell me! You know I'm like a guru when it comes to matters of the heart.'

'Hmm, usually you just tell me to chuck my phone in the sea and get stoned,' I said. 'Besides, looks like you've got more sweeping to do.'

'Yeah, but the sweeping goes so much faster if you regale me with your cringeworthy dating tales while I'm doing it.'

I looked up to see he'd threaded his broom across his shoulders and was letting his hands dangle over each end, like a scarecrow. Or a sort of hippy Jesus.

'Okay, fine,' I sighed dramatically, closing the app and shoving the phone in my pocket. 'I'll give you a hand.'

I opened the van door, swung my legs round and hopped out onto the promenade. While Charlie swept, I went and wiped down the tables with an anti-bac wipe before setting each with a metal box of napkins.

'So, did you hook up last night after the hen?' Charlie asked after about five seconds.

I glared at him.

'Ohhh, something did happen, didn't it!' Charlie smiled, before miming something unspeakable with the broom handle and his mouth.

'Please don't do that to company property,' I said flatly.

'What about this?' He turned the broom upside down,

poked the handle down his jeans and through his open fly, and started wiggling it about.

Rolling my eyes. I took out my phone and quickly snapped a photo.

'How about you stop messing about, or I post this on the Cuppacino Twitter feed?'

'Okay, and how about I report *you* to HR?'

'Unfortunately for you,' I said, 'I'm your HR rep, on-site therapist and line manager all in one.'

Charlie stood to attention, using the broom as a makeshift rifle.

'So, basically, don't mess with me,' I said.

'Is that an order?' he smiled.

I nodded sharply, and he made a mock salute and went back to sweeping. When he put his head down, his curls licked his eyebrows and threatened to cover those big brown eyes and he could've competed for the position of office dog himself. Well, office puppy maybe. He certainly seemed to be behind Rocco in the cafe hierarchy. While he was distracted, I snuck a look at my phone screen to see if Parker had replied. *Nothing*. Normally, I was super chill about guys taking hours to reply. So why was this guy making me feel so anxious?

'Oh, don't tell me he's ghosting you, is he?' Charlie asked, spotting me shove my phone back in my pocket.

I didn't answer. To be honest, the phrase *ghosting* had taken on a whole new meaning after this morning's events.

'I knew it!' he said. 'He totally ghosted you!'

'Honestly, I am not in the mood for this today, okay?' I snapped, shoving a chair under a table so hard it knocked the little pot of wooden cutlery off. Charlie's goofy grin slumped into a frown, and as I knelt to pick them up, he bent down next to me. When I picked up a spoon, he put his hand over mine.

'Gwen, is everything okay?' he said softly.

He looked straight at me, his brown curls flopping in front of his large, hopeful eyes. To be honest, his eyes always looked like that, like a docile cow waiting to be milked.

I sighed, shook off his hand and stood up.

'The police came round this morning,' I blurted out.

'Woah! Really?' he cried, dropping the broom. 'What did they want?'

'Remember that guy I went for drinks with last week, Rob? Well, they found his body. His *dead* body. And you know the guy I went out with after that? Freddie? Well, he's dead too. So yes, okay, I am hung-over, but I am also freaking out just a little bit here.'

'What the hell, Gwen?' he said. 'Two of your exes are dead?'

I glared at him. 'Careful, I'm not sure they heard you in Brighton.'

Even though – as usual – there were no potential customers in a 100-mile radius, I wasn't wild about Charlie broadcasting the rocketing death rate of my dating history to the entire county.

'Okay, okay, sorry,' he said, almost in a whisper. 'But what do you mean, dead?'

'I mean dead, as in not breathing, distinctly un-alive and probably murdered.'

'Oh shit,' Charlie said, his voice softening. He pulled out a chair and motioned for me to sit on it. 'I'm sorry, Gwen.'

'Don't be,' I said, flopping down. 'I barely knew them.'

'So why did the police want to speak to you?' Charlie asked.

'Connector,' I said. 'My messages were on both of their phones. So I guess maybe they were just checking on everyone who'd seen them recently?'

I left the question hanging, hoping he'd confirm to me that, yes, this was all just part of totally normal police work.

'Wow,' Charlie said after a moment, his previous concern for me replaced with an enthusiasm I found hard to share. 'You could be on one of your nerdy true crime podcasts.'

'Charlie! This is serious!' I said, hitting him on the arm with a spoon. To be fair, the thought had crossed my mind. I'd spent many a bus journey imagining being gently probed by the treacly-voiced host of *Danger Land*. I liked to imagine that one day, I'd witness a thrilling crime and they'd invite me on the show to recount the exact details to thousands of listeners, with a little added panache of course.

'I know, I know,' he said. 'But like you said, you barely knew them.'

'Still,' I said. 'They had families, people who cared about them.'

'Hey, how do you know? Maybe they were orphans with no friends.'

'No, Rob told me on the date. He said he had... two brothers, I think?' I thought for a second. 'Actually, maybe three. I don't remember.'

'Wow, sounds like you were really paying attention as usual,' Charlie said. 'Or were you just calculating the number of drinks you had to finish before you could escape?'

I folded my arms and scowled at him. 'Don't you have some oat milk to restock or something?'

'Alright, sorry,' he sighed, holding his hands up. 'But seriously, you okay, boss?'

'I'm fine,' I said. 'It's just a weird coincidence, you know?'

He looked at me slack-jawed as the gears turned in his clockwork brain and I waited patiently for his thoughts to make their way to his mouth.

Eventually, he leant towards me and lowered his voice.

'So who's next?' he asked dramatically.

'What do you mean, "who's next?"'

'Well, so far the first two guys you dated on Connector have been found dead,' Charlie said. 'So, who did you meet next?'

I froze. I hadn't even thought of that.

'Wait, you think someone else is going to get hurt?' I asked.

'Maybe, maybe not,' he said, pulling out his vape pen again and taking a slow draw.

'Shit,' I said, thinking back over the last couple of weeks. 'I don't know, who was it after Freddie?'

'You don't remember? Jesus, Gwen, were there that many? Wasn't it the one who looked a bit like Chris Hemsworth?'

'No,' I said, trying to think. 'He came later. And FYI, he looked *nothing* like Chris Hemsworth in the flesh.'

'Hmm, okay, was it that bloke with the tiny hands?'

'Josh? Yeah, I think it was,' I said. 'We went to play crazy golf and he tried to convince me that immigrants were going to start mooring their dinghies off Eastbourne Pier.'

'Oh yeah, that clown. Whatever happened with him anyway? Did you ever hear from him again?'

'No,' I snapped, a little too quickly. 'Never.'

Charlie looked at me and cocked his head to one side.

'Did something bad happen on that date, Gwen? I remember you said it was in your top ten worst evenings of all time.'

'No,' I said, avoiding his gaze and staring very intently at the back of a spoon. 'I just really, really don't like losing at crazy golf.'

I thought back to that night and felt sick. What if Charlie was right, and someone was going to come after Josh? What if he was already dead?

'I should at least check on him, right?' I said.

'And what are you going to tell him? A psychopath is coming after all your exes, and he's next? He's gonna love that.'

'They are not my exes!' I snapped. 'I went on one date with these guys, one!'

'Then stay out of it, Gwen,' Charlie said. 'Like you said, you barely knew them. Let the police worry about Josh. And all of these losers. Besides, chasing after them is only going to make you look suspicious.'

'What do you mean?' I cried.

'Hey, I'm just saying, if this *was* a true crime podcast, you'd be the prime suspect!' He began imitating a clichéd podcaster voice. '*Rejected by every man in Eastbourne, beautiful twenty-something Gwen Turner finally snapped and took her bloody revenge…*'

'You're about two sentences away from being fired,' I warned him.

He was being a complete knob-end, but maybe Charlie had a point. Besides, even if I wanted to warn Josh, I never even took his number, and after our date, I had immediately blocked him on the app. Even if I hadn't, there was no way in hell either of us was going to contact the other again, not after what really went down at the crazy golf course.

'I mean, you've got enough problems, right?' Charlie continued. 'If you don't find a new flatmate, you're going to be sleeping in the van. And, if we have another month selling one cappuccino and a cheese toastie a day to Jamal, you're gonna have to sell the van. So then you're gonna be sleeping on the beach, and trust me, that is not as fun as it sounds in the middle of February.'

'Wow, thanks Charlie,' I sighed. 'You should pop some of these motivational quotes on Instagram over a nice sunset backdrop, they're so inspiring.'

'I'm just saying—' he began.

'Shush now,' I said, pointing down the promenade. 'Customer.'

I turned to see Jamal striding towards us, laptop under one arm and clutching Rocco in the other.

'Grande cappuccino and a toastie, please,' he smiled as he rummaged around in his pockets for change.

I climbed into the van, fired up the coffee machine and slammed my fist on our ancient till, the only way to get the drawer to spring open. Despite his designer labels and fashionable thick black-rimmed glasses (which I suspected had no lenses), Jamal would always pay in cash, usually in fresh notes and shiny pound coins and fifty pence pieces.

'Thanks,' he said as I cupped the coins into my hand and dropped them individually into their corresponding compartments in the till.

'Here you go, boy,' I said, scraping the crispy cheese from the edge of the toastie machine and placing it on my open palm for Rocco to lick up appreciatively.

'Most loyal man I know,' I smiled.

I watched them amble back down the beach while I considered testing the resilience of my stomach with a lunchtime Mr Whippy. As I reached for the lever, I saw my phone flashing at me from the counter.

New message from Parker.

Oh, *now* he wanted to chat. Finally, I could find out why he sent that stupid link and relax. I swiped the screen to see the message.

Parker: Two down.

And I swear my heart stopped beating.

TWELVE

Two Down? What the hell did that mean?

I typed out 'Two Down? What the hell does that mean?' but then, thinking better of it, quickly deleted everything but the '?' and pressed send.

I stared at the screen, waiting for his response. When nothing came, I read his message again, over and over, trying to work out if it was just a weird autocorrect, and he'd actually meant to type 'Gwen you're totally amazing and I'm sorry for being a complete weirdo.'

Suddenly, a new message popped up.

Parker: what?

What? What was 'what?' supposed to mean? Was he playing with me? Or was he just being thick?

'What do you mean "two down"?' I typed back, assuming the latter.

Three dots appeared on the screen, meaning he was typing something. They seemed to sit there for an eternity, taunting me.

'Come on, you bastard,' I whispered, staring at the screen, trying to physically force the message to appear. Finally, it did.

Parker: Two strikes out of three. I flaked last night, and then sent you that link. Sorry, that must have freaked you out. But you'll give me one more chance for a date, right?

A wave of relief washed over me. Maybe it was me who was being dumb. All this police stuff must have been making me paranoid. Still, I was not in the mood for another round of clumsy flirting.

'I'm a one strike and you're out kind of girl,' I typed back.

Parker: Well I think I deserve another.

I paused, momentarily thrown. Maybe I was misreading the tone, but that felt wrong, almost menacing, and I didn't have the energy to play stupid games. But just as I was about to close the app, an emoji popped up on the screen. Of course, it was the fucking winky face, my least favourite of all the emojis, the text equivalent of yelling 'not!' after a sentence.

'I'll think about it,' I typed quickly. 'But if you don't want a third strike, tell me why you sent me that link.'

And then for good measure, and because I didn't know what else to do, a smiley emoji. The one with little jazz hands, just to hammer home my *extremely* breezy, non-antagonising tone.

I chucked my phone on the counter and flopped down on a box of Kettle Chips. Squeezing my hand through the Sellotaped flaps, I pulled a packet out. As I crunched on a baked goat's cheese and caramelised onion veg chip, I silently cursed myself for only stocking the posh hand-cooked ones. Deep inside, my heart longed for the sweet, dusty orange delight of a Wotsit.

I stared at my phone, waiting for its silly little face to light up again. Maybe Charlie was right. I should delete that stupid app, chuck my phone in the sea and sort my stupid life out. Yes, that's exactly what I was going to do. I stood up and grabbed my phone, but just as I did, it started ringing.

'Dandy Lyons' the screen read.

I almost dropped it in shock. God, what did *he* want? Now I had to add 'the police' to the list of people who actually still called me, which currently consisted of my mother and the Deliveroo driver when he had somehow managed to deliver my pad thai to a business park in East Croydon.

My finger hovered over the green 'pick-up' symbol, but Charlie was just outside, leaning on his broom and vaping, so I let it ring out and waited for the inevitable voicemail notification. When it came, I shut the van door, nestled myself between the bags of coffee beans and dialled 121. I held the phone to my ear, and listened to Lyons's muffled message.

'*Gwen, uh sorry, Ms Turner, this is Detective Lyons, from, um, this morning. I wanted to talk to you about a... development in the case we spoke about. I wondered if you could come into the station at your earliest convenience. Thank you.*'

'Shit,' I whispered.

The word 'development' sounded ominous. 'Development' sounded like something bad had happened. If they had found the killer – or killers – why would I have to come into the police station? Or had they tracked down Josh already, and he'd told them what really happened on our date? I knew I should go in, tell them all about Josh, and the others. Tell them about these weird messages from Parker. Tell them everything. But if I did, would they ever let me go?

I stuffed my phone back in my pocket and pulled a napkin from the shelf behind me. With the pen from my order pad, I scribbled down the names of all the guys I'd dated since my break-up.

Rob

Freddie

Josh

Dev

Seb

Two of these men were already dead. I dragged my pen through their names.

Two down, I thought. *Is that what Parker meant? Were the others on the list in danger?*

I paused for a second and then carefully wrote down one more name at the bottom of the napkin. But when I looked at that final name, scribbled there in black and white (or rather, blue biro), my stomach turned.

No, I thought, not that one.

Not him.

Very carefully, I tore the end off, the part with the sixth name on it, dropped it in the bin, and stuffed the napkin in the back of my jeans.

And then I pulled out my phone and texted Lyons.

Gwen: Can we talk?

THIRTEEN

I leant on the counter, watching as a cold wind blew across the beachfront, knocking over the pots of cutlery on the tables. I'd sent Lyons a location pin and asked him to meet me, and with a complete absence of any more customers, all I had to do was wait.

Eventually, a familiar figure appeared in the distance, walking down the promenade towards the van. I watched him slowly make his way through the plastic tables to the van window, and noticed that, despite the way he hung his head like he was permanently trying to solve a difficult crossword puzzle, he had a good physique: tall and broad chested. As he approached, Charlie put his broom down and turned to greet him.

'What can I get you, mate?' he asked.

'I'll take this one, Charlie,' I said. 'This is Dandy, an old friend of mine.'

'Detective Lyons,' he corrected me.

When he said that, Charlie's eyes widened and he grabbed his baseball cap, pulling it down over his curls.

'Right, ah, well, I'll leave you two to it then,' he said. 'I'll take my break, boss, see you in twenty.'

With that, he threw his apron off and started down the seafront. Lyons watched him head towards the arcade, and when he'd finally disappeared from view, he turned back to me.

'So, this is the famous van, huh?' Lyons said. 'The "Mystery Machine"?'

'The Mystery Machine? From *Scooby Doo*? Wow. You really need to update your references,' I said. 'This is Alfredo. Me and my ex were going to take him on the road, round every festival in the country. Then maybe Europe next year, then…' I tailed off.

'Then the world?' said Lyons.

'Well, that was Noah's dream, to sell overpriced hot milky drinks to muddy hipsters around the globe. Guess it's up to me now though, as soon as I find someone to split the petrol money with.'

I jolted myself out of a daydream I didn't want to wallow in.

'So, what's this development?' I asked. 'Did you find a connection between Rob and Freddie?'

'Yes. They were both making quite large payments in cryptocurrency to the same anonymous account. Our working theory is that these men were mixed up in organised crime, probably drug related. There's been an influx of class-A dealing in Eastbourne.'

'Oh right,' I said. 'So it's nothing to do with me?'

'No, we don't think you're connected, Gwen,' he said. 'This is a small town. Rob and Freddie probably dated a lot of the same women.'

A wave of relief washed over me for a second. Then I remembered the napkin in my back pocket.

'Hey, why don't you take a seat and I'll make you a

coffee?' I motioned to the plastic chairs scattered across the promenade.

'I've already had one, thanks,' he said.

'Tea then?' I offered. 'Hot chocolate? Wait, don't tell me you're a Mr Whippy man, Detective Lyons?'

'Uh, tea's fine,' he said, taking a seat at one of the tables.

'Good choice,' I said. 'Gimme a minute.'

He sat down and I brought over a cardboard cup of tea and a packet of crisps.

'So,' I said. 'You couldn't have told me that "development" over the phone?'

'Uh, well, these things are always better face to face, if you, uh, know what I mean,' he stuttered.

I cocked my head at him and narrowed my eyes.

'Okay, well, if you're going to be hanging around, I should know your real name. Your first name, I mean, unless you want me to keep calling you Dandy.'

'Aubrey,' he said.

'Aubrey?' I repeated.

'Yep, Aubrey,' he replied.

'Sorry, I thought for a second you said Aubrey.'

'That's right. Aubrey's my name.'

'Ahhh yeah, that's not gonna work, sorry.'

He looked at me blankly.

'That's your actual real name?' I said. 'Sorry, I thought you were joking. No wonder we gave you a nickname.'

'Homicide detectives don't really do jokes,' he said.

'I noticed,' I said. 'I'm dying on my arse here.'

'No pun intended?' He raised an eyebrow.

'All of my puns are intended,' I told him. 'If we're going to get along, you should know that about me.'

Lyons squinted at me.

'Do you ever think all this joking around is just a defence mechanism?' he asked.

'Could be,' I nodded. 'Or, it could just be that I'm naturally hilarious.'

Lyons didn't say anything, but he blew on his tea as I sat down opposite him.

'So what gives?' I said. 'At school you were always the sensible older brother, now all of a sudden you're, what, some sort of seaside Luther?'

'It's been a long time since school,' he said.

'Tell me about it. You look so much…' I tailed off.

'What?' he said.

'Older,' I replied.

'We're both older, Gwen,' he said.

'Yeah, but you're like, a proper grown-up. How did you end up doing,' I waved my hand at him, 'all this?'

'I actually moved to London after uni, started teacher training, was all set to be an English teacher. And I was for a bit. But then, uh, I met my wife and, well, things changed.'

The word 'wife' seemed to hang in the air for a moment, like an unwelcome seagull.

'I signed on to the National Detective Programme about eighteen months ago,' he went on. 'You know, the graduate scheme? When I finished the programme, they sent me down here. Once I've worked a few cases, I might get a chance with the Met.'

'Happy to hear we've got the crack team on the case,' I said. 'So this is like, your first ever murder then?'

'No,' he replied defensively. 'Second. They don't just let us loose straight away, you know. It's a lot of hard work and training. The scheme is meant to encourage more graduates to join the force. Not that many people want to be police officers these days.'

'So they just let high school teachers investigate homicides now?' I asked. 'I cannot imagine Mr McHallis hunting down serial killers.'

'Who's Mr McHallis?' he asked.

'Our old maths teacher!' I said. 'Remember? Bad breath, even worse taste in corduroy. I'm not sure he'd be much use to you.'

'Oh yeah, Mr McHalitosis,' Lyons said, a faint smile crossing his face. 'I dunno, maybe he would be a great detective, he seemed to have a sixth sense when it came to us bunking off.'

He reached over to the bag of crisps and placed one gingerly on his tongue.

'It's not laced with ricin, don't worry,' I said. 'Although, murder by Kettle Chip would be a great episode of *Danger Land*...'

Lyons looked at me and swallowed. I took a crisp from the packet and chucked it in my mouth, just to prove they were harmless.

'Listen, are you *sure* these deaths aren't related to my, you know, dating history?' I asked.

'I told you, Gwen, it's just a coincidence, you mustn't—'

Before he could finish, I pulled the napkin out of my back pocket and slapped it on the table.

'Look at this,' I said. 'These are the guys I met on Connector. In this exact order. Rob, Freddie, Josh, Dev, Seb. The first two are dead. Still think it's just a coincidence?'

Lyons flattened out the crumpled paper on the table until the names were legible.

'You couldn't have printed this out?' he asked.

'No, because no one's "printed anything out" since 2007, detective,' I said, looking at him like he'd suggested I chisel the names into Beachy Head. 'Besides, I've got really neat handwriting. Anyway, forget that – you need to find these guys and make sure they're safe.'

Lyons picked up the napkin and squinted at it. 'And you met *all* these men in just the last few weeks?'

'Um, yeah, Judgy McJudgerson, I did,' I said. 'So what?'

'What happened here?' Lyons asked, pointing to the end of the napkin where I'd torn off a piece.

'Spilt a mocha on it,' I said quickly.

Lyons looked at me quizzically, opened his mouth to say something, but then seemed to change his mind.

'These remaining names here – Josh, Dev and Seb – do you have their phone numbers?'

'Well... no, I don't usually swap numbers unless we go on a second date,' I said.

'You went and met random strangers without getting their phone numbers?'

'Hey, I didn't want them hitting up my WhatsApp with endless aubergine emojis at 1 a.m.! They weren't complete random strangers, anyway, I did my due diligence. I stalked them online. And Sarah insists that I text her screenshots of their profiles.'

'Alright,' Lyons sighed. 'And I'm guessing none of these went well enough to get a second date?'

I shrugged at him. 'Nope,' I said. 'Full disclosure, I'm pretty picky.'

'Can I see their Connector profiles?'

'Um, I blocked them,' I said apologetically.

'Oh, this just gets better and better.' Lyons put his head in his hands.

'Hey, they were almost exclusively total dicks!' I cried. 'I'm so sorry I didn't have the foresight to see they were going to be stalked by a serial killer at the time.'

'Let's not jump to conclusions.' Lyons sipped his tea. 'Do you know how many *actual* serial killers there have been in England in the past decade?'

He paused for effect.

'One.'

'Doesn't that mean we're about due another?' I asked.

Lyons stopped mid-sip to consider that, as if it wasn't something he'd thought of before.

'I do know a few things about serial killers, you know, I've listened to literally hundreds of hours of *Danger Land*.'

'What is this *Danger Land* you keep talking about?' Lyons raised an eyebrow.

'It's a podcast,' I sighed. 'I take it you've heard of them? Come on, you're a thirty-something-year-old man, right? I'm surprised you don't have one yourself.'

'I see,' Lyons said. 'And you think listening to a podcast qualifies you to play detective, does it?'

'Well, technically you've only worked on one more case than I have. Did you even solve that one?'

'That's not relevant,' Lyons said firmly. 'Let's focus on this case for a moment, shall we?' He picked up the napkin and examined it again. 'Have you upset anyone recently, anyone who might want to hurt you?'

'No!' I cried. 'I'm almost completely 100 per cent

inoffensive. I'm a people pleaser. Don't have a single enemy. Well, unless you count Kelly Sanchez, but I haven't seen her since sixth form prom.'

'Kelly Sanchez? I remember her. Isn't she the one who you punched in the mouth after she kissed your date?'

'Slapped,' I said. 'I *slapped* her. After she threw a wine glass at my head.'

'Wait, she threw a glass at your head?'

'Well, yeah, a plastic one.'

'God, that must be more than ten years ago now,' he said.

'And yet, I myself have only aged five years,' I said.

Lyons shook his head. 'Let's try and keep focused here, Gwen. It sounds like the only people you've upset are the spurned men on this napkin. Unless... what about this ex you mentioned?'

A jolt went through me, kind of like that feeling when you realise you've left your passport at home when you're halfway to the airport.

'No way, he's not part of this,' I said defensively. 'I've not heard from him since we broke up.

'Was it amicable?'

'The break-up? Incredibly amicable,' I said.

'Really?' Lyons asked, arching an eyebrow. 'I'm getting the impression that maybe there's some unfinished business there?'

'That detective training is really coming in handy, isn't it? Alright, fine. It wasn't exactly an absolute classic for all involved,' I said. 'But no break-up is, right? Noah is one of the good guys. When I tell you he's not mixed up in any of this, you can believe me. Right now I'm just trying to forget about him, get some distance, and, you know, move on with my life.'

'Well, for what it's worth, I'm sorry, Gwen. I know separations can be hard.'

'Sounds like you're speaking from experience?' I ventured.

Lyons sipped his tea again.

'This isn't about me. And I'm still not sure it's about you either. It's about Rob and Freddie and making sure nobody else gets hurt.'

I saw his eyes flicker sideways for a split second. I knew enough about body language to know that meant he was recalling a memory. I wondered if it was a good or a bad one. I studied his face for more clues, and noticed he had somehow grown up to bear a passing resemblance to Tom Hardy. He may not have had the bad boy demeanour and tattoos, but there was definitely some pain behind those eyes.

'Okay, so you'll do it then? You'll track down the names on this napkin?' I asked.

'I still think it's very unlikely that any of these deaths have anything *directly* to do with you or your boyfriends.'

'They're not my...' I began.

'Just guys you dated, I know,' Lyons said. 'Well, let me reassure you, the fact that you happened to have gone out with two unrelated victims is more than likely just a coincidence.'

'Yeah, and to be fair to me, there are plenty of guys I have been out with who *haven't* been murdered.'

Lyons hesitated a moment before taking the cup and pressing it to his lips. When he tipped the cup upwards and drained the liquid into his mouth, I could see a well-defined jawline beneath his grainy stubble.

'That's good to know,' he said.

I didn't want to tell Lyons, but actually, I didn't have the greatest track record with guys. When I was a kid, my parents had always seemed so together, so solid, and oh so sensible. Then, during my last year at university, we lost my dad. Sudden heart attack. It came out of nowhere, and it was like someone had swung a demolition ball through our lives. I abandoned everything for a while – uni, boys, sleeping. It was only thanks to Sarah that I got through it. But after that, the whole idea of a serious relationship seemed stupid. If someone you loved could just be taken away in an instant, then what was the point? So while it was true I didn't have many dead exes, I didn't exactly have many alive ones either.

Lyons took a deep breath, threw a final gulp of tea down his throat and pushed his chair back.

'Alright, I have to get back to the station,' he said, standing up.

'Wait, so that's it?' I said. 'I just stay here and wait?'

'A few names on a napkin isn't a lot to go on, but I'll talk to Forrester and see what we can do, okay? Just sit tight and let us do our job. Goodbye, Gwen.'

He began walking off towards town.

'But how long is that going to take?' I called after him. 'I can't be part of a murder investigation, I've got a business to run, a wedding in three days where I am maid of honour…'

Lyons paused for a moment and looked back at me.

'I have to go,' he said. 'I'll call you if there's any further developments.'

'Wait,' I said, reaching for my phone in my pocket. 'I got these—'

I was pulling out my phone to show him Parker's messages

when something suddenly stopped me. I felt stupid. What would I say? Sarah was right. All I had was yet another creepy message from a creepy guy. Lyons would just think I'd listened to too many crime podcasts.

'What?' he asked.

'Nothing,' I said. 'Just, uh, you didn't finish your tea.'

'Right.' Lyons took the cardboard cup off the table and lifted his hand to wave goodbye.

I watched him walk away, with his half-drunk cup of tea and my life in his hands, and somehow I wasn't filled with confidence that an ex-English teacher turned cop and his bushy-faced friend were going to get very far. I sat at the table, watching the napkin dance in the wind. I put my phone on it to stop it blowing off down the beach and, as I scanned the names again, a shiver ran through me. Could they really be in danger? Lyons didn't seem to think so, but what if he was wrong?

Suddenly, my phone lit up with a Connector notification, jolting me from my thoughts. My mouth went dry as I read the message.

Parker: ready for strike three?

I swallowed hard, the last traces of cold saliva trickling down my throat as I grabbed the napkin and shoved it in my back pocket.

This time, I wasn't going to respond with a jovial emoji. I didn't know if Parker was just yet another exhausting Reply Guy or something worse, but I'd had enough of these games. So as much as I never wanted to see Josh ever again in my

life, if the police weren't bothered about tracking him down, maybe I was going to have to do it myself.

There was only one problem, I had absolutely no idea where to find him.

FOURTEEN

So, like any sensible person, I do my fair share of pre-date stalking. Sarah was always telling me I should at least have a cursory google of Connector guys before I met them, just to be safe. And she was right. Unfortunately, when I'd typed 'Josh Little' into the search engine, all I'd learnt was that Josh shared his name with a major league baseball player from San Francisco. And while I was super impressed that this Josh Little had, apparently, scored forty-four home runs last season and had a really neat goatee, that information was not incredibly helpful right now.

I scribbled a 'Back Soon' note for Charlie, unlocked my bike from the back of the van and pedalled towards Jolly Jungle Crazy Golf, the scene of my disastrous date with Josh. I figured if he'd booked our session online, they'd at least have an email address for him. Built as a kids' attraction about ten years ago, Jolly Jungle Crazy Golf had recently been repurposed as a sort of hipster hangout, where grown adults seemingly found it hilarious to smack tiny balls past giant polypropylene animals into tiny holes.

When I arrived, I went up to the booth at the entrance and knocked on the glass.

'Hi,' I said, trying to get the attention of the teenage attendant hunched over a laptop inside.

He didn't look up from the screen. Peering through the glass, I could see he was in the middle of a hand of online poker. I rapped on the window again.

'Hey,' I said, more loudly this time.

With a sigh, the boy looked up to meet my eyes. Despite what I opined to be a terrible haircut and even more questionable facial hair than Josh Little (the baseball one), he had kind eyes and looked cosy in a chunky puffer jacket.

'Four pound fifty,' he mumbled. 'The clubs are down there.'

He gestured to a metal container full of putters.

'No, I don't want to play, thanks. I need your help. My friend, Josh Little, made a booking here. Can you look him up on your computer there?'

'We don't do that sort of thing, sorry,' he replied.

'Oh really, not even for me,' I scanned his puffer jacket in vain for some sort of name tag, 'um, mate?'

'Stephen,' he said indifferently.

'Okay look, Stephen, the truth is, me and Josh had an amazing first date here, and then I went and lost my phone! So I just need his number so I can tell him how much I enjoyed it. He probably thinks I'm ghosting him. I'm like, so totally into him, you know? You don't want to stand in the way of true love, do you?'

I gave him my best Sandra Bullock goofy smile.

'Wait, you were here on a date last week? Think I heard about that. Weren't you the one who...'

'No,' I interrupted. 'That wasn't me. We had a *great* date.

That's why I need his number, email address, anything. Please. I really need to get hold of him. You must have all the booking information stored there somewhere.'

'I should get the manager,' he said.

'No, no, wait a second. Listen a sec, Stephen. I own the coffee van out on the promenade,' I said. 'I'll give you free hot chocolates for a week if you help me out here.'

He paused for a moment.

'With those little marshmallows on top?'

'Uh, yeah, sure, with the little marshmallows. Just look up Josh Little on your computer there for me, will you?'

Stephen started tapping on the laptop in front of him.

'Right, here he is. I have an email address and a contact number here,' he said, turning the computer screen to face me.

As I pulled out my phone and started copying it down, Stephen eyed my battered phone complete with the grinning sparkly unicorn on the back suspiciously.

'It's ironic,' I told him.

'Didn't you say you lost your phone?'

'Yeah, I did,' I told him. 'I dropped it in the bath. Then I got a new one.'

'Doesn't look new,' he said.

'New phone, old case,' I told him.

Stephen narrowed his eyes at me and shook his head. He reached up and swung the laptop screen away from me.

'Hey! What are you doing?' I cried. 'I'm not finished.'

'I'm sorry, I really think I should get the manager,' he said, picking up his phone.

'Wait, wait, do we really want to involve the manager with this, Stephen?' I said. 'He's probably really busy, right? I'm sure he doesn't have time to hear about his under-age staff using the company computer for gambling, right?'

Stephen shifted in his seat and looked guiltily at the computer.

'So, tell you what,' I went on. 'Since you like a bet, I'll make you a deal.'

'Go on,' he said through gritted teeth.

'Okay, if I get a hole in one on the crocodile hole,' I said, pointing over at the course, 'you give me the number. I miss, you get the free hot chocolates for a month. With the marshmallows. Plus a muffin.'

Stephen considered the offer for a second.

'You won't make that shot,' he said, looking me up and down. 'No one does. That's the hardest hole on the course.'

It took all my strength not to tell him it was a seaside crazy golf course filled with unrealistic monkeys, not the links at St Andrews. But I bit my lip and forced a smile. The hole consisted of a gigantic plastic green crocodile with an opening and closing mouth. In order to do it in one shot, you had to hit your ball down the green and through the mouth when it opened, which would then send it running all the way down his tail and into the hole.

'Well, you have nothing to lose then,' I said, sticking my hand through the window of the booth.

'Whatever,' he said, taking it and shaking firmly. 'Knock yourself out.'

'Great.' I picked up a club and went over to the hole. A few yards in front of me, the jaws of the massive plastic crocodile slowly opened, and then, with a loud click, snapped shut. I placed my ball on the white spot at the start of the hole and watched the crocodile's mouth carefully as it opened and clamped shut again. Then, I closed my eyes.

'I haven't got all day,' Stephen called from the booth.

I ignored him and carefully counted to three, before tapping the ball towards the crocodile's mouth. I'd timed it perfectly. It reached the jaws just as they opened, and rolled past the gleaming white teeth into the beast.

'Yes!' I shouted. But then I watched in horror as the ball bumped up against something and trundled back towards my feet.

'What?' I cried. 'No way! There's something wrong with the crocodile.'

'Sorry,' Stephen said. 'You lose.'

'I am not having this,' I said, marching down the Astroturf fairway to the crocodile. I poked my mini club inside the mouth. I could feel something blocking the way through.

'There's something in there. I demand another turn!' I said, bending down to investigate. I peered in the crocodile's mouth to try and see what it was.

As I poked the club in between the jaws again, something flopped out.

I stifled a scream.

It was a hand.

FIFTEEN

An hour later, I was sitting on a swivel office chair with a blanket around my shoulders, sipping a lukewarm tea out of a chipped Jolly Jungle Crazy Golf mug, while Detective Lyons stared angrily at me. Police officers and forensic teams swarmed across the golf course, stretching yellow tape over the crocodile and photographing everything.

'Tell me again,' Detective Lyons said slowly, 'why you decided to come here?'

'I was trying to help,' I said quietly.

'I told you to sit tight while we handled this,' he said.

'You call this handling it?' I hissed, pointing to the body bag being hauled onto the green.

Several officers turned to look at us.

'Gwen, listen—' Lyons started.

I held my hand up to stop him. The last thing I needed was a lecture. I closed my eyes and all I could see was Josh's hand, covered in splashes of deep red blood. The only dead body I had seen before was my dad's, lying still in a hospital bed, and that wasn't very frightening. Just horribly, heart-achingly sad. But Josh's stiff, crooked fingers looked like a bloody, broken doll.

'Whoever did this obviously wanted the body to be found, Gwen,' Lyons said, more softly this time.

It occurred to me that Lyons was probably quite used to murder. He must've thought about them all day – well, at least from nine 'til five, anyway. I actually had no idea what hours a junior homicide cop worked.

'They wanted me to find it?' I asked, my voice beginning to wobble.

Lyons shook his head. 'Anyone could have found it. Now, focus, this is important,' he said. 'Did you see anyone else on the course when you came in, anything suspicious?'

'Just the guy in the booth,' I said. 'No one else.'

'Okay. We're talking to everyone who works here and checking the CCTV,' Lyons said. 'Someone must have seen something.'

I nodded and sipped my tea. Lyons knelt down next to me.

'It doesn't exactly look great that you were at the scene,' he said in a low voice so the other officers couldn't hear.

'What do you mean? I was at work all morning, the body was in the fucking crocodile, how could I…' I tailed off.

I could feel tears welling up behind my eyes. With everything that had happened, it was only just dawning on me that these circumstances might make me look a teeny bit, well, guilty.

'We're still ascertaining exactly when and where he was killed,' Lyons said, still quietly.

'The blood was still pouring out of him!' I cried.

The officers looked round at us again.

'It's possible the body was hidden somewhere previously,

and the killer placed it on the course at some point last night,' Lyons said.

'Oh right, so you're saying I dragged a dead, bleeding body onto a crazy golf course in the middle of the night, then turned up this morning so I could be here to find it? Is that what you reckon, *detective*? I think maybe you need to ask for a refund on that training programme.'

'Gwen, slow down, what I am trying to explain is—' he began.

'Don't bother,' I said, standing up. 'I need to go home.'

I was shaking, and on the verge of crying, but I didn't want him to see it. I needed to get away from this horrible place and home to Sarah.

'Sit down, this isn't over,' Lyons said. 'This is a major investigation. We have a team in Lewes working round the clock on this now. The Met want to get involved. We need to know where you are at all times.'

'Why, so you can make sure I don't murder anyone else?' I snapped.

Now all the other officers were *really* staring at us.

'It's okay,' Lyons said gently, pronouncing each word carefully. 'No one is accusing you of anything. We just need to make sure you're okay.'

'Fine, I'll be at home, I think you know where that is, don't you?' I said, and defiantly downed the rest of my tea.

'I'm sorry, Gwen, I really am,' he said. 'But we're going to need you to come to the station and go through a few things.'

I looked at him, trying to work out if this was just excellent police aftercare, or this was some sort of low-key stealth arrest.

'Do I have to?'

'I think it would be best if you did,' said a voice from behind him.

I looked up to see the pug-faced DCI Forrester looming above Lyons, and my heart sank.

SIXTEEN

I don't know if you've ever had to go to a police station. Newsflash: turns out it is not fun. I suppose it's never going to be for a good reason, but I always thought it would be at least a little bit exciting. It isn't. In fact, the Eastbourne police station was as mundane as any other workplace, not at all like a cool cop show with officers running about and shouting at each other in between dipping doughnuts in black coffee. It was more like a doctors' surgery, filled with miserable-looking people huddled on plastic chairs and a bored desk clerk who took my details and told me to wait.

After fifteen minutes, she called my name and I was led through security doors into another horribly plain room with a small TV screen hanging on the wall. A tape recorder sat on a table, ominously. I took a seat on yet *another* plastic chair and someone unmemorable brought me a cup of tea in a Styrofoam cup. After a minute of staring at it, DCI Forrester came in, carrying a laptop, followed by Lyons, who sat down opposite me. He managed an awkward half smile in my direction before pressing a button on the machine on the table and reeling off the time and date in a cold, official tone.

'We're just going to run through the timeline for the tape, Ms Turner,' he said. 'Don't worry, it's just so we have a record of everything.'

I shrugged.

'You remember Detective Chief Inspector Forrester,' Lyons continued, motioning to the man on his left with a swing of his Bic biro. 'I should tell you this interview is being recorded and you're free to leave at any time.'

DCI Forrester looked at me blankly, as if I was just another piece of luggage on the airport conveyor belt that wasn't his.

'Okay, hi,' I said, and then, leaning into the tape recorder: 'You can call me Gwen, by the way.'

'Thank you, Gwen,' Lyons said.

I realised I was shaking, and gripped my hands around my cup of tea. The heat that seeped through the Styrofoam pricked my fingers, but the pain was a good distraction.

'We're going to ask you some questions about what happened to Josh Little.'

'Wait, shouldn't I have a lawyer here or something?'

'You're entitled to a lawyer if you want one,' Forrester said, with absolutely zero emotion in his voice.

'It's okay, Gwen,' Detective Lyons said. 'We're not accusing you of anything, and you're not under arrest. We simply need to establish your whereabouts so we can eliminate you from any inquiries.'

I'd heard that line before. On TV, that's what the cops always said to the person they thought did it.

'I really don't know anything about Josh,' I sighed. 'I met him once, it was fine, we had some drinks. End of story.'

'When?' Forrester asked.

'Um, last Wednesday, I think? 8 p.m.'

Forrester leant towards me and spoke slowly. 'And where did you go?'

'Jolly Jungle Crazy Golf,' I said.

Lyons's eyes flicked towards his boss, who gave him an almost imperceptible nod.

'Who won the game?' Lyons asked.

'I don't remember,' I said.

'You don't remember?' Forrester said. 'I thought this was a good date?'

'I said it was fine,' I said.

'What time did you leave?'

'Around nine. I don't remember exactly.'

'Nine is early,' said Forrester.

'We didn't really hit it off,' I said.

'You didn't get on?' Forrester asked, arching an eyebrow.

Shit. Why the hell did I say that?

'I mean, look, we weren't a good match, so I made an excuse and got out of there,' I said.

Okay, so maybe that wasn't the whole, complete, *absolute* truth. But this wasn't the time for that. Right now, I was in damage-control mode.

'And where did you go afterwards?' Lyons asked.

'I got on the bus and went home. My flatmate, Sarah, ask her. She can vouch for me. We stayed up and watched TV.'

'What did you watch?'

'*The Real Housewives of New Orleans*. We always watch that.'

Forrester scribbled in his yellow lined pad.

'You're writing *that* down? You're writing *The Real Housewives of New Orleans* down?' I said. 'Why are you writing that down?'

'Did you hear from Josh again?' he asked, ignoring me.

I hesitated. I gripped my cup even tighter and took a sip, being extra careful not to spill it down my face, and tried to choose my next words just as carefully.

'Um, yeah, I think he messaged me to say thanks for coming out, or something like that,' I said.

'What time?' Lyons said.

'I'm not sure.'

'Can you check?'

'Well, I blocked him on the app,' I said. 'So no, I can't check.'

'You blocked him?' Forrester said, arching that bloody eyebrow so high that I thought it was going to fly off his head.

He scribbled something else down on the pad in front of him.

'Yes,' I said. 'Like I told you, it wasn't a good match.'

'And can you tell us why you went back to the golf course today?' Forrester asked.

'I told you, I was worried about Josh, I was worried someone might hurt him.'

'Can you think of a reason anyone would want to hurt Josh?' Lyons asked.

'I can't think of a reason why anyone would hurt anyone.' My voice was getting louder now. 'It's not something that would ever occur to me, because newsflash: I. am. not. a. murderer.'

There was a short silence.

'We'd like you to take a look at this,' Forrester said. He clicked the mousepad on his laptop and a screenshot appeared on the TV screen. 'These are messages we found on Josh's phone that we recovered from the crime scene.'

The image on the screen showed mine and Josh's chat from Connector. Staring me in the face was my last message to him. As I read it, my stomach flipped like it was rehearsing for next summer's Olympic gymnastics final.

Josh: You broke my hand, you crazy bitch

Gwen: If I see you again, it'll be your balls. Fuck off and die.

I looked at the screen, taking in my own words.

'Anything you want to tell me?' said Lyons.

I tried to compose myself.

'Well, number one, I am not crazy, I resent that. And number two, I gave him a *light* slap. If he thinks that's painful, then he has no idea what being hit by me really feels like.'

There was another silence.

'Gwen, do you want to take a minute,' Lyons said.

I leant into the tape recorder again. 'Yes, sorry, can we strike that from the record please.'

'That's not how this works,' Lyons said gently. 'This is a police station, not a courtroom, and only the judge gets to say that…'

'Okay, right. I know this looks bad, but I…' I stuttered. 'Fine, I hit him, but he asked for it.'

This time both officers scribbled in their notebooks hurriedly.

'Wait, look, just… just stop writing! This isn't what it looks like.'

'I think you better tell us what happened,' Lyons said, putting down his pen and looking me in the eyes. 'Right now.'

SEVENTEEN

'I'm at the bar, want a drink?' the text read.

Yes, of course I want a drink. I just got completely soaked while getting lost finding this stupid place, despite the seven-foot plastic gorilla hanging off the entrance. Get me a big f-off drink right now.

Sarah's just reminded me she's moving out at the end of the month, after she gets back from honeymoon in Vancouver, and there's no way I can afford to pay the full rent myself. Of course, I'd known this was coming for ages and had made only the most cursory attempts to find a new flatmate. But I had other much more important things to do, like googling 'do cats understand when you miaow back at them' or 'how old is the world's oldest egg'.

So it's fair to say I'm not in the most romantic frame of mind, but to be honest, the Jolly Jungle Crazy Golf is not one of Eastbourne's most romantic attractions. Sure, I suppose it could potentially be a fun place for a date, if you were feeling particularly ironic, in an amazingly good mood or bone dry. Reader, I am none of those things.

Tonight, Jolly Jungle Crazy Golf is full of people who are, and, after I push my way through them, I spot a man who looks, hmm, at least 80 per cent like Josh Little.

'Josh?' I ask, sticking my head into his field of vision and giving a little wave.

'Gwen!' he says, a broad smile spreading across his face, which is considerably less ruddy and damp than mine. 'Sorry, I just got served.'

He motions to a pint of lager sitting on the drip tray in front of him.

'Oh right, okay, no problem,' I say, immediately trying to catch the server's eye as she scuttles to the other end of the bar.

Please give me that pint right now, my brain is screaming. But my mouth says, 'I'll get myself one, no worries.'

Josh's app profile had informed me he was 34 and worked in recruitment. His hair was cropped close to the scalp, his skin was slightly shiny and he had the thick, knitted eyebrows of a Gallagher brother. Tonight, he is wearing what looked like a fresh-out-of-the-box dark green shirt, smart trainers and skinny jeans. I take a breath and compose myself. I need to chill out and have a good time, and not take my frustrations out on poor, dry Josh with his lovely big full pint.

Eventually, I manage to order a bottle of Corona and we squeeze our way through to the crazy golf course.

'So how was your day?' I ask, handing him one of the mini-sized clubs. 'On a scale of one to ten?'

'Uh, five, I guess,' he says. 'I sit in front of a computer all day, so it's pretty much the same every day to be honest.'

'How long have you been, um, recruiting people?' I say. 'That's right, isn't it? Recruitment?'

'Shit, probably more than ten years now,' he says. 'I started there straight out of school actually. It's not very

exciting but the pay's alright, and we get reduced gym membership.'

I place my day-glo orange golf ball on the marker at the start of the first hole. The aim seems to be to get it through the mouth of a large crocodile, which, if done accurately, would send the ball winding down its tail before depositing it neatly into the hole.

I knock my ball towards the crocodile, but it bounces off his jaw just as it closes, and trundles back towards me, ending up pretty much where it started.

'This place is cool,' I venture, watching my ball come to a stop at my feet. 'Good choice.'

'Yeah, my office is just round the corner, so it's really convenient for me,' he says.

'Oh right, it's actually quite far from me. I'm on the other side of town.'

'We come here after work on a Friday for a drink sometimes,' he continues. 'Can get pretty messy!'

'Oh yeah? Like dancing on the tables and snogging the head of accounts kinda messy?' I ask.

'Oh, I wish,' he says. He takes a gulp of his beer, leaving a half moon of foam across his upper lip, and smiles at me.

I look at Josh's almost-full pint and sigh inwardly. Despite having at least ten minutes head start on me, it looks like he's barely touched it 'til now. I wait to see if he would ask me about my day, or what I did, or at least ask what my favourite pizza topping is. But he doesn't, so instead we continue to sip our drinks in silence for a bit. I begin to think that this could turn into a very long night.

Josh picks up his club to take his turn against the grinning crocodile that has rocketed to number four on my list of all-time top nemeses. He waits until the crocodile's mouth closes, pauses, then sends his ball straight through its jaws. The ball runs through the tail, pops out the other end and plops straight into the hole.

'Hole in one!' he smiles.

'Wait, how did you do that?' I ask.

'There's a trick to it,' Josh says. 'It's all about timing. I've played this hole a hundred times, and you can get a hole in one every time. You wait 'til the crocodile closes his mouth, count to three, and hit the ball.'

A hundred times? How many women has he taken here, I wonder.

'So is this how you impress all your dates?' I ask.

'Hey, don't go telling everyone the secret,' he says.

'I'll take it to my grave,' I tell him.

We move on to the next hole, which involves knocking the ball through the legs of a giant tarantula, and set our drinks down on the little table by the tee.

'Now, with this one you just have to bounce it off her back leg there…' he begins, lining up his shot.

'Have you always lived in Eastbourne?' I interrupt before he can continue his tutorial.

'Yes,' he says. 'My parents are from here, and my grandparents too. I'd hate to grow up around here now though.'

'Why?' I ask.

'Too many immigrants these days.'

I study his face carefully for any micro-expressions that might have indicated it was just a misguided joke. I don't know what to say, so I say nothing, which turns out to be a mistake, as he takes that as a signal to carry on.

'It used to be quite a nice area until about five years ago,' he says. 'But they began to house a lot of refugees in the estate around the corner, and it all went downhill after that.'

'That sounds a little, um, racist, Josh,' I say.

'No, it's not like that,' he says, putting his club down. 'I'm not saying they're bad people. We've got one at work right now. Weird little geezer. I just think it's a mistake to let too many foreigners into the country, especially if they can't contribute.'

'What do you mean "can't contribute"?' I say. 'They get jobs and they pay their tax.'

'Yes, they do get jobs – they get our jobs.'

'I didn't picture you as a Russian Twitter bot,' I say, trying to force a laugh.

'Don't be facetious,' he says, looking a bit pissed off. 'I'm just saying we need to protect our borders.'

'Protect our borders?' I snort. 'They're not invading. These people need our help.'

'We need to look after our own people first. British people who live in tiny council flats in run-down estates. British people who are struggling to survive on Universal Credit and food banks. We can't all grow up in a nice middle-class, three-bedroom semi with nice parents and a nice school,' he says. 'That's you, right? Am I close?'

Annoyingly, he's actually not far off. Before Dad died, pretty much everything about my childhood had been 'nice'. My own bedroom. Two overprotective older sisters. One cat (okay he didn't last long, but that was an accident). Happily married parents who'd enjoyed the sort of benign, suburban romance that belonged to the last generation to marry young and stay together for the sake of the kids. As grateful as I was to them for providing such a stable home life, I did sometimes wonder if they were ever bored out of their minds. But none of this meant I didn't care about people who had a less advantageous start than I did.

'It's funny that you presume to know everything about me,' I say. 'Even though you haven't asked me a single question all night.'

'Oh, here we go,' he says. 'Don't tell me you're one of those women.'

'Those women?' I spit. 'What the hell is that supposed to mean?'

'I mean,' he says, taking a deep breath like he'd had to explain this a thousand times. 'Every woman I meet on Connector, you're all the same: privileged snobs with plenty of opinions, putting the world to rights while Daddy pays your rent.'

Those words cut through me, tearing open an old wound.

'I forked out a lot of money for these matches, and all of you think you're too good for the likes of me. I should ask for my money back,' he mutters.

'What are you talking about? It's a free app,' I tell him.

'Yeah, right,' he snorts. 'Free for you, maybe. I bet you can get as many matches as you like, no problem. Some of us aren't so fortunate.'

I can feel the heat rising through my damp cardigan as all the blood in my body rushes to my cheeks.

'I just thought we could have a nice chat and a round of golf, rather than you giving me a lecture on my own life,' I say. 'Look, let's just go back to knocking tiny balls past plastic animals, okay? I mean, you went to all the trouble of planning such a glamorous evening for us, I'd hate for us not to make the most of it.'

'Here we go again,' he says, almost under his breath, but deliberately loud enough for me to hear. 'Little Miss Better Than Everyone Else.'

'Excuse me?' I snap.

I was about to be evicted, my business was hanging on by a thread and this prick was telling me I was Eastbourne's answer to Kendall Jenner.

'Calm down,' Josh says. 'We're just having a conversation, like you wanted, right? It's people like you that make it so hard for guys like me to get a date in this town.'

'This is what you call a conversation?' I say. 'Because the last time I checked, conversations usually involve two people.'

I take a breath. I am actually about to lose my shit, and in danger of giving him all the evidence he needs to tell his mates I was an over-emotional woman who couldn't handle a little robust debate.

'Sorry, Josh,' I say calmly. 'I've had a really long, bad day and I don't think I'm in the mood for this. I'm going to go. Thank you for the drink.'

Then I remember.

'Oh, that's right, you didn't get me a drink,' I say. 'Have a nice night.'

I pick up his pint of beer, drain the last of it into my mouth and turn to leave.

'Hey, wait,' he says. 'Don't be stupid, we just got here.'

I don't answer. Is this guy nuts? Has he just wiped the last ten minutes from his memory? I start walking.

'I'm going home,' I say sharply.

'Jeez, you're so hormonal,' he says, standing up and placing a hand on my waist. 'We haven't even finished the hole yet. No wonder you're single.'

'Get off me,' I say, loudly this time. The place goes quiet as stunned faces turn to look at us.

'Jen, will you just sit down and discuss this,' he says, like he's speaking to a child. 'If you disagree with me, that's fine, but at least let's debate it like adults, instead of having a tantrum.'

'It's Gwen,' I say. 'And no.'

'Stop making a scene. You're embarrassing me,' he hisses.

Before I know it, I feel his hand on my wrist, grabbing me – not tightly, but firmly enough to make a fiery rush of adrenaline shoot through me. It's like his fingers burn my skin. I spin round, shaking him off.

Maybe it's because I've just downed the best part of a pint of overly strong pale ale, or maybe it's because I'm tired and cold and fed the fuck up, but in that moment, something breaks.

'I said get off me.' I lift the golf club above my head and swing it down hard. I see his mouth drop open in fear as the club collides with his forearm with a dull thud.

'Fuck!' he screams.

I turn around and walk out into the sleet without looking back. Each drop cools me down, and by the time I've stomped to the bus stop, my heart rate has just about returned to normal. Predictably, before I even reach my front door, he's already messaged me.

Josh: You broke my hand, you crazy bitch

I let him know exactly where he'll be bleeding from next if he ever messages me again, block him and go to bed.

EIGHTEEN

The two detectives looked at each other. I didn't know what to say, but saying nothing made me look pretty guilty. And I definitely knew I didn't want to throw up again.

'I know how this looks…' I started.

'It looks like he took you out for drinks, and in return you hit him with a golf club,' Forrester stated.

At that moment I really despised Detective Chief Inspector Forrester's squashed-up, angry, unloved face. I wanted to say that no, Josh *didn't* take me out for drinks, it *wasn't* my job to make sure he felt better about himself, or my responsibility to educate him.

Thankfully, I didn't say any of that out loud.

'Yep, that's about it,' I said instead.

Forrester wrote that down in his silly little notepad.

'Look, he was just a prick with a chip on his shoulder. I lost my temper and…' I started. 'It was nothing, okay? A light tap.'

'We'll speak to the staff there to verify that,' said Forrester.

'They'll verify he's a little prick, for sure,' I grumbled.

'Was,' said Forrester. '*Was* a "little prick".'

'Right,' I said, suddenly remembering. 'Was.'

I slumped back in my chair, defeated. Josh was a prick, but he didn't deserve to end up dead inside a plastic crocodile. Nobody did.

'So,' Lyons ventured. 'Is there anyone else, besides Josh, who might have a grudge against you?'

I thought for a second. 'There's this guy I matched with on Connector, Parker. He's been sending me weird messages. He knows something about these murders.'

'What makes you think that?' said Forrester.

'He's said some pretty out there stuff,' I said.

'I see,' said Forrester. 'What sort of "out there" stuff?'

'I mean, well, he knew what happened to Rob, you know?' I tailed off.

'What do you mean, he knew about it?'

'He sent me the news link,' I said. 'You know, about the body in the park.'

'Right, so he read about Rob Hamilton's death on the internet after it happened,' Forrester said. 'It was reported widely, Ms Turner. Hardly very "out there".'

'But Parker didn't *know* I'd been on a date with him,' I said. 'Don't you see? He had no reason to send me that.'

'Have other men sent you strange messages on this app?'

'Well, yeah, sure, I mean, once this guy asked me if I could shave his back, but—'

Forrester coughed into his fist. 'I mean threatening messages, Ms Turner.'

'Well, actually yes, I get sent a load of passive- and not-so-passive-aggressive crap on pretty much a daily basis,' I told him. 'Guys demanding dates, or getting pissed off if I dare to stop chatting to them. And then there's the really charming ones who tell me I look like a slut in my profile pictures.'

Forrester's face blushed. 'Well then,' he mumbled. 'So strange messages aren't out of the ordinary.'

'But I'm telling you, there's something different about this Parker guy. Something bad, if you just—'

'And exactly how many men have you been chatting to on this app?' Forrester interrupted.

'Um, well, depends on how you define "many",' I said, making air quotes with my fingers. 'Let's call it "a few".'

'We'll need their full names and phone numbers, please,' Forrester said.

'That's not really how it works—' I started.

I could see the blood rushing to Forrester's face as he grew more and more impatient with me. Lyons looked over at his colleague.

'I think what Ms Turner means is that the app doesn't provide her with that sort of information,' he said.

'Right, well, just the ones you've met up with then,' Forrester huffed.

'There was only a couple after Josh – the ones on the list I showed Detective Lyons, Dev and Sebastian,' I said. 'But, well, we didn't exactly, um, part on good terms either.'

'What does that mean?' Forrester barked.

'I ended up blocking them too.' I shrugged. 'Sorry.'

Forrester took a deep breath, like he was swallowing down a lifetime's worth of exasperation.

'We think it would be best if we examined your phone,' Forrester said. 'There were a number of threatening messages on Rob and Freddie's phones from the same unknown number.'

'Wait, you think I'm the one threatening these guys?'

'We know you threatened Josh Little,' Forrester said.

'It may be that someone else has a grudge against these men,' Lyons said. 'Do you have any ex-boyfriends who might be unhappy that you're dating?'

'Only my ex, Noah, Noah Coulter, I guess,' I said. 'But he's not capable of anything like this.'

'Are you sure about that?' Forrester asked.

'Of course!' I cried. 'If you met him, you'd see. He's... well, he's kind of amazing, really.'

'Has he contacted you recently?' Lyons asked.

'No,' I said, a hint of regret in my voice. 'I haven't seen or heard from him in weeks. Why? Are you going to speak to him? He's nothing to do with this.'

'It's just part of our inquiries, Ms Turner,' Lyons said.

'So he has no reason to be angry at you?' Forrester asked.

'No,' I lied. 'And anyway, he doesn't even know I'm dating. Or probably even care.'

'I spoke to your old manager at Delicioso,' Forrester said.

'You what?' I cried. 'Why?'

'We're just crossing the t's and dotting the i's, Gwen,' Lyons said.

Digging through the personal business of an innocent woman didn't sound like standard police paperwork to me, but I bit my lip and let him carry on.

'He told me you quit your job shortly after he offered you a big promotion,' Forrester went on.

'Yeah, I told you, me and my ex were starting a business together,' I said.

'Your boss said the promotion was a pretty big deal, and

you'd been working hard for it for months, campaigning for it, even.'

'Yes,' I said. 'So what?'

'That just seems like unusual behaviour,' he said, adopting a childlike tone, like he was intentionally playing dumb, trying to lure me into a trap. 'To work so hard for a promotion, then turn it down and dump your boyfriend.'

'I never said I dumped him,' I said.

'So he dumped you?' Forrester asked.

'Why does this even matter?' I said, my voice rising. 'People are getting murdered and you want the tea on my relationship?'

The room went quiet for a moment.

'Just answer the questions, Ms Turner, if you would,' Forrester said calmly. 'I should tell you, I tried to pay a visit to Noah Coulter this morning, and no one was home. Do you know if he's left town for any reason?'

'I told you,' I said quietly. 'I haven't heard from him since we split. Maybe he went to visit his mum. She's been sick.'

There was another silence while Forrester scribbled that down in his notebook.

'So, ah, who else would know the details of your dates?' Lyons asked eventually. 'Perhaps someone who felt protective towards you?'

'Well, there's Charlie. I usually give him a full debrief after a date the next day at work.'

'Charlie?'

'Charlie Edwards. He works with me in the mobile coffee van on the seafront.'

'And is he on this Connector app too?' Lyons asked.

'Oh God no. Charlie wouldn't go near dating apps. I think he just relies on Cosmic Ordering to bring him girlfriends. Probably why he's still single.'

'I see. Anything ever happened between the two of you?' Lyons looked straight at me, and I noticed his eyes weren't quite blue after all. In this light, they were almost grey.

'No,' I said. 'We're just friends. He's cute, I guess, and funny, and well, he's a nice guy and everything but a total space cadet.'

The two officers looked at each other.

'Your phone, if you wouldn't mind, Ms Turner,' Forrester said.

'Really? Isn't that a breach of data protection laws or something?' I said.

'Is there a reason why you don't want us to see your phone, Ms Turner?' Forrester fixed me with another one of his icy stares.

'Fine.' I pulled it out of my pocket and slid it across the table. 'The code is 1234.'

The two men exchanged a glance, and I started to wish I'd changed that stupid day-glo yellow phone case with a picture of a grinning unicorn on it.

'Has anyone else had access to this?' Forrester asked, picking up the phone with two fingers, like it was something his dog had just deposited on the pavement, and dropping it into a clear plastic zip bag.

'No,' I said. 'I'm the only one who knows my code. Well, Noah, he knows it. But, I told you, I've not seen him for months.'

'Your code is 1234, Ms Turner, it's hardly Fort Knox.' Forrester tapped the zip bag with his Bic.

'What about your flatmates? Family? People at work?' Lyons asked. 'Could they have used your phone?'

'Nope,' I replied. 'Ah, well I let Charlie use it to update the Cuppacino Twitter feed. And I sometimes lend it to Jamal, our regular, to FaceTime his mum because he says he doesn't have a smartphone. But that's it. Oh, and I left it at the pub on New Year's Eve for two nights because I lost it down the sofa cushions.'

'Right,' Forrester said, dropping his pen on the table and leaning back in his seat with a sigh.

I looked around the room, which I could confidently say was the worst room I'd ever had the misfortune to be sat in. Off-white paint was peeling off the bare walls and the tick of the solitary clock that hung behind Lyons was the only noise for a moment.

'Listen to me, you're wasting time,' I said eventually. 'I'm telling you, you need to find Parker. He's probably the one threatening these guys.'

Forrester coughed loudly through his thick moustache.

'We'll look into that, Ms Turner,' Forrester said. 'But right now, you need to stay put and let us do our job.'

'Totally fine by me,' I said. I'd seen quite enough dead bodies for one day. 'Can I go now then?'

'Yes, but we're going to ask you to remain in town,' Forrester said.

'Wait, does that mean I'm a suspect?' I asked.

Forrester coughed again. Lyons shifted in his seat.

'No, we call it a person of interest,' Lyons said. 'It just means that we need to eliminate you from our inquiries.'

I could feel the bile in my stomach rising again.

'You can eliminate me right now,' I told them, standing up. 'This has nothing to do with me.'

Neither man said anything. Eventually, when I started walking towards the door, Forrester mumbled something into the tape about terminating the interview. Lyons stood up.

'I'll see you out,' he said.

I ignored him and headed past the front desk, through the revolving door of the station and into the cold air, gulping it down like I'd been held underwater for too long.

NINETEEN

Outside, I walked down the concrete steps of the police station, sliding my hand over the cool railing. I stopped on the last step for a second to collect myself. All I wanted to do was call my mum, tell her everything. But I didn't know where I would even start.

'Gwen,' a voice said behind me, interrupting my reassembly. I turned around to see Detective Lyons.

'Nope,' I said and began walking away.

'Just wait for a second,' he said. 'Look, I know that was rough in there, but we're just making sure we have all the information. It's going to be okay.'

'Really?' I said. 'Is that your professional opinion?'

I didn't quite believe him, thanks to the sensation that my heart was about to hammer its way out of my ribcage.

'Yes,' he said, looking at me without blinking. 'Yes, it is. I promise you, one way or another, we'll get to the bottom of this thing.'

Thing. I thought that was a weird way to refer to what was fast amounting to a massacre of Eastbourne's entire population of single men, but fine. I sat down on the step and stared at my trainers.

'I know this seems crazy right now,' he went on. 'But I'm on your side. Let me give you a lift home. It's been a hell of a day.'

He motioned to an unmarked car parked by the station.

'No, I can walk,' I said. 'It's like, ten minutes from here.'

'Sure? Looks like rain.' Lyons squinted upwards at the clouds like the sky had asked him a difficult riddle.

'Nope. No. No way, it is definitely not going to rain,' I told him. 'I'm walking.'

'You haven't changed, have you?' Lyons said, shaking his head. He went over to the car, opened the door and paused. 'You can call me, I mean, you know, if you remember anything that might help.'

'Yeah, if I ever get my phone back.' I shrugged and began trudging back toward the flat in a daze. As specks of rain began to pepper my face, I silently cursed Lyons and his lovely dry Ford Fiesta. But I stamped onwards, trying to make sense of the last three hours.

When I finally turned into my road, I saw Sarah tugging a wheelie case out of our front door.

'Hey!' she chirped. 'I was worried I was going to miss you! Where have you been? I've been calling you.'

'Hiya,' I said, looking down at my now damp Converse.

'Gwen? You okay?' Sarah let go of the case handle and rushed towards me.

As soon as she reached me, I suddenly grabbed her in a hug and held tight.

'You look like shit,' she said, releasing me from her embrace and looking me up and down. 'What happened?'

'Thanks!' I said, trying to smile. 'I've, uh, I've been with the police. They think Rob's death wasn't an accident.'

'What the fuck?' she gasped. 'The wet lad? Why are they asking you about that?'

'They just wanted to know what happened on the date, when I last spoke to him, you know, that sort of stuff.'

I looked back at my feet. It felt bad lying to her, but what could I do? Tell her I just found a dead body in a plastic crocodile, and I was now the number one suspect in a murder inquiry? That would *really* dampen her wedding celebrations. She'd cancel everything and there was no way I was letting that happen. But once this was all over, I swore to myself I'd tell her everything.

'Bloody hell, Gwen,' Sarah said. 'I hope you told them the guy was a total loser and you never wanted to see him again.'

'Yeah right, that's exactly what I said, Sar. Turns out the police absolutely *love* it when you tell them how much you couldn't stand the victim.'

She made a face at me.

'What's with the suitcase anyway? Where are you going?' I asked.

'Me and Mum are hitting the spa, remember? She insisted on a pre-wedding pamper.' Sarah rolled her eyes at the thought of spending hours trapped, naked, in a steam room with her mother.

'Oh yeah, of course, I totally forgot,' I mumbled. My heart sank a little. I'd hoped we'd stay together tonight and drink cheap wine in front of some trashy romcom I'd seen a hundred times before.

'Richard's gone off to Brighton with the mountaineering lads for a couple of nights. I've told him to stay out of trouble.'

'I'm not sure how much trouble you can get in playing Settlers of Catan,' I said, attempting a smile.

Sarah narrowed her eyes at me and touched my arm. 'Gwen, are you okay? Usually when you're making lots of terrible jokes, it means you're trying to pretend everything is okay.'

'I'm just exhausted,' I said.

'Want me to cancel? We can get a bottle of plonk and just talk, if you like?'

'No,' I said firmly. 'No, no, no. You need a pamper for God's sake, look at you.'

She laughed. 'Okay, if you're sure?'

'Yeah, don't worry. Honestly, all I want to do is eat a Pop Tart in the bath and go straight to bed,' I said. 'Oh, hey, now *that's* a treatment they should offer at the spa.'

Sarah didn't smile.

'You know I can postpone the wedding, right?' She looked me in the eye. 'Never leave a sister behind, right? You're more important to me than some silly big dress and a piss-up.'

'Really?' I said. 'You'd do that?'

'No, of course not,' she smiled. 'I've got a three K deposit on the catering. But I am worried about you, Gwendolyn. You've been through a lot lately.'

'It's fine. I'm honestly *fine*,' I said. 'The police have finished with me, it's over. I can't wait for next week, it's going to be perfect.'

The wedding was going to be a predictably lavish affair, thanks to Sarah's uncanny ability to organise the living shit out of everything. She'd booked (with minimal input from Richard) a beautiful converted eighteenth-century church on Eastleigh Island, about fifteen miles off the coast, for

Valentine's Day. We'd gone for a nose round together after New Year, and it was like something out of *Rebecca*, or as Richard commented, 'a James Bond villain's evil lair'.

Sarah gave me another hard stare, as if she was trying to decipher if I was telling her the truth, and if I *wasn't,* then working out if arguing with me was worth it.

'Call me if you need anything at all, okay? Or you could even come join us. I'm only forty-five minutes away. I'm sure I can skip an hour of being lectured on my weight by my mother while being vigorously massaged by an old Greek woman.'

How could I tell her I wasn't allowed to leave town and didn't even have my phone? Say what you like about Sarah, but she was twice the friend I could ever be. With my dad, with Noah, she was always there to put me back together when my world fell apart. But this time, I wasn't going to let my problems spoil her happiness.

'I'm really going to miss you when you move out, you know,' I blurted.

Sarah looked at me quizzically again.

'Now I know something's up!' She smiled. 'Don't go all soft on me, Gwendolyn. I'll be just down the road. And you're far too busy dating anyway. You won't even notice I'm not there.'

'Yeah, I know, but…' I hesitated. 'You are totally, totally sure Richard really is The One?'

Sarah's face soured for a second.

'For the millionth time, of course I'm sure. He's the love of my life. I know that's hard to hear, after everything that happened with Noah, but—'

'It's not, I'm fine,' I said quickly. 'It's just—'

I stopped, and we stood there on the street in silence for a moment. I opened my mouth to say something else, but as I did, the heavens began to open.

'Look at this, I'm going to get soaked,' I said, holding my hand skywards and letting fat drops of rain splash into my palm. 'Go.'

She grabbed her case and shoved it in the back seat of her car, hugged me and climbed in the driver's seat. Before she closed the door, she turned to me as she clipped in her seat belt.

'Here if you need, remember?' she said.

'Ditto,' I said. 'Have fun. Don't forget to nick all the Molton Brown – we're almost out.'

'Gwen, when I move out, you know you're going to have to steal your own toiletries, right?' Sarah said as she slammed the car door.

I stuck my tongue out at her as she drove off, then went inside and collapsed up the stairs to my bed. After ten minutes of lying there with my eyes closed, listening to the rain lashing against the windows, I gave up making any sense of what had happened over the last forty-eight hours.

I took the napkin out of my pocket and smoothed it out on the duvet. I grabbed my lipstick from the bedside table and a cold shiver trickled through me as I dragged a thick red line through Josh's name. Three dead men, all of whom had been on a date with me in the past couple of weeks. Surely there had to be another connection, right? I mean, other than all being wankers.

I stared at the names again.

Rob. Freddie. Josh. Dev. Seb.

And, of course, there was the name I'd torn off the end of the napkin. Yes, they were all total knobheads, but none of them deserved to die.

I ran a bath and ransacked the flat for any rogue snacks. With zero Pop Tarts to be found, I loaded a plate with barely in-date cheese, half a bagel and the last scrape of Branston pickle and gingerly poked my foot into the bubbles. My heart sank. The water was only lukewarm, but I was committed now, and I lowered the rest of myself in. As I sat, unsatisfied, in the bath, I couldn't stop thinking about Parker, and why anyone would want to do this. I optimistically twisted the hot tap with my big toe and held my foot under it, hoping the water would warm up. It just got colder.

After a good few minutes of sitting in tepid bathwater scooping the remains of the pickle into my mouth, I got out and wrapped myself in a towel. As I dried off, I stared at the unrelenting rain from my bedroom window. By the glow of the street lamps, just down the road, I could see a car parked up by Mrs Bradshaw's house. Which was weird, because she always left it empty in the winter while she decamped to Benalmádena for Christmas. I rubbed away the condensation on the window and pushed my face up to the glass. I could just about make out a figure sitting in the driver's seat.

Someone was watching me.

TWENTY

'That fucker,' I snarled, pulling on my dressing gown.

I stomped out into the pouring rain, and when I reached the blue Ford Fiesta, I rapped my knuckles repeatedly on the driver's window. It took a good thirty seconds before Detective Lyons shook himself awake. When he did, he looked up to see my wet, angry face, partially obscured by a sodden fluffy dressing gown hood. A medley of emotions ran across his face: first confusion, then realisation and finally acceptance. Reluctantly, he wound down the window.

'Uh, Gwen, listen…' he mumbled.

'This your first stakeout, huh?' I asked.

'It's not a—'

'Don't even start,' I said. 'I'm not an idiot. Are you out here watching me?'

'No, not watching you exactly, I'd say it's more like watching out for you,' he said.

'Uh huh, and how exactly does that work with your eyes closed?' I asked.

Lyons ran a hand across his face. 'It's been a long day.'

'Then go home, *Dandy*,' I said. 'Is this even in the rules?

Are you allowed to just follow me around? I don't care if I'm a suspect, this is not okay.'

'You're not a suspect—' he started.

By now my dressing gown was heavy with cold rain. I leant against the car door and looked in at Lyons.

'Yeah, yeah, I know, I'm not a suspect, I'm a "person of interest". Well, I'm telling you, for a so-called person of interest, I'm really not that interesting. Go home to your wife.'

'I'm not married,' he said. 'Not any more.'

'Well, go home and jerk off then,' I said. With that, I turned and walked back into the flat with the utmost dignity, my pink dressing gown dragging in puddles behind me.

'Gwen, wait,' he shouted after me.

I got to my doorstep, walked inside and slammed the door behind me.

I sat on the sofa, furious, and went to text Sarah, before remembering I didn't have my damn phone. No phone, no snacks and now an increasingly damp sofa. I went upstairs and rubbed a towel roughly over my head, as if I was trying to rub out the thoughts in there.

Why were the police watching me? Did they really think I was capable of any of this? Or did they think I might be in danger?

Just then, there was a knock at the door. I knew who it was and no way was I going to answer it. But after three minutes of banging, I gave in and opened the door to see Lyons on the doorstep, looking wetter than I did.

'Don't you get issued with a standard police umbrella?' I asked.

'I was ringing the bell for quite a while,' he said, ignoring my question.

'It's broken,' I said. 'A bit like your code of ethics.'

Lyons stared at me, getting damper by the second.

'Look, I just came to give your phone back,' he said.

'And?' I asked. 'Did you find proof on there that I'm a bloodthirsty serial killer?'

'I know you didn't send those threatening messages, Gwen, but someone did.'

'It's Parker, I told you,' I said.

Lyons pinched the bridge of his nose. 'Parker,' he sighed. 'Whoever this Parker is, there isn't any indication that he's got anything to do with these murders, other than reading about them on the news. He's more than likely just another weirdo on the internet.'

I looked at him standing there, his hair flattened by the downpour and a hangdog expression on his face, and I couldn't help but feel a little sorry for him. Say what you like, but at least he *wasn't* a weirdo on the internet.

'If you really want to make sure I'm not a murderer, why don't you come inside. Case the joint. That's what you guys say, right?'

I stepped aside and motioned for him to enter.

'Here,' I said, taking the damp towel from around my shoulders and holding it out to him. He took it, despite looking at it like I'd just handed him a rotting carcass of a ferret, and came inside.

'Thanks,' he said, gingerly rubbing the towel across his head.

'I believe you're familiar with my lounge,' I said, as Lyons hung his sodden jacket on the coat stand and made his way into the front room.

He eyed his surroundings suspiciously. I noticed his white

shirt was slightly damp, and parts of it clung to his body, leaving the skin visible underneath.

'Take a seat,' I said, patting the sofa. 'Although your car is probably more comfortable than this piece of junk.'

If this sofa could talk, the tales it could tell. Sure, mostly tales of takeaway pizzas and spilt makeshift cocktails, but some genuinely exciting trysts too. Then I remembered that Richard and Sarah had probably had sex on this sofa on more than one occasion and I grimaced at the thought of it.

'So, are you going to tell me what the hell is going on, Aubrey?' I asked. 'I thought I wasn't a suspect? Do you really think I'm going to hop on a ferry to France and go on the run or something? That Forrester creep really thinks I'm something to do with this, doesn't he?'

'He thinks there's something you're not telling us,' Lyons said.

I looked down at my feet.

'Is there something you're not telling us, Gwen?'

'Is that why you're hanging around outside my house watching me? Because you think I'm lying to you?'

'I wasn't spying on you,' he said. 'I wanted to make sure you were safe.'

'Are *you* safe, that's the question?'

Lyons frowned at me, wiped the remaining drops of rain from his forehead and handed me back the towel.

'I should go back to the car,' he said.

I looked at his sad little face and shook my head.

'Nah, you're good,' I said. 'You should know, me and Grace used to go through your bedroom drawers all the time when you were out. I already know all your secrets. And I could use the company, to be honest.'

I fetched the emergency bag of Quavers from the kitchen and splayed the packet open on the coffee table. Lyons looked at them suspiciously before reaching into his pocket and pulling out my phone.

'Nice case, by the way,' he said.

'I keep telling people, it's ironic. So, um, did you look through all the chats on my Connector?' I asked sheepishly.

'Yes,' Lyons answered plainly. 'There were, well, quite a lot on there.'

I felt my cheeks blush.

'The guys on the napkin,' I said. 'I met them all on Connector. Can't you ask the people who made the app to give you their contact details?'

'They're based in Amsterdam,' Lyons said. 'We've put in a request but they're dragging their heels. There's a lot of data protection red tape to get through.'

I slumped down beside him on the sofa.

'Do you really think I'm in danger?' I asked.

'Well, if you're right, whoever is doing this is killing the men you dated in the order you dated them. So it's Dev who's in immediate danger.'

'But what happens when he gets to the end of the list?' I asked.

Lyons took a crisp and crunched it slowly.

'It won't get to that. We have a lead on Dev, Forrester is probably with him right now.'

I felt a wave of relief.

'What about Seb?'

'He's proving a little more tricky to track down,' Lyons said. 'It might have been easier if you hadn't blocked him.

Could you try and match with him on Connector again? There can't be that many profiles on there.'

'Um, no,' I said. 'That's not how it works. Once he's blocked, he's blocked. And there are literally *thousands* of people on there, Aubrey.'

'Really?' he sighed.

'Honestly, you have no idea what it's like on the dating scene. It's bloody hard work. You have to put the hours in, talking nonsense to hundreds of bellends in the vain hope that one of them turns out to have vaguely more personality than a baked potato.'

I loaded up Connector and showed him the screen.

'This is what I'm up against here,' I said, scrolling through a few random guys. 'Here, check it out.'

Lyons took the phone and began jabbing at the screen, flipping through profiles with his index finger, like he'd only just discovered touch screens.

'Jesus, Aubrey, you really have never been single, have you?'

'I have been single,' Lyons said. 'I *am* single. I've just never used these things before. You're right, there's too many profiles on here. How do you even choose one?'

'Slow down before you hurt yourself,' I said, taking my phone back off him. 'Here, look I'll show you.' I sat up, turned towards him and pushed my hair down over my face. 'Yes or no?'

'What?'

'I'm Jenny. I like going out to pubs and the cinema but equally lazy Sunday mornings with the papers. Swipe yes or no.'

'No,' he said.

I wiped my palm across my face, pulled my hair back and made a new expression.

'I'm Denise. I like lasagne and dislike Mondays. Yes or no?'

'Isn't that Garfield?' he said.

'Who's Garfield?'

'Gwen, you know who Garfield is,' he sighed. 'The big orange cat!'

'A big orange cat who likes lasagne?' I said. 'Sounds made up. Okay, last go.'

I wiped my palm across my face again and pouted.

'I am Gwen,' I said. 'I like pizza and solving murder mysteries. Yes or no?'

'Hmm, is there a "maybe" option?' Lyons smiled.

'No!' I shoved him in mock indignation.

'Alright, I'll think about it,' he said. 'But seriously, is dating really this shameless now?'

'Totally. One guy sent me a dick pic with a sepia filter, like it was from the Victorian era.'

Lyons looked faintly disgusted.

'Hey, it's not all bad,' I shrugged. 'You get to drink, flirt with cute boys and then never text them again. No commitment, no promises, no jealousy, no arguments, and no visiting in-laws. I get to spend my bank holidays in bed like you're supposed to. It's the perfect crime!'

'Don't you want something serious though, one day?' Lyons asked. 'Marriage and all that?'

'Doesn't seem like that worked out so well for you,' I said.

Lyons suddenly found the packet of Quavers very interesting.

'And Dev,' Lyons asked, changing the subject. 'Was he one of the good ones?'

'Yeah,' I said quietly. 'I guess he was, for a bit, anyway.'

'Hey, don't worry, we'll find him,' Lyons said, seeing my frown. 'What did you guys talk about on the date? Anything you can tell us might help speed up the search.'

'I don't know.' I said. 'The usual rubbish: star signs, the weather, public transport.'

Lyons looked at me in disbelief.

'He had really good hair, I remember that,' I said. 'And he's a Taurus. I think.'

'Star signs? That's what people talk about on dates now?' he said.

I thought hard.

'Okay, okay, wait, be quiet for a second, let me focus,' I said. 'I had to drink through most of these dates, to be honest. They all merge into one another. A lot of the time they were explaining the Marvel Cinematic Universe timeline in excruciating detail, or simultaneously patronising or insulting me while I—'

I stopped, catching myself. I remembered the thick lines dissecting Rob, Freddie and Josh's names on my napkin.

'I guess I didn't really know anything about any of them,' I said, realising as I said it that it was true. A lot of useless small talk, but nothing real.

Lyons took a deep breath. 'Just start from the beginning.'

TWENTY-ONE

Normally, I never would have swiped right on a profile like Dev's. A link to his Insta in the bio. A photo where he'd clearly blurred out his ex. Topless in 66 per cent of his photos and surrounded by women in the other 34 per cent. But, I had to admit, he was very good looking, with a cocky smile that said: I am at once confident, charming, quite probably amazing in bed and a complete bastard. But surely he can't be as bad as the last three guys. And who knows, perhaps he was hiding a winning personality under those rock-hard abs?

So when he sends me a faintly amusing opening gambit ('Come here often?'), I reply, and, after a couple of days of back and forth, it seems, despite all evidence to the contrary, Dev might actually possess the heralded trifecta so rarely found in the men of Eastbourne: funny, handsome and not a total dickhead.

Eventually, Dev had asked if I wanted to meet up.

Dev: How about bowling tonight?

Gwen: Yes! Sounds great. Love bowling.

Now, never tell anyone, but secretly, I hate bowling. But, luckily for Dev, I am willing to take one for the team and embarrass myself for an hour. By the time I get home from work that night, all I have to do is shower, find a suitable outfit and practise my best 'please tell me more about your podcast idea' face.

Shouting 'hi' to Sarah and Richard as I rush upstairs, I set about pulling some options from my wardrobe, aiming for that sweet spot between 'couldn't care less' and 'trying far too hard'. After choosing a denim playsuit, which I decide is both practical and cute, I sit cross-legged in front of the full-length mirror in the hallway to do my make-up while sipping a tequila and tonic and chewing on a piece of toast (sure, pre drinks were important, but so was lining my stomach).

Next, armed with a wide-toothed comb and my ghds, I drag my stubborn blonde mane in different directions for five minutes. I stare at the angry lion in the mirror (an angry lion who admittedly had totally nailed a smoky eye with flicks), defeated. It was getting late, so I scrape it up with both hands in desperation, then pull it back into a messy ponytail and make do.

On my way out, I present myself to Sarah, who deems me acceptable. It's hard comparing myself with her sometimes. With her long black glossy hair and always flawless make-up, Sarah looks like she has a secret second career as one of those models on hair dye boxes. Especially when sheathed in a tight cream polo neck, as she so often was at this time of year. It seems such a waste when she and Richard were permanently attached to the sofa these days.

'So this is your date night?' I ask, waving my hand

over the detritus of half-eaten Thai takeaway boxes and freshly filled wine glasses that basked in the glow of the TV screen.

'What?' Sarah says, not taking her eyes from the screen. 'We're living in the golden age of television!'

'Uh huh, well I guess you can regale your grandchildren with tales of Narcos *season five,' I say.*

'Actually, season two is the best season,' Richard pipes up.

'Good to know,' I say as I head for the door. 'Don't wait up.'

'We won't,' says Richard. 'I think I'll be just about ready to turn in after this episode.'

Sarah rolls her eyes and kisses Richard on the cheek as I mime putting a gun to my head and blowing my brains out.

Richard was the sort of man who would pray for a leaking tap just so he could drag Sarah on a three-hour circuit of B&Q on a Saturday. And let me tell you, pre-Richard Sarah wouldn't be caught dead near a B&Q. You'd more likely find her draining a bottle of Sauvignon Blanc in the pub next door. But the most thrilling part of an average evening in Richard's life was the 'da dum' that announced another night of Netflix. I always felt you could measure a person by whether they liked surprises or not. And Richard fucking hated them.

'Talking of getting horribly murdered,' Sarah says. 'Don't forget to pin me your location when you get there, just so I know where to send the police if he turns out to be a psychopath.'

'Hey, maybe a psychopath would make the perfect plus-one to the wedding,' I said. 'Imagine your mum's face when he starts stabbing everyone with the cake knife.'

'Gwen, that's not funny...' Richard began.

'I am officially rescinding that plus-one! I told you, I don't want some random arsehole at the wedding just cos you ran out of time and had to bring an estate agent,' Sarah says.

'What have you got against random arseholes? Some of my best friends are random arseholes,' I said, glancing towards Richard.

'Hey, wait a second—' Richard starts.

'Sorry, gotta go!' I say, opening the front door. 'Love you!'

With that, I step out into the cold air, my stomach full of butterflies. When I arrive at the trendy bowling place in the Hampden Park mall (all neon-lit alleys, American-diner-style booths and old-school rock and roll tunes), I'm pleased to see Dev in a crisp white T-shirt, tight black jeans and brogues.

In person, he's just as good looking as his pictures, with thick black eyelashes circling big, deep eyes almost the colour of dark gold.

'You look great,' he says, pecking me on the cheek when I make my big entrance.

'You too,' I say. 'You look like a fifties throwback.'

'Well, the choices for us guys are pretty limited,' he said, 'It's basically jeans, and then the choice between a shirt or a T-shirt.'

'Oh, how come I didn't get the shirt option then? Not classy enough for you?'

I once overheard a customer saying that if a guy showed up on a date wearing a T-shirt, she'd know they were splitting the bill. But me, I liked guys in T-shirts.

'I wanted to show off my biceps,' he smiles.

I glanced at his arms. I had to admit that, sure, there was some definition there.

'What do you think of my shoes?' He points to his feet.

'I genuinely could not give a shit about your shoes, Dev.'

'I thought the first thing a woman looks at is a guy's shoes?'

'There is nothing more boring than a man's shoes,' I tell him.

It was true. If I've seen one tan leather brogue, I've seen a million. No, make that two million because there's always two of the fuckers. When it comes to shoes, as long as it's not made of plastic and I can't see your feet through it, I'm happy.

'Drink?' he offers.

'Sure,' I say. 'Tequila and soda, please, with some lime if they have it.'

We stand at the bar and exchange the usual small talk about our days. I tell him I've spent all morning cleaning the flat and my hands are already weakened.

'Therefore, my bowling prowess will not be up to its usual excellent standards,' I tell him.

'That's good, because I am a terrible loser,' he says.

'Aw, don't worry, even with a weak hand, I'm still going to thrash you,' I say, stroking his arm.

'Oh, I don't think so,' he smiles. 'I take all my first dates here, so my aim is getting pretty good.'

'Oh really, and where do you go on second dates?' I ask.

'I've never got that far,' he says. 'Yet.'

I can already tell this guy is going to drive me crazy, but I'm not sure if it's going to be in a good or a bad way.

'Okay, let's put a bet on it,' he says. 'Loser buys the winner any drink he wants from the bar.'

'He or she,' I point out.

'Nah,' he says. 'I think I had it right the first time.'

We swap our footwear for ill-fitting bowling shoes and take our drinks over to the lanes. Impressively, Dev had pre-booked and even ordered milkshakes and fries to be brought over to us. As I chuck balls down the gutter and chips into my mouth with equal abandon, he tells me about his job in an advertising agency.

'It's a really small firm, Thoughterfall Media.'

'Thoughterfall. What, like a waterfall?'

'Mmm, yeah, but instead of water, it's a waterfall of amazing thoughts,' he laughs. 'Okay, look, basically, I have to think up slogans to sell toothpaste and pet food.'

'Oh, so you're like Eastbourne's answer to Don Draper then?' I ask.

'Sure,' he says. 'Only without the alcoholism and misogyny.'

I laugh, just as I was throwing a ball, and for once it wobbled into the centre of the lane, knocking down most of the pins.

'See, told you I was going to beat you,' I say, trying to hide my surprise.

His dark fringe flops adorably over his eyes as he studies the scoreboard on the screen above our alley.

'Hmm, not sure maths is your strong point either,' he says, pulling his hair back and squinting. 'I make that 46 to 99.'

I throw a chip at him. I always find throwing food at boys to be a good flirting tactic.

'Don't worry, another two strikes and you might catch up,' he says.

I throw another ball down the lane. It drifts off to the left and drops into the gutter with a disheartening clunk.

'Guess I'm a one strike kinda girl,' I say with a shrug.

'Is that right? And how many strikes do I get?' he smiles.

'We still talking about bowling here?' I ask.

He pops a chip in his mouth and picks up his ball. With one graceful swing, he sends it flying artfully into the centre pin, sending them all crashing over. He winks at me, annoyingly.

I dip a chip into my strawberry milkshake and eat it.

'That's gross!' he says.

'I call this "sending a potato on holiday",' I tell him.

'I call it incredibly disgusting,' he says.

'But also incredibly sexy?' I ask.

After destroying me at bowling, we're ejected from our lane by an apologetic usher, and head to the bar. Luckily, the alley has a limited selection of premium drinks, so he settles for a double of a cheap bourbon as his prize.

'So how have you found dating on Connector?' I ask.

'Mostly terrible,' he laughs. 'In fact, you're the first person I've met who actually seems normal.'

'I'm not sure that's a compliment,' I say.

'Okay, well, your bowling is not normal, if that helps?' He smiles. 'But the rest of you seems pretty good.'

'So, you've been on a lot of bad dates then?' I ask, innocently sipping on my beer bottle.

'Connector is wild, if you know how to use it right,' he says. 'But I guess the law of averages means if you go on a lot of dates, you're going to get a few bad apples. One woman ordered a bottle of champagne to the table and then didn't even split the bill at the end of the meal,' he says. 'Another one tried to stick her hand down my pants in full view of the whole pub.'

'What do you mean "know how to use Connector right"?' I ask.

I wasn't aware there was a way to 'use Connector right'. But up until tonight, I'd managed to pick a run of absolute creeps, so maybe I had been using it wrong all this time.

'Let's just say that my profile required a little fine-tuning before I got it just right,' Dev says, his eyes narrowing as if he's working out if he can trust me. 'Anyway, what about you, have you been on many dates?'

'One or two,' I say. 'I was seeing someone up until not that long ago.'

'What happened?'

'I guess I freaked out,' I say.

'Freaked out?' he asks.

'Um, yeah. I mean, we were going to travel the country together, give up our jobs, the whole thing. It was his idea, his dream, but it was never mine. I wanted to do it for him, you know? In the end, it was just too much. I couldn't go through with it.'

The truth was a little more complicated than that. When Noah's mum got ill, he changed. Not in a bad way, but before that, he'd always been the sensible one, which gave me licence to be the stupid one, making rash decisions and running off head first into everything without thinking. He got this newfound sense of 'life is too short' just when I was starting to, I dunno, settle down a bit?

'Note to self, don't propose to Gwen on the first date,' Dev smiles. 'So newly single and dipping your toe back in the world of dating?'

'The last time I was single, people only used dating apps for hook-ups,' I say. 'Now everyone seems to be meeting their future husbands on them.'

'Ah, so this isn't a hook-up then?' he smiles.

I blush and suddenly find the label on my bottle incredibly interesting.

'Depends if you play your cards right,' I say, getting up. 'Excuse me a minute.'

In the bathroom, after checking my make-up and cursing my stupid hair, I text Sarah.

Gwen: Just thrashing him at bowling, and now having a victory drink. He's actually pretty nice!

Sarah: He definitely let you win, didn't he? Be careful. Don't let him take advantage of you.

Gwen: Chill your beans, he's far too hot to be a psychopath.

Sarah: Wait, you're not planning on bringing him home tonight are you, you reprobate?

Gwen: Not if you and Richard are still on the sofa surrounded by takeaway boxes, no.

She replies with an eye-rolling emoji (her favourite).

I quickly dismiss the four Connector alerts on my screen demanding attention, and stuff the phone back in my pocket. When I sit back down at our table, Dev has ordered another round. I'm already more than a little tipsy, but for the first time in ages, I'm attracted to someone, and I feel like I can let my guard down. It's weird, but it feels a bit like a betrayal. Like I'm taking the first step towards leaving Noah behind. Part of that scares me a little, and part of it excites me.

'Cheers,' I say, picking up my bottle and chinking it against his whiskey glass. 'So how long have you been single?'

'Who said I was single?' he laughs. 'Maybe I have a harem of lovers back home?'

'So you're telling me you're a polyamorous Don Draper bowling champion?' I say. 'I really have hit the jackpot.'

'Let's play a game,' he says.

'Another one?' I ask. 'I'm not sure I'm up for another thrashing tonight.'

'Oh really…' he begins, raising an eyebrow.

'Stop that right there.' I smile, holding up my finger. 'That's quite enough of that. Tell me, what's the game?'

'Let me see if I can guess your star sign,' he says.

'Don't tell me you believe in that shit?' I scoff.

'No, but I reckon I'm about 6 per cent psychic so let's just try, shall we?' he says. 'You, Gwen, are a classic Gemini.'

'Wrong. Hah!'

'Cancer then.'

'Lucky guess,' I say. 'I wish it wasn't though. I hate my star sign. For a start, it's called cancer, which absolutely nobody wants, and two, it's a freaking crab! Who wants to be a crab?'

Dev gets his phone out and begins typing something into Google.

'Okay, let's see if you're a typical Cancer,' he says, and starts reading aloud. 'Hmm, says here, you should be generous, empathetic and innovative.'

'Those are true, actually!' I say. 'Hang on, what bad things does it say?'

'So, according to ZodiacRevealed.com, you're extremely secretive, scared to be alone and terrified of taking anything seriously.'

'Charming,' I say. But to be fair, the guys at Zodiac Revealed were kinda spot-on.

'Hmm, maybe there is something to this stuff after all,' I say.

'Well, that's interesting,' Dev says. 'Because I was actually reading out the traits for Gemini. So, looks like maybe I was right to begin with…'

I wish we still had chips so I could throw another one at him. But knowing him, he'd probably catch it in his mouth.

'Fine, what star sign are you then?' I say.

'Hang on, let me just check,' he says, tapping on his phone. '"What sign is most sexually compatible with a Cancer…"'

'I don't think we need ZodiacRevealed.com to tell us that,' I say. 'It's the little known constellation in the southern hemisphere, "The Douchebag".'

Dev laughs and tips the rest of his whiskey down his throat before setting his big brown eyes on me.

'Shall we go?' he says.

As we walk out, side by side, he suddenly takes my hand and pulls me into a dark corner next to the fire exit. Shielded from the crowds, he puts his hand on my waist. I push him towards the wall and he kisses me. I kiss him back, harder.

'Sorry for the diversion,' he says. 'Couldn't help myself.'

'I love a diversion. Let's get out of here,' I say.

'Here,' he says, pushing open the fire door behind us, and we slip into the mall. The noise of balls crashing into pins fades behind us.

We rush, giggling like truants, to the escalator. He stands on the step in front of me, so his head is level with mine, his eyes look directly into mine and our lips line up perfectly.

Turns out this one really is six foot one. I can feel the heat of his body as he leans closer, until our mouths are so close, all it would take is a knock from someone coming past us and we'd be kissing again. As it happens, I don't wait for that. I slip my fingers through his belt loops and pull him towards me, closing the gap between us.

We're still kissing when the escalator tips us off into the car park. Outside, where the air is cold and fresh, he presses me against the wall. I can feel his hands moving towards the buttons on my playsuit. He moves his lips down to my neck, and gently undoes the top button. When I feel him slip his hand inside and over my bra, I'm more impressed than surprised.

'Let's go somewhere warmer,' I say, pulling up the Uber app on my phone.

'Your place?' he asks.

'We could do, but my flatmate and her fiancé are there,' I say. 'What about yours?'

There's a beat.

'Give me one second,' he says, checking his phone. 'Okay, yeah, my roommate is away tonight. We can go to mine.'

I hand him my phone and he taps the address in. When the Uber arrives, the driver has to beep his horn to interrupt us kissing, and we break off long enough to climb in the back seat.

I've only just managed to pull my seat belt on when Dev starts running a hand up my thigh.

'You're going to ruin my 4.5 star rating,' I say, glancing at the driver in the rear-view mirror.

'On the contrary,' he smiles, reaching over to kiss me again. 'I think this is going to get you that extra half star.'

Just then, a ringtone sings out and breaks the moment. Dev pulls away and fishes in his pocket for the offending phone. As he goes to decline the call, he pauses for a moment. I can see his eyes glint in the darkness as they register the name on the screen. He taps the red button and drops the phone on the back seat. Moments later, the screen lights up again with a message. Dev's face contorts in what looks like fear.

'I'm really sorry, something's come up. I can't... you know. Can we do this some other time?'

'Wait, what?' I say. 'Is everything okay?'

'Yeah, um, it's my, it's just my, uh, roommate,' he mumbles. 'I gotta get back, sorry.'

'I thought he wasn't there?'

Dev doesn't say anything, instead he looks out the window. The atmosphere in the car changes in an instant. It's gone from a sauna to a plunge pool in here. I catch the eyes of the driver in the mirror again, and I swear he can feel it too.

'Can you make an extra stop?' I ask him, doing up my buttons as my heart rate tumbles.

'Sorry, I can only drop off at the address you put in the app,' he replies.

'Okay fine, um, don't worry, I'll get out at the next traffic lights.'

The Uber pulls up to the kerb, and I flick off my seat belt.

'Gwen, wait,' Dev says, leaning over to kiss me on the lips. 'I had a great time.'

'Me too,' I say, climbing out into the cold. And it's so very close to being true.

As I begin trudging back to my flat, I send Dev a message – 'hey, let me know if everything's okay' – but by the time

I've completed the twenty-five-minute walk home, there's no reply.

It's only after I get home and fall dramatically onto my bed that I notice I still have my bowling shoes on.

TWENTY-TWO

'And you never heard from him again?' Lyons asked after I'd finished.

'I tried messaging him, but the app wouldn't let me. He must've blocked me,' I said.

'He ghosted you, is that how that works?'

'No!' I said. 'Not *necessarily*. He looked terrified when he got that message in the cab, like he was in serious trouble. Just like Rob did in the park. What if someone was threatening him? What if that message was from Parker? What if the reason I never heard from him is because he's… dead?'

I couldn't hide the panic in my voice.

'Gwen, it's okay. Dev is not dead,' Lyons said, placing his hand on my shoulder. 'DCI Forrester and our team are probably at his address right now.'

'Probably isn't good enough! I warned you about Josh and look what happened. You need to find Dev, now. In case you hadn't noticed,' I said, overenunciating the words to make sure he really got the point, 'People. Are. Dying.'

'I am well aware of that, *Ms Turner*,' he said, with a hint of annoyance in his voice. 'Rest assured, we are working around the clock on this, and we'll keep you informed of developments.'

'Round the clock, huh? Yeah, so I noticed,' I said.

'Gwen, that's not—' he started before being interrupted by his mobile ringing. He gave me a hard look as he answered it and walked off into the kitchen area.

I watched from the sofa, scoffing the last of the Quavers as I tried my best to listen.

'Well?' I asked when he came back into the lounge.

'That was Forrester,' Lyons said. 'It's not good news. Apparently Dev hasn't come home. I have to go.'

'Wait, he's missing?' I said. I looked at the time on my phone, it was almost 2 a.m.

'Forrester spoke to Dev's wife,' Lyons said. 'She hasn't seen him since he went out with a friend for a quick drink earlier this evening, and he's not responding to calls or messages.'

'I'm sorry, his what?'

'His wife,' Lyons said.

TWENTY-THREE

Dev was married – that made perfect sense now. There was no 'emergency.' He wasn't getting some sinister message from Parker or anyone else. It was his wife who had texted him on our date. But if no one was threatening him, then where the hell was he?

Lyons left quickly after his call with Forrester, and I'd eventually fallen asleep. The next morning I woke up far too early and tried desperately to go back to sleep. When that didn't work, I wrapped myself up in the duvet, a makeshift cocoon, and closed my eyes. I hoped that maybe when I opened them this would all be over, and I would emerge as a beautiful butterfly. When that got boring, I poked my hand gingerly out of the covers and retrieved my phone from the bedside cabinet. I jabbed at the screen to see if there were any new messages. Nothing.

Rather than spend the day in bed staring intermittently between the ceiling and my phone, I dragged myself out of the flat, picked up my bike and cycled to work. When Charlie saw me pedalling towards the van, he quickly stuffed his vape pen in his pocket.

'Just opening up, boss,' he said.

'Don't bother,' I said. 'Gimme a puff of that. You're not going to believe what happened.'

We sat down, leaning our backs on the van, and watched the sun finish its ascent over the beach. Charlie grabbed a couple of yesterday's unsold sandwiches as I filled him in on everything that had happened.

'A dead body?' Charlie gasped. 'This is too much, Gwen.'

'Well, technically I only saw a dead *hand*, not a whole dead body,' I said.

'Still, that's pretty wild,' Charlie said.

'And worse, now Dev is missing,' I said. 'This is awful, it's all my fault and I have no idea what to do next.'

'And you think this Parker dude has something to do with it?'

The name made me shiver. I pulled out my phone and checked Connector again. Still nothing.

'I honestly don't know what to think any more,' I sighed, fishing the cucumber out of a soggy chicken salad bap that had been languishing on the counter all night. I'd stupidly let Charlie take first pick, and I think he took some perverse delight in forcing me to eat sandwiches full of cucumber (officially the world's lamest vegetable).

'The police don't buy it. They think it's just some drug deal gone wrong, but I swear to you, there's something off about Parker. Somehow he's involved in all this.'

'Let's have a look at this potential serial killer then,' Charlie said.

I handed over my phone, and Charlie flicked through Parker's profile pictures.

'Dude looks uber basic, Gwen.'

'Yeah, well they all do when you reduce them to a Top Trump card!' I said. 'Does he seem like a murderer, though? That's the gazillion dollar question.'

'Well, statistically, if you insist on swiping right on every prick in Eastbourne, then you're going to hit on a psychopath eventually.'

Charlie had been single since I'd known him, and didn't seem very interested in changing that. He always said he was waiting for the right person to find *him*, and whether it took months or decades, it would arrive when they were both ready. I thought that was so much zodiac bullshit.

'That is not helpful right now, Charlie,' I said, flinging limp slices of cucumber onto the cold concrete promenade.

'There's a bin right there!' he tutted, watching as I narrowly missed hitting a bemused seagull.

'Chill out, Greta, they biodegrade,' I told him.

He rolled his eyes and went back to looking at my phone. The seagull began pecking suspiciously at the cucumber, as if it was a strange delicacy from a foreign land that he felt under obligation to try.

'What does Sarah think about all this?' Charlie asked.

'Not told her,' I said.

'You've not told your best friend that you're the number one suspect in a murder inquiry?'

'The wedding, genius,' I said. 'It's days away. I can't ruin it for her, whatever happens.'

'Oh yeah, Eastbourne's most glamorous couple, finally tying the knot at the wedding of the century,' Charlie groaned.

'Aw, you *still* not over not getting invited?' I rubbed his floppy mop of hair.

'Richard was my mentor!' Charlie said. 'He taught me everything I know about Java.'

'Yep, until you jacked it all in to take over the world in an ice cream van with me. And now you're going to miss Richard's epic speech about wooing Sarah with a PowerPoint presentation in a Milton Keynes conference centre.'

Charlie snorted.

'He never met her at a work conference,' he said. 'Richard told me once – Sarah swore him to secrecy – they met on Connector.'

'What?' I cried. 'She never told me that! She was always so proud of how they met in real life, like proper old-school boomers.'

'Nope, never happened,' said Charlie. 'Sarah just wanted people to think that. I think their first date was in the Nando's on the high street.'

That stung a little. Actually, more than a little. Sarah normally told me *everything*.

'Wow,' I said. 'I'm shocked. Not about Nando's, I mean, we all know Richard does love a Nando's, but I can't believe Sarah never told me that. She's always telling me to get off this app.'

'Ah, you know Sarah, her whole life is a fairy tale. She'd die before admitting she met the love of her life in a chicken shop. She'll swear blind she stumbled into Prince Charming in an enchanted forest or something.'

'I'm not sure there are many enchanted forests off the A26,' I said. 'But yeah, you're right, Nando's is totally off-brand for Sarah.'

'And she was right about Connector,' Charlie said. 'It's bad news, boss. This Parker dude could literally be *anyone*. We should reverse image search his profile pictures and find out who he *really* is.'

I shivered again. I didn't want to say, but the idea of coming face to face with Parker terrified me.

'That's a job for the police,' I said quickly. 'But maybe I should try and find Dev.'

'Going looking for your exes didn't work out so well last time, did it?' he said.

'For the last time, they are not my exes—' I started.

'Anyway, if anyone deserves to die, it's that guy. Cheating bastard.'

'Charlie!' I cried. 'First of all, no he doesn't, and second, what about his wife? If he hadn't gone on a date with me, he never would be mixed up in any of this.'

'Well, maybe he shouldn't have screwed around then,' Charlie said. 'Besides, you just said the police think this is all some sort of drugs deal gone wrong.'

'Whatever it is, I can't just sit around here serving cappuccinos while he's out there, God knows where…'

'Look around, boss, we aren't serving anything to anyone.'

Just then, a cold wind blew across the beachfront, knocking over the pots of cutlery on the tables. I shivered. Dev could be in danger *right now.* I couldn't just let him end up like Josh, could I? The police seemed more concerned about me skipping town, or some mysterious seaside drug cartel of Eastbourne fuckboys, than they did about finding Dev and Seb. It was my fault Parker was after them. I couldn't just wait for them to die.

I got out my phone to call Lyons, but there was a Connector notification blinking at me.

New message from Parker.

I ran my thumb across it and it popped up on the screen.

Parker: You're ignoring me now? I told you I was sorry. Do you really need me to prove to you how sorry I am?

A sort of acrid bile rose in my throat, a cocktail of fear and anger burning up from inside of me. Parker knew something about all this, I was sure of it. I couldn't just sit here and wait.

'Look after the van for me for a couple of hours, will you?' I said.

'Where are you going?' he asked. 'You have no idea where this Dev is.'

'His address will still be in my Uber app,' I said. 'I can start there. Speak to his wife.'

'Oh, she's gonna *love* that,' Charlie said.

'I have to do something,' I said, getting up and unlocking my bike. 'The police said that Dev went out for a drink with a mate last night. What if that mate was Parker? I can show Dev's wife his profile picture, and maybe she'll recognise him.'

Balancing my phone on my handlebars, I cycled through the town centre to the nice, slightly posher part of Eastbourne. The statue of the Duke of Devonshire divided the two parts of town, with the nicer bits towards the west, and the rest, including me, to the east. Eventually, I rode up outside a nice semi-detached in Holywell. I stood on the doorstep and repeatedly rang the bell.

No answer.

I lifted the letterbox and tried to peek through.

'Hello?' I shouted. Even if she was home, I didn't know what the hell I was going to say to her.

I looked down and noticed the doormat had 'Burglars, my neighbours have better stuff' written on it in multicoloured stencilled letters. Rolling my eyes, I stepped back and looked up at the house. Dev lived here? I was expecting a stylish flat somewhere, but this reminded me a bit of my parents' place – a proper grown-up house, with ivy crawling up the brickwork and a pebble driveway and everything.

After knocking on the door and ringing the bell again, I peered through the lounge window, straining to see past the partially closed curtains into the darkness of the front room. It didn't look like anyone was home. I briefly considered calling a locksmith, but if Dev's dead body was lying in the hallway, well, that was really going to be hard to explain.

Finally, I heard some footsteps approaching, and the front door swung open to reveal a very pregnant woman.

'Can I help you?' she asked, a hand resting protectively on her belly.

I couldn't reply immediately as my jaw was hanging somewhere around my knees. Dev had not only been cheating on his wife, he'd been cheating on his heavily pregnant wife.

'Um, hi,' I said eventually. 'Are you Dev's wife?'

She was beautiful, ticking all the clichés a pregnant woman is supposed to: glowing skin, lush hair and a wary look in her eyes that says 'I will kill you if you come between me and my family'.

'Why?' she said, her voice rising an octave. 'Have you seen him?'

'Ah, no, sorry,' I said. 'So, um, you don't know me, but I'm a, well, I'm a friend of Dev's from work. And I've been looking for him, and I, er, I thought he might have gone out with this colleague of ours.'

I got my phone out and held up Parker's photo.

'You work with Dev?' she asked.

'Yeah, that's right, at the…' I stopped as my brain hurriedly tried to remember where Dev said he worked. 'At the advertising agency! I'm the one who writes everything on the big whiteboard when we do the brainstorms. I'm basically in charge of the marker pens. It's actually a really intrinsic role…'

Dev's wife didn't wait for me to finish before taking the phone from my hand and peering at the image.

'I've never seen him before. Who is he?' she said.

'Uh, Parker,' I said. 'Does that name mean anything to you? Did he say who he was going out with?'

'Sorry, what did you say your name was again?'

'Gwen,' I said. 'My name is Gwen. It's lovely to meet you.'

I looked down at her bump and twenty thousand pinpricks of guilt pricked me, like I was being subjected to the world's shittest acupuncture session.

'He didn't say who he was meeting,' she said. 'But last time he went out drinking with a friend, he came back absolutely plastered, wearing those.'

She pointed at the shoe rack by the door. There, alongside several pairs of shiny brown brogues and some women's trainers, was a pair of bowling shoes.

TWENTY-FOUR

Ten minutes later, I was cycling up to the mall as fast as my legs would allow. It wasn't yet nine, so nothing was open, and I stashed my bike in the empty car park.

Of course Dev hadn't gone out for a drink with a 'mate' – he'd gone on a date. He'd told me that he always took his dates to the bowling alley, and if that was true, I could find him here.

I went up the escalator to the front entrance only to find the door of the alley swinging wide open. Poking my head inside, I felt around for the light switches near the door. When the hall flickered into view, I was hit by a smell of disinfectant mixed with sweaty bowling shoes.

'Hello?' I shouted, my voice echoing off the polished fibreglass of the lanes.

It was weird seeing the place completely empty, and I had an acute sense of being somewhere I shouldn't be.

I poked my head into the cloakroom, which, with a random collection of forgotten coats and a nice handbag from the mid-2000s, bore a distinct resemblance to my own closet. I walked past the bar where Dev and I had got drunk, and ran my hand across the plywood. It didn't seem that long ago that we'd been sitting here chatting shit about horoscopes.

Suddenly, there was a loud noise from the direction of the bathrooms. It sounded like something falling over.

'Dev?' I called out, my voice shaking. 'Is that you?'

I looked around for anything I could use as a weapon, but my choices were limited to a half-empty vodka bottle or a bowling ball I could barely lift. So I went over to the men's bathroom door and placed my ear against it.

Nothing.

Gulping down the cold saliva gathering in my mouth, I pushed the door open slowly with my shoulder. The lights flickered on automatically, revealing nothing but a grubby urinal and a row of three stalls. One by one, I kicked open the doors of each stall and peered inside. When I got to the last one, I pushed the door open gingerly with my foot.

I looked inside and gasped.

'Jesus Christ,' I said.

Sitting on the toilet, his legs bound with a cable tie and his hands behind his back, was Dev.

A cloth gag was pulled tightly around his mouth, and his hair was damp and matted with sweat. He looked unconscious.

'Dev, are you alright?'

There was a gash on his right temple, and he was bleeding quite heavily.

'Dev!' I grabbed his face with both my hands. 'Wake up!'

His eyelids fluttered open and he looked straight at me.

'Are you alright?' I asked.

He grunted back incomprehensibly, but I figured it was probably a 'no'.

'Come on, let's get out of here,' I said.

I noticed something was Sellotaped to his chest. I leant in and pulled it off. It was a grainy black-and-white photo showing an ultrasound of a tiny baby. I felt like I'd been punched in the stomach.

'Dev, is this yours? This is your baby?'

He spluttered through the gag, trying to speak.

'What?' I asked, leaning in closer. 'I can't understand you, let me—'

Suddenly I saw his eyes widen and he began grunting wildly.

'Give me a second!' I said. 'Hold still and I can try and—'

I pulled the gag from his mouth.

'Get away from me!' he spat.

'What are you talking about?'

'You're going to kill me because I cheated on my wife? You're crazy!' he garbled.

'I'm not going to do anything!' I cried. 'Just hold still and I'll untie you.'

As I fiddled with the cable ties, I heard the noise of a door creaking from behind me. I froze.

'Just let me go, please, I'll never—'

'Shut up a second, will you? I think someone's here.'

'Help!' Dev started shouting.

'For fuck's sake, Dev, I am trying to help you! Whoever did this to you might still be here, just be quiet, please.'

I pulled the gag back around his mouth and he began grunting again. The effort seemed to exhaust him, and eventually his head slumped forward onto his chest. He'd lost consciousness again.

I stood up and poked my head out of the stall. The bathroom looked empty – maybe I'd just imagined the noise?

But whoever had done this to Dev clearly hadn't finished the job, so it stood to reason they might still be around. I walked to the sinks, pulled out my phone and scrolled to Lyons's number. Just as I was about to press dial, the lights went out. The bathroom went pitch black.

In that moment, my phone lit up with a Connector message.

Parker: Fancy seeing you here.

A cold spike of adrenaline shot through me as I spun around in the darkness.

'Where are you?' I cried out, my voice cracking.

Suddenly, I felt someone grab me from behind. A strong arm squeezed round my throat, gripping me so tightly I couldn't turn around. Something sharp poked into my back.

'Why are you doing this?' I croaked.

I could feel his cold breath around my ears. I tried to twist around, but whatever sharp implement it was dug harder into me. I felt something pierce the fabric of my shirt and cold metal touched my skin. Slowly, Parker turned me around to face the rectangular window at the back of the bathroom. I squinted hard, trying to see his face in the reflection of the glass, but my head obscured his, and a face mask covered his mouth and nose.

'What do you want?' I asked quietly. I swear I could hear the thud of my heartbeat reverberate around the tiled walls.

Instead of answering, he leant his face into mine, and through his face mask I felt his lips press against my cheek.

Fury boiled up inside me, eclipsing my fear. I took a deep breath and slammed my heel down hard on his foot. As he jumped back in pain, his grip loosened in shock and I yanked myself away. I spun around to look at my attacker. He was dressed in black, with a hood pulled down to shield his eyes. In the darkness, I couldn't see enough to work out if I recognised him.

'If this is about me, then let him go,' I panted, hoping he didn't see how much my hands were shaking.

He waved the knife towards the stall, where Dev was still slumped on the toilet. Reaching inside, he pulled him out of the stall and threw him onto the tiled floor. The figure knelt over Dev's unconscious body and placed the knife against his throat.

Deep down, I wanted to run. But I thought about Dev's wife. I thought about the little, curled-up grainy black-and-white baby in that photo.

'His wife, she doesn't deserve this,' I said.

The hooded figure reached into his pocket and pulled out a phone, and, using his thumb, began typing. Seconds later, my phone buzzed with his message. Tentatively, I looked down at the screen.

Parker: Does she deserve this piece of shit?

I looked up to see him pointing the knife at Dev's temple.

'He did a bad thing,' I said. 'But one bad thing doesn't make him worthless. Just let him go, Parker.'

The hand holding the knife wavered slightly.

'I'm sorry we never got to meet for that drink,' I went on. 'But maybe we could have a chat now, you know, get to know each other a bit better?'

I held my hands up and carefully took a step closer.

'Why don't you explain to me why you're doing this?' I said softly.

Instead of answering, he typed out another message. When I read it, my hands started to shake.

Parker: One more step and he's dead, bitch.

I swallowed hard and tried to shuffle my Converse forward, just an inch.

As I did, Parker pressed the blade into Dev's throat. Specks of blood popped from his neck like beads of crimson sweat.

'Okay, okay,' I said, freezing on the spot. 'But what's your endgame here? We're in a bowling alley bathroom. I'm standing in front of the only door out of here. So what's your next move?'

He growled quietly, and pressed the knife harder into Dev's throat. I needed to distract him, otherwise Dev wasn't leaving this bathroom alive.

'Wait, stop, stop,' I begged. 'Maybe you don't care about Dev, but there's something you don't know.'

He hesitated a moment.

'Just let me send you something,' I said, lifting up my phone. 'You might change your mind when you see this.'

Slowly and carefully, making no sudden movements, I chose the last picture in my camera roll, the photo of Charlie sticking a broom out of his flies, and sent it to Parker.

Seconds later, his phone flashed, and as he looked down at it, I took my chance. I threw my arm back and hurled my phone at him with all my remaining energy. It smashed into the side of his head with a crunch. He yelled in shock and dropped the knife, sending it skimming across the tiled floor.

Quick as a flash, I bent down and grabbed it, but by the time I looked up, he'd jumped up and scrambled out of the bathroom window. I collapsed down next to Dev, pressing my hand over the wound on his throat.

'Come on, come on, wake up,' I pleaded.

After a few seconds, he blinked his eyes slowly at me and gurgled.

'You're okay, you're going to be okay,' I told him.

From the floor, I reached over and picked up the ultrasound photo. It was speckled with blood, but I wiped it off on my hoodie sleeve and pressed it into his hand. His fingers slowly curled around the photo.

Suddenly, the lights flicked on, and my heart nearly burst out of my chest. I looked up, half expecting Parker to be brandishing a bowling ball at the doorway, but it wasn't him. It was Lyons, pointing a Taser at my face.

'Gwen! What happened?' he shouted. His eyes flicked to the knife in my hand.

'What are you doing here?' I panted. 'It's Dev, he's been hurt. Put that thing away and call an ambulance!'

Lyons put the Taser into the holster hung around his chest and pulled out his phone. He made the call as he knelt down next to me.

'It was Parker. Parker was here,' I panted. 'Tell them.'

'He was here?' Lyons said, placing his hands over mine and applying pressure to Dev's neck. I noticed Lyons wasn't wearing the blazer he'd had on last night, just a white T-shirt, which was now splattered with Dev's blood.

'Yes, he was here,' I cried. 'Look around you!'

'Connector...' Dev mumbled, his eyes rolling back.

'We're losing him,' Lyons said. 'Keep your hands there. The ambulance is on its way.'

My hands were gradually turning red as blood seeped through my fingers.

'Where did he go?' Lyons asked.

'Parker? Through there.' I nodded to the window.

'Keep the pressure on,' he said, getting up and going over to the open window.

'Go after him,' I ordered. 'I'll stay with Dev.'

'No, I'm not leaving you again,' he said.

He came back and crouched next to me, pushing my hair away from my face.

'Are you okay? Did he hurt you?'

'I'm fine,' I said angrily.

I wasn't fine, my heart felt like it was going to burst out of my chest, and I was fairly sure I was sitting in someone's day-old piss.

'Did you see his face?' Lyons asked.

I hung my head. 'I couldn't, I tried...' I tailed off.

Lyons put his hand on my arm. 'It's okay,' he said gently. 'We'll get him.'

Every inch of me wanted to shove him off, but I was terrified that if I let go of Dev's throat, we'd both be covered in gushing blood.

'What are you even doing here?' I asked. 'You were following me, weren't you? Again?'

Lyons's mouth tightened.

'I'm glad I was,' he said. 'You could've been hurt, Gwen. Or worse.'

'For fuck's sake, Aubrey,' I cried. 'It's not me you should

be worried about, it's this Parker. Do you believe me now? We need to go after him, otherwise someone else is going to get hurt.'

'What we need to do,' Lyons said carefully, 'is stay here until the ambulance arrives. Forrester is on his way. We'll send out a search party.'

'It'll be too late,' I snapped.

Lyons put his hands over Dev's throat, and his eyes fluttered open.

'It's going to be okay,' Lyons told him. 'Hang in there, mate.'

I stood up. 'This is about me. This is my fault. I have to go after him.'

'It's too dangerous. And you'll never catch up with him now,' Lyons said.

'The fire escape,' I said, remembering my date with Dev. 'I can get out the back and cut him off. Stay here with Dev, make sure he's okay.'

'Gwen, wait—' Lyons said.

I ignored him and ran out of the bathroom to the fire door, slammed the bar, and didn't look back.

TWENTY-FIVE

I practically skidded down the escalator and out into the car park. There was no sign of Parker among the handful of shoppers beginning to arrive at the mall. It must have just opened, and apart from a young couple wrestling a pram from their car boot and a few teenagers mooching around the entrance, the car park was empty. Then, in the distance, I saw a lone hooded figure, running. *It had to be him.*

I grabbed my bike from where I'd chucked it by the entrance and started pedalling furiously towards the figure, silently cursing all those times I'd stayed in bed instead of going to those Wednesday morning spin classes. I had no idea what the hell I would even do if I caught up with him. He must have heard my increasingly loud panting, as I saw him turn around. His hood was up, and he was too far away for me to make out any distinct features, but I swear he looked me in the eye and knew I was coming for him.

As I gained on him, he reached the barrier at the end of the car park and squeezed through the gap into the skate park next door. I jammed my brakes on, skidded up to the barrier and jumped off my bike.

I looked around frantically. My heart sank. My field of vision was filled with a sea of hooded teenagers, trundling down the half pipes and ramps, smoking dubious-looking cigarettes on the bench and watching each other fall off their boards as they attempted jumps off the handrails. Whoever it was, they were lost in a sea of identical-looking hoodies.

'Shit,' I panted.

Defeated, I wandered back to my bike. I picked it up and leant it against the barrier. I could see an ambulance in the car park, and paramedics were swarming around the entrance to the mall. My heart jumped as Lyons emerged, followed closely by Dev on a stretcher.

'Is he okay?' I asked, running over.

'He'll make it,' Lyons replied. 'What happened to Parker? Did you see him?'

'I thought I did,' I muttered. 'But…'

'Right, just stay here, will you? DCI Forrester will be here in a minute,' he said. 'We'll need to take your statement.'

'My statement? I already told you what happened. You're wasting time. Look at Dev,' I said, pointing to the ambulance crew as they loaded the stretcher on board. 'You need to find Parker before he does *that* to anyone else.'

'No,' Lyons said firmly. 'You need to slow down. You're in shock. We have zero leads on Parker. Forensics are in the alley now, and we'll speak to Dev when he wakes up. But right now, that's all we can do.'

I was about to argue with him when a white-jumpsuited forensics officer approached, holding a transparent bag. Inside was a black hoodie, just like the one Parker had been wearing, and I could make out spots of dark red blood on it.

'We found this outside the back window,' the officer said to Lyons.

'That's his,' I said. 'That's Parker's.'

The skateboarder I chased must have been just that – a kid in a similar hoodie.

'Probably dumped it as he ran off.' Lyons took the bag and held it up to his eyeline. 'Or maybe it got caught in the window when he climbed out.'

'How'd he get away so quickly?' I said, scanning the car park again.

'Could have had a car here,' Lyons said, noticeably shivering in the cold morning air. 'We'll check the CCTV.'

'You can run tests on that, right?' I said, motioning to the hoodie. 'DNA or something?'

Lyons stared at me, barely hiding his exasperation. 'Why don't you wait for DCI Forrester in the lobby,' he said, as politely as possible.

The last thing I wanted to do was go back inside that place, so I wandered back to my bike and kicked the wheel in frustration. I closed my eyes, and all I could see was Dev, gurgling on the bathroom floor. When I opened them again, my hands were shaking. Fuck it. I didn't have time to be in shock – people were in danger. I took a deep breath, then another one, until my heart rate returned to a vaguely normal level and my hands were steady(ish).

Lyons was right. I had no idea who Parker was. All I knew about him was the sum total of his Connector profile: his favourite flavour of ice cream (rum and raisin) and his second favourite movie (like 98 per cent of all other 34-year-old, *Inception*). I didn't know his surname, or where exactly he worked, or which part of town he lived in. All his bio said was Parker, 34 and an obligatory height boast: six foot one.

Then something hit me. A six-foot-tall person could not have squeezed through the window in the bowling alley toilets. Now, I know from bitter experience that six foot one on a dating profile normally translates as five foot ten or under – but even in the dark, I could see Parker wasn't even that. It made me wonder what else about his profile might not be true.

I pulled out my phone, which was littered with missed call notifications from Charlie and about seventeen WhatsApp messages from Sarah about personalised napkins for the top table. I knew I should call them and explain where I'd been, but there was no time for that now. Instead, I bashed 'data analyst' and 'Parker' into Google. A box appeared on my screen and demanded to know if I was a robot or not.

'How many times do I need to tell you, Google, I am not a robot,' I snapped.

The prompt asked me to pick all the images of boats I could see.

'Could a robot do *this*?' I said dramatically, and quickly clicked on the four images of boats.

A message popped up: 'Please try again.'

By the time I finally passed the stupid test, I was predictably met with approximately one billion pages of results. I scrolled back through his profile, looking for anything that might help narrow it down. Parker did IT for a PR agency, but there was nothing more specific than that. In fact, I noticed he'd carefully avoided saying anything specific about his life at all.

There was an old episode of *Danger Land* where the police disproved someone's alibi after spotting the suspect in the back of a Facebook photo. Maybe I could find some clue in Parker's profile that would lead me to him. I flicked through it again, trying to work out if maybe I'd seen him somewhere before, or recognised any of the places in the photos. Pinching the screen, I zoomed in on the backgrounds, looking for clues, but it revealed nothing but generic bars and soft furnishings.

The only other photo with another person in it looked like it was taken at some sort of awards ceremony. Parker was standing next to an older woman who looked a bit like Claudia Winkleman but with even more eyeliner, if that was at all possible. They were holding some sort of ghastly glass trophy. When I zoomed in, I could just about make out the words 'Best Brand Strategy' etched into the glass, and 'Rosemary Da...'. The rest of the surname was obscured by his ridiculously bling cufflinks. I added 'brand strategy award' and 'Rosemary' to my Google search and clicked on the images tab. I scrolled down until I saw a familiar face. 'Rosemary Daniels, Senior Graphic Designer, Pentangle PR.', the caption read.

Bingo.

I quickly googled Pentangle and called the number. A softly spoken woman answered the phone.

'Is Rosemary there, Rosemary Daniels?'

'Rosemary Daniels? I'm sorry, she hasn't worked here for ages,' the woman said.

'What about Parker? Is he around?'

'Sorry, who is this?'

'I'm Parker's girlfriend,' I said. 'He does work there, right?'

'Parker? You mean Colin? Colin Parker?'

Okay, so Parker was his surname?

'Um, yes, yeah, that's right, Colin,' I said.

'Girlfriend, you say? Are you sure?' she asked.

'Well, it's complicated,' I said. 'But it's an emergency, is he there?'

'Well, all the senior managers are in a meeting right now,' she said. 'They just went in, so it'll be about an hour I expect. Should I go in and get him, if it's an emergency?'

'No, no, don't do that, I know how much he, likes, um, meetings. Tell you what, I'll come and speak to him in person, thanks for your help,' I said, hanging up and getting on my bike.

'Gwen, where are you going?' I heard Lyons shouting from across the car park. 'Wait!'

I didn't listen, I just pedalled.

Cold air blasted into my face as I raced down the Grand Parade. Clutching my phone in one hand for directions and steering badly with the other, I headed down Channel View Road. Five minutes later I was staring up at a tall, mirrored building. I stashed my bike in a side alley and ran into reception, where a young receptionist eyed me suspiciously over his horn-rimmed spectacles.

'Colin Parker,' I panted at him.

'What company?' he asked, flicking his eyes away from my ruddy face and towards his computer screen with an air of disgust.

'That one,' I managed to spit out, pointing to the word PENTANGLE, next to a large number two, in big silver metallic letters behind him.

'Have you got an appointment?' he asked dryly, fully knowing that of course I damn well didn't.

I shook my head.

'I'll call up and let him know he has a… visitor,' the receptionist said, enunciating the word 'visitor' like I was a particularly clingy STD.

He punched a few numbers into the phone and I waited, leaning over on the desk.

'Sorry, no answer,' the receptionist said after a few moments, looking down disdainfully at the drops of sweat dropping from my forehead onto his very shiny desk.

Just then a tall bearded man in ripped jeans and, bizarrely, a shirt and tie walked through the revolving doors behind me. Flashing his ID at the receptionist with a smile, he headed straight past and beeped his card on the reader by the lifts.

'Fuck this,' I mumbled.

'Excuse me?' the receptionist said.

'I said, "Thanks for this". I really enjoyed our time together.'

He gave me a sarcastic smile and went back to pretending to work on his computer.

I watched the tall man stepping into the lift. If I timed it just right, I reckoned I could make it there before anyone could stop me. Out of the corner of my eye, I could see the lift doors just starting to close.

'Bye!' I said to the receptionist, and made a dash for it. Just before the doors slid shut, I jumped inside the lift beside Ripped Jeans Man and jabbed the number two button.

'Late for a meeting,' I beamed, as he looked suspiciously at my sweaty cheeks and hoodie.

Through the crack of the closing doors, I could see the angry face of the receptionist as he punched more numbers into his phone. When the lift dinged at floor two, I yelled 'See ya!' to the bemused man and rushed out into a sea of desks. Bored-looking workers jabbed away at their computers.

'Colin!' I shouted across the office. 'Colin Parker!'

No one even looked up. I ran to the nearest person and spun their chair round to face me.

'Where does Colin sit?' I asked.

'Colin Parker?' the man said. 'He's in a meeting right now. Can I help you?'

'I really need to speak to him urgently,' I said.

'Sorry… who are you?'

'I'm just a friend, um, his best friend, actually. His girlfriend. Look, it's an emergency, I need to speak to him.'

'What sort of emergency?'

'I don't know, the big kind. Somewhere in between a tornado and a zombie apocalypse. His dog's on fire. I'm not sure. I just really need to see Colin Parker right now, okay?'

'It's a very important meeting. Have you tried emailing him?' the man said.

'Yes, I've sent him many, many emails,' I said. 'Now, please, where's the meeting room?'

The man gestured towards a glass-walled office in the corner.

'Great, thanks,' I said, taking a step towards it. But as I did, I felt a heavy hand on my shoulder. I turned around to see a very large man in a security guard uniform, and the receptionist smirking behind him.

'You have to leave – now,' the security guard said slowly, his voice low and considered.

'Okay, look I'm going, alright?' I said. I held my hands up, as if to show I was totally harmless.

'Yes, you are,' the guard said, turning me round and leading me gently towards the lift.

'Wait, wait,' I pleaded. 'Just one second.' I turned back to the guy at the computer. 'What's the number of the conference call speaker in the meeting room?'

'That's extension 221,' he said.

'Don't even think about it,' the guard said, but before he could stop me, I grabbed the phone on the desk, pulled it towards me and jabbed the numbers in.

'Colin Parker! This is an emergency, please leave the meeting immediately and return to your desk,' I managed to yell into the receiver before the guard pulled it away from me. He slammed down the phone and gave me a look like he was about to roll me in a ball and dunk me into the waste-paper bin.

'Just give me a second, please,' I begged him. 'This Colin guy could be a wanted criminal. You can arrest him and be a national hero.'

Through the glass office walls, I saw a man stand up, look out at us with a shrug, and open the door. As he walked towards me, I squinted at him. He looked like Parker, for sure, but significantly more round, grey and annoyed looking.

'You're Parker?' I said. I noticed he had a wedding ring on his finger.

It was definitely the same guy from the app, but visibly much older.

'Colin Parker, yes,' he said. 'What's going on here? Do I know you?'

'You tell me,' I said, pulling out my phone. 'Have you been messaging me?'

I held up Parker's profile in front of his face.

'What?' he stuttered.

'Is this you?' I said, showing him the awards ceremony photo.

'Yes, that's me,' he said. 'But that photo is from about twelve years ago. In fact, it's from exactly twelve years ago.'

He pulled out something from among the debris of paper on his desk.

'Look,' he said, holding up a shiny onyx trophy with the words 'Best Brand Strategy 2011' inscribed across it. My mouth fell open.

'Looks like you've been catfished,' the receptionist crowed from behind the security guard's shoulder.

'You didn't send me these messages?' I asked, scrolling through the Connector chat.

'I don't think my husband would be very impressed if I did,' he said.

I stood there, deflated, the office workers staring at me like a gaping salmon that had flopped onto dry land.

'Wait, someone's been using my photos on their dating app?' Colin asked.

'Yeah, you might want to update your Facebook privacy settings,' I told him. 'If you wanna, you know, avoid future office invasions.'

'Alright, that's enough,' the guard said. 'I'm calling the police.'

'Yes, good idea,' the receptionist said, a sarcastic smile on his face.

'Go ahead,' I said. 'Call them! They need to see this. Ask for Detective Lyons.'

The guard eyed me suspiciously as he tapped the number into his phone and waited for someone to answer.

There was an awkward silence as the three of us stood

by the lift. The office workers eventually stopped staring and went back to their precious spreadsheets, and Colin Parker sloped back into his meeting. The receptionist and I exchanged pleasantries: he gave me a sarcastic smile, and I gave him the finger.

'He's on his way,' the security guard said eventually. 'I filled him in on what's been going on here.'

As we waited, I got out my phone and typed 'Colin Parker' into Facebook, and clicked on the 'mutual friends' tab.

There was only one friend we had in common, and when I saw it, my mouth went dry.

Charlie Edwards.

TWENTY-SIX

Eventually, there was a loud 'ding' and the elevator doors slid open to reveal a very angry-looking Lyons.

'I'll take it from here,' he said to the security guard, flashing his ID.

He motioned me into the lift with a tilt of his head, and didn't speak to me until the doors closed. He turned to face me with a serious expression. I mean, his face was *always* serious, but now it was properly stern.

'What the hell are you doing, Gwen? Going after Parker on your own was incredibly dangerous.'

'If you had believed me in the first place, I wouldn't have had to,' I replied. 'I told you there was something wrong about Parker, and this proves it.'

'This isn't the time for "I told you so"s. And all you've "proved" is that Parker is a fake account.'

We stood in silence for a moment, only interrupted by the soft ding of the lift bell as it made its way through the Pentangle building.

'Dev's going to be okay, by the way,' Lyons said, watching me out of the corner of his eye. 'In case you were wondering.'

'Thank God,' I said. 'Was he able to tell you anything? Does he know who Parker really is?'

'He didn't see anyone, Gwen, except for you. All we could get out of him was that he went on a date to the bowling alley, and then someone jumped him in the toilets. Next thing he knew, you were stuffing a gag into his mouth.'

'*Back* into his mouth!' I said. 'I was trying to get him to shut up!'

'The fact is,' Lyons interrupted me, 'you were the only person seen at the crime scene. And not for the first time.'

'Okay, so we should track down whoever he was on the date with,' I said. 'Maybe she can—'

'Gwen, stop. This isn't *Danger Mouse* or one of your podcasts.'

'*Danger Land*,' I corrected him. '*Danger Mouse* is something completely—'

He gave me a sharp look.

'Anyway,' I went on. 'I need to tell you something about Colin, listen—'

'Gwen, please. Just listen to *me* for a moment.' Lyons put his hand up to stop me talking. 'Forrester wants me to bring you in, take a statement, probably read you your rights.'

'What? He still thinks I've got something to do with this? How the hell? I literally just saw the killer slice a man's throat!'

'And you were the only one who did see it,' Lyons said. 'When I found you, you were holding a bloody knife. Can you blame Forrester for being suspicious?'

'Yes, I can blame him!' I cried. 'He should be giving me a freaking medal, not arresting me! You can check the messages Parker sent me in the alley, he was going to kill Dev! If I hadn't found him in time, well, God knows what would have happened.'

Lyons considered this for a moment, pursing his lips.

'For what it's worth,' he said, his voice softer now, 'I think he's wrong.'

'Thank you,' I said. 'So let's—'

'But I'm still taking you in,' Lyons said bluntly as the lift came to an abrupt stop on the ground floor.

I followed Lyons out to his Ford Fiesta, and he held the passenger door open for me. I sat sulkily, fiddling with the glove compartment while he got in the other side and started the car. Suddenly it sprang open, depositing a slew of old Fiesta manuals and paperwork onto my lap.

'What are you doing?' Lyons snapped.

'Looking for snacks!' I said. 'Haven't you got any crisps or something in here? Just FYI, this car is a tip.' I began ordering the contents of the glove compartment neatly into a pile.

'Just leave it alone, will you?' he said.

We both stared out the windscreen saying nothing for a few moments. It had started raining, and the rhythm of the wipers and the warmth of the car heater had lulled us into a silence.

I couldn't stop thinking about Charlie being Facebook friends with Colin. Was that just another coincidence? Colin's profile wasn't private, anyone could have nicked his photos. But it was odd. Really odd. Could Charlie really be Parker? It didn't make sense – he had no reason to hurt any of the men on my list.

The rain lashed on the windscreen faster than the wipers could whip it off. I shoved my hands deep in my pockets and focused on the white lines of the road, disappearing as quickly as they appeared on the horizon. I looked over at Lyons, who was still staring straight ahead, a look of something in his face that reminded me of a cornered animal. I pushed my hands deeper into my pockets. At the bottom, I found a packet of gum. With my fingers, I traced the outline of the wrapper. There were two pieces left.

'Gum?' I offered, and Lyons reached over without taking his eyes off the road. I squeezed a piece out of the crumpled packet into his open palm.

I popped the last piece in my mouth, and let it sit lifelessly on my tongue. The low squeaking of the rubber wipers against wet glass that filled the car only accentuated the awkwardness.

'So…' I said eventually. 'If Forrester wants to arrest me, then where is he? Why'd you come after me on your own?' I asked.

'Let's just say I'm working a hunch here.'

I spat out the gum into the empty wrapper and rolled it up into a ball. I dribbled the silver foil ball around my palm with my finger before flicking it at him.

'Forrester doesn't know, does he?' I said. 'Don't tell me you're going rogue here, Dandy?'

'Please stop calling me that.' Lyons tapped his fingers on the steering wheel.

'Really?' I said. 'You're telling me you actually prefer Aubrey?'

'Detective Lyons is fine,' he said, still not taking his eyes off the road. 'And no, I'm not going rogue. But I'm not convinced you're guilty of anything. Which means someone else is.'

'Of course I'm not guilty!' I cried. 'For God's sake, *Detective Lyons*, I'm a twenty-nine-year-old barista with nothing to her name but a clapped-out ice cream van, two maxed-out credit cards and, right now, the beginnings of what feels like the mother of all migraines. Do I seem the sort of person who could be bothered to plot an overly complex killing spree on a whim?'

'Gwen, calm down,' Lyons said.

I slumped back into the seat and crossed my legs. If there was one thing guaranteed to make me *not* calm down, it was being told to calm down. If anything, it was just gonna make me calm *up*.

'You're not doing anything! We need to do something. There are still names on this napkin. Parker is real. And he's out there somewhere, with a grudge against me. People are dying and it's my fault.'

He took a deep breath and, without saying a word, Lyons swung the car sharply into a side road and pulled on the handbrake.

'Okay, listen,' he said, exhaling through his nose. 'I do believe you, Gwen. And I think you may be right. Parker is still out there, and I need your help to figure out who he might be – fast. But if we're going to do this, you can't keep running off on your own, okay?'

I nodded.

'Alright,' he went on. 'We need to work out why anyone would want to kill your dates.'

I thought about Charlie being Facebook friends with Colin. If I told Lyons that, he'd be off on another wild goose chase. I needed him to stay focused on finding the real killer.

'I think Parker wanted me to find Dev at the bowling alley,' I said. 'Like he wanted me to find Josh. He's trying to frame me for all of this.'

'But why?'

'I don't know. He's been harassing me for a date and I kept fobbing him off,' I said.

Lyons looked at me and shook his head.

'I don't think that's quite enough to frame you for murder.'

'You don't know what some of these guys on Connector are like,' I muttered.

'What about the photo? Dev had an ultrasound photo in his hand.'

'It was pinned on him when I found him,' I said. 'His wife is pregnant.'

'But why would Parker pin that on him?' Lyons asked.

'To make it look like I'm some insanely jealous murderer,' I said. 'He wants it to look like I dated Dev, found out that he was cheating on his wife – his *pregnant* wife – then sliced his throat.'

'Let me see these messages,' Lyons said. 'Maybe he gave something away, something that tells us who he really is.'

I handed him my phone and he scrolled through the Connector chat between me and Parker.

'Doesn't give much away,' he said. 'He could be anyone.'

'But somehow he knows who've I've been dating?' I asked. 'You think he's been stalking me?'

Lyons studied the phone screen the way some dogs stare at a washing machine doing a spin cycle.

'If Parker somehow had access to the Connector data, he'd be able to see all your chats on there and know who you'd been dating.'

'You think he hacked the app?' I asked. 'Can people do that?'

'It's possible. I arrested a hacker last year, calls himself "Maestro" for some reason. Started off his criminal career by hacking dating apps for kids in his sixth form, then progressed to hacking his head teacher's dating profile and matching him with half the students' single parents. By the end of the year, he'd moved on to hacking celebrities' Twitter profiles, changing the passwords and holding them at ransom. Got off with a suspended sentence as he was only eighteen. Pretty smart guy if I'm honest.'

'Aubrey! You've totally got yourself an inside man. Just like a real detective. This Maestro guy can hack Connector and find out who Parker really is, right? Or at least help us track down Seb. What are you waiting for? Do you want that promotion to the Met or not?'

He shook his head. 'One, we will not be hacking anything. That data is protected and we have to go through the proper channels. Two, Maestro lives "off the grid" in a yacht on the dock now, and I do not want to know how he paid for that. Maybe I should take you back to the station, at least there you'll be safe.'

'So Forrester can just keep interrogating me until everyone on this list gets murdered?'

Lyons looked at me and sighed deeply. It was all I could do not to grab his shoulders and shake some sense into him.

'Listen, *we're* not going to hack anything, The Mysterious Maestro is,' I said. 'The docks are five minutes from here, and you'll need my phone to show him Parker's profile. There's no time to go through the proper channels, and you know it. Let's stop pretending you're taking me back to the station. You need my help, you said it yourself. So, come on, why don't you and me go nail this bastard?'

Lyons pulled the handbrake off and started the car. 'I'm beginning to see why none of those guys wanted a second date with you,' he muttered.

TWENTY-SEVEN

I usually felt kind of peaceful around moored boats. There was something exciting about the possibilities of pulling up the anchor and sailing away without a second thought. Once they set sail though, I was suddenly less keen.

The boats lined up in the Sovereign Harbour Marina were not cheap. Most of the gleaming sailboats looked more expensive than the crumbling flats that lined the seafront. Lyons had called Maestro on the way over, and he'd agreed to help us.

'Apparently it's called *The Nautilus*,' said Lyons, as we walked down the thin walkway across the water, looking for the right boat.

Nestled in between the towering sailboats was a much smaller, wooden-panelled fishing boat.

'That's *The Nautilus*?' I asked, pointing to the name, painted in an italic font across the bow. 'I thought you said it was a yacht!'

Lyons shrugged and we stepped onto the deck. I knocked on the small cabin door, but without waiting for a reply, Lyons pushed the door open and stepped inside. The cabin

…it up only by the glow of a laptop screen and rows …, blinking lights that made up a large bank of servers. In …t, there wasn't much in the tiny cabin that wasn't blinking, or making a low whirring sound.

As I followed Lyons in, steadying myself against the gentle rocking of the boat, I felt something wet brush my ankle. I looked down, half panicking that we were sinking, and saw something small and hairy licking my leg.

'Rocco!' I squealed. 'What the hell are you doing here?'

'No toastie for you today, mate. Leave her alone,' I heard a familiar voice say from the back of the boat. Rocco stopped trying to eat my Converse and trotted towards it obediently.

'Gwen, this is Jamal Childs, aka Maestro,' Lyons said. 'He's going to have a little snoop round Connector for us.'

'In a totally legit and legal way, of course.' Jamal smiled, spinning around in his swivel chair to greet us. 'Nice to see you again, Gwen.'

'Wait, you two know each other?' said Lyons.

'Yeah, he hangs out at the van to leech my Wi-Fi.' I looked around the cabin. 'So *this* is where you live?'

'Well, after your friend here,' he pointed to Lyons, 'got me off with a suspended sentence, my parents kicked me out. So this is my new "base of operations".'

'And you're really Maestro, the master hacker?' I scoffed. With his suede loafers and a smattering of artfully crafted facial hair, he looked more like an own-brand ASOS model than a cybercriminal. 'So that's what you've been using my internet for then, hacking into the Bank of England? No wonder it's always so slow.'

'I'm really more of a hacktivist than a cybercriminal—' Jamal started.

'Sorry to break up your little reunion, but we don't have time for this,' Lyons interrupted. 'Jamal, we have reason to believe someone might be using the Connector app to conduct criminal activities.'

'Whoa, slow down there,' Jamal said. 'That kind of talk ends in a lawsuit. Developers like Dragon, who make Connector, can't be held responsible for any harm that comes to users of the app. It's all in the terms and conditions.'

'Three people have died, Mr Childs, and one is currently in intensive care,' Lyons snapped back. 'I'm not interested in terms and conditions; I'm interested in saving lives.'

My little pep talk in the car must have worked, because I was witnessing a whole new side to Dandy Lyons. One I kinda liked.

Jamal shifted slightly in his chair. 'I'm sorry. Where are my manners? Piece of fruit, detective?' he said, gesturing to a bowl of apples and bananas on his desk.

Lyons ignored him. I held up my phone and showed him Parker's profile.

'We need to find out who made this profile,' I said.

Jamal squinted at the screen, then looked back at Lyons.

'Are you sure this is police business?' he asked. 'I'm not sure I should be doing this, with my suspended sentence and all…'

Lyons tilted his head at him. 'Talking of police business, maybe I should tell DCI Forrester exactly what you've been up to in your little offshore command centre?'

'Look, I'm just a tech guy, mate. I fix bugs,' Jamal said, holding his hands up.

'Really, and exactly what have you been using Gwen's IP address for, hmm?' Lyons asked.

Jamal fiddled with his glasses.

'Listen, any data Dragon keeps on its users is protected by strict data protection laws. It would be totally illegal to pull that sort of info.'

'Okay Jamal, we get it. Now we've got all the disclaimers out of the way, can you help us, or do I have to start pulling out some plugs around here?' Lyons said.

Jamal picked up an apple from the fruit bowl and took a large chomp. 'Short answer: no,' he said. 'I mean, I wish I could, but it's not that simple.'

'What are you talking about?' Lyons said. 'When we nicked you, you were matching all your little mates with Instagram models. I know you can hack the app, "Maestro".'

'Well, that's altogether different, my friend. I simply learnt how to manipulate the algorithms, thus making my associates highly desirable, resulting in a greater ratio of elite matches.'

'In English please,' Lyons said.

'He's saying he increased his mates' chances of matching with certain people,' I said.

Lyons thought for a minute. 'So someone could have manipulated the app to give Gwen specific matches?' he asked.

I pulled out the napkin and showed him the biro-scribbled names. 'Like these guys?'

'Well, not quite,' Jamal said. 'Look, all these dating apps work off algorithms. Sure they all look a little different, but under the surface of amusing fonts and cupid logos, they're all the same. You're shown a random selection of profiles of people that meet your criteria – age, location, gender – and then you can simply swipe "yes" or "no". If two people both say "yes" to each other, that's a match and you can chat. The mechanics are simple.'

'We know how dating apps work, Jamal,' Lyons said firmly.

I coughed loudly and gave him a sharp look.

'Of course you do,' Jamal continued. 'Like any app, they're gamified to make it addictive and keep you coming back. The apparent randomness of which profiles you see adds an exhilarating element of chance, and the notion that – just like the movies – romance is a magical power that only St Valentine himself can control. "The One" could be just around the next corner, or in this case, the next swipe.' Jamal took another bite of apple. 'But in reality, they all have a secret algorithm built in that's designed to keep you trapped in this Kafka-esque nightmare. It throws all the most attractive, most liked people at you when you first open the app, lulling you into thinking the city is full of beautiful singletons desperate for two awkward drinks in a noisy bar. The endorphins that shoot through your brain when you get that "match" message flash up on your phone keep you swiping, like lining up three cherries or getting Mario to jump on one of those mushrooms.'

'So who decides who's attractive or not?' I asked. 'Who gets to be the judge of the beauty contest?'

'Companies like Dragon Ltd created a universal definition of attractiveness. They're able to use deductive reasoning to rank you on a desirability scale.'

'A what now?' I said.

'It's called an Elo Algorithm,' Jamal went on.

'Ah yes, I've heard of it,' said Lyons. 'Same thing they use to rank chess players.'

'I knew it!' I cried, punching him on the arm. 'I knew you had a nerdy hobby.'

Jamal finally finished gnawing on his apple and threw the

core out the open window. I heard the plop as it hit the water. He swivelled round in his chair and reached for the fruit bowl.

'Here, let me show you,' he said.

He picked out some bananas from the bowl. There were three greenish yellow ones, and the rest were beginning to brown. He mixed them up and laid them in a vertical line on his desk. Rocco looked up at them hopefully.

'Which one would you pick?'

I pointed to one of the yellower ones.

Jamal moved it to the top.

'And what would you say to this one, detective?' Jamal waved another yellow banana at Lyons.

'I'd eat it,' Lyons said.

Jamal put that banana under the one I chose.

'Everyone starts with the same score,' he said. 'But if someone likes you, and swipes right, that lets the computer know you're attractive, and you get a point.'

Jamal picked up one of the browning bananas and placed it at the bottom.

'And if they think you're gross, and swipe left, you go down the rankings.'

'Why did my banana go underneath Gwen's?' Lyons asked.

'Your score is weighted by the attractiveness of the people that swipe yes to you. So if you get a yes from Ryan Gosling, it's worth more points than, say…'

'This guy,' I said, jerking my thumb towards Lyons.

He ignored me.

'And so on,' Jamal said, taking the rest of the yellow bananas and moving them to the top, one by one. 'Until this.'

He gestured to the row of fruit. All the yellow ones were at the top and the browns were at the bottom.

'Ugh,' I grimaced. 'So the more people that swipe right on you, the better score you get?'

'Yes,' said Jamal. 'And if you have a low score, and you swipe on someone with a high score, not only do they go up the ranking, you go down. The good stuff rises to the top, like with these bananas here.'

Jamal swivelled back round to his laptop and began tapping away.

'The algorithm will pigeonhole you based on who you swipe right on,' he went on. 'And if you swipe right on everyone, you're penalised heavily cos you're not selective.'

'So if I am swiping away, thinking all these guys I'm seeing are gross, it's because the app thinks I'm not attractive and is serving me people who are rated the same?' I asked.

'You need to have a specific taste that they can quantify,' Jamal said. 'In an Elo system, it's very, very difficult to climb the rankings once you've got a bad score.'

'So the app only works if you're young, good looking and happy to show off your boobs?' I scoffed. I don't know why I was surprised. These apps were all coded by middle-class, heterosexual men, so of course they were going to cater to their tastes. 'Basically, if you don't fit the stereotype of conventional attractiveness then you're screwed?'

'Sure. But it's not just Connector,' said Jamal. 'All dating apps work like this. A six-foot-one model with washboard abs will always outrank a funny, interesting, normal person. That's why you wouldn't catch me on this thing.'

I felt slightly offended.

'Think of it this way, imagine the person you love most in the world,' Jamal said.

I couldn't help but think of Noah.

'Now, could you reduce that person to five pictures?' Jamal went on. 'Could you sum up everything you love about them to just a handful of photos?'

He pushed his glasses up on the bridge of his nose.

'You can't, but these apps have to reduce people to their most basic qualities. That's because our brains are designed to only select between five and ten options. In the wilds of the Serengeti, Homo sapiens didn't have a hundred options, they had about five, and four of those would kill you. That's why humans have a negative bias. The brain is built to be suspicious, to play it safe. To swipe left. Because back then, pretty much anyone could be a predator, even the people you thought were your friends. You *had* to be vigilant, because if you weren't...' Jamal drew a finger across his throat.

'So what sort of profiles do well?' Lyons asked.

'According to Dragon's research, the top three things singles look for are nice teeth, good grammar and confidence. Teeth show you're healthy, correct spelling shows that you're educated, and, by extension, your class. And self-confidence proves you're psychologically stable. So any profiles that exhibit those traits tend to rise to the top.'

'Psychological stability?' Lyons raised an eyebrow.

'Basically, human beings are attracted to people that are happy,' Jamal said.

I flashed them my best smile.

'Give me a second,' Jamal said. His laptop hummed quietly as he ran his hand over the keyboard. A few minutes later, a spreadsheet full of names and numbers appeared on the screen.

'Here, take a look at this,' he said. 'This is every profile on Connector within a thirty-mile radius, along with their rating.'

'Their rating?' I asked.

Jamal picked up one of the yellow bananas from the desk and started unpeeling it.

'You've all got a rating,' he smiled. 'Your surname is Turner, right?'

I nodded.

He tapped on the keyboard and suddenly my name popped up on the screen.

'Here we are,' he said. 'Gwen Turner, 1004, not bad.'

'What the hell does that mean?' I asked. 'I'm the one thousand and fourth most popular woman on Connector?' I wasn't 100 per cent sure if that was very good or very offensive.

I put the napkin on the desk, folded my arms and thought for a moment. 'Wait, am I a yellow banana or a brown banana?'

Jamal smiled. 'Look, you're 1004th in the whole county, that's probably top ten in Eastbourne.'

I considered this, and was slightly less offended.

'Wait,' said Lyons, grabbing the napkin. 'Are these names on your spreadsheet here?'

'I'll need a little more than just their first names,' Jamal said.

I got out my phone and showed him the screenshots of the profiles.

'Let me see what I can do,' said Jamal and span back around to face the computer.

He tapped away for a few minutes before leaning back and scratching his chin.

'Well... they're all very high, towards the absolute top actually,' he said thoughtfully as he studied his screen. 'But that doesn't mean they didn't earn that ranking. Maybe they're just super hot guys with nice teeth and perfect spelling?'

Lyons looked at me.

'Nope,' I said, shaking my head. 'And none of them seemed that psychologically stable, either.'

'You've just explained – at length – how only the best profiles rise to the top, how our brains naturally reject anyone who seems suspicious. So don't you think it's a little strange,' said Lyons, 'that the five people on this list, three of which are dead, are at the top of this spreadsheet here, Mr Childs?'

'I'm telling you, the system can't be hacked by just anyone,' said Jamal.

'But let's just say, if someone *did* artificially put these five people at the top of the rankings, then there's a massive chance I would have seen them,' I said.

'Seen them, yes, but there's no guarantee you would match,' said Jamal.

'Hmmm well, yeah, but to be totally honest, I wasn't being too choosy who I swiped yes to,' I said.

'You bypassed your brain's negativity bias, Gwen. And by going on a date with just about everyone you matched with, all "Parker" had to do was watch and see what order you met them in,' Lyons said to me.

'Um, okay, it wasn't "everyone",' I scowled at him.

It occurred to me that all this time, I thought I was picking complete losers, that I just had terrible judgement, or I somehow magically attracted knobheads, like that was all I deserved. But no, they were being served up to me, by men who were playing the system to meet women.

Lyons turned back to Jamal. 'Speaking of Parker, is his profile on your spreadsheet here?'

I held up my phone in front of Jamal's face to show him.

'Let me see, fairly unusual name,' Jamal said, tapping a few keys on the computer. Three profiles called 'Parker' popped up on the screen and he picked the one with the same profile pic.

'Here he is,' Jamal said. 'Nice looking guy.'

'What information is on there?' Lyons leant forward urgently. 'IP address, bank account details? Anything?'

'Just the email address he used to sign up to the app.'

'What's the email?' I asked.

'PrinceCharming007@rajakov.net,' Jamal said.

'Wow,' I said. 'Was "GodsGift69" taken?'

'Could we use that to get into his account? Guess his password?' Lyons asked.

Jamal shrugged. 'You could try. Most people choose obvious passwords, something personal to them, something they love that's easy to remember. What else do you know about this guy?'

'Um, he likes rum and raisin ice cream and Christopher Nolan movies?' I offered.

'Everything on his profile is likely fake,' Lyons said. 'We don't know anything about him.'

'I could have a look at his activity on the app, see what else he's been up to on there…'

Jamal tapped a few more keys and more numbers scrolled across the screen.

'Weird, says here he's only got one match,' he said, pressing enter.

Suddenly my face filled the screen.

'Oh,' said Jamal. 'It's you.'

TWENTY-EIGHT

Jamal tapped away as I stared at my own gormless face, grinning and holding my tequila aloft without a care in the world.

'So not only did this Parker guy only ever chat with Gwen, he never even swiped "yes" to anyone else. Says here that his distance parameters were always set at 0.5 miles, the minimum the app allows. I'd have to say, it looks very much like he was looking to match with one person.'

'Me,' I said quietly, stepping back from the computer. I suddenly felt colder than I had outside.

Lyons pulled up a chair and sat next to Jamal.

'So it's someone who knows her?' he said.

'Or someone who *wants* to know her?' Jamal replied. 'You know, like, maybe he clocked her in a bar, liked what he saw and checked to see if she was on the app. And bingo, she was.'

'Does it tell you when he swiped yes?' Lyons continued.

'No, only when he and Gwen matched, February 9th, eight fifteen in the evening. He could've swiped yes at any time before that.'

Rocco sniffed at my leg as I stared out the window of the boat. This wasn't getting us anywhere.

'Jamal, can you check one more name for me?' I asked.

'Go for it,' he said.

'Charlie Edwards.'

Lyons's eyes flicked towards mine, but I avoided his gaze and watched as Jamal tapped away at the computer.

'No profile registered under that name,' he said. 'Sorry.'

I turned away from the screen and began to walk out of the cabin.

'Hey, where are you going?' said Lyons, leaning over his shoulder.

Out on the dock, I watched the sun begin to dip below the horizon. The riggings of the sailboats rattled in the wind and I zipped up my hoodie. I didn't feel any warmer. The thought of someone watching me, following me, hurting people because of me, made me dizzy. Seconds later, Lyons followed me out.

'We done?' I asked.

'Yeah,' he said. 'Sorry, that must have been a bit weird for you.'

'This whole thing is weird for me,' I said. 'And it doesn't seem like we're getting any closer to Parker. Do any of those spreadsheets actually help us?'

'Well, we know that the men on your napkin each have extraordinarily high rankings on Connector.'

'Higher than they should have,' I said. 'Trust me, they were *not* that great.'

'They could have manipulated their rankings somehow. Jamal said it was possible.'

'And so what if they did? So what if they cheated the app? The app was cheating everyone! It's a horrible system that rewards superficiality. It deserves to be hacked.' I started to walk away from him up the dock.

'So says Ms One Thousand and Four,' Lyons said.

I turned and scowled at him.

'Anyway, Jamal said you'd have to be like, a master hacker to do it,' I said. 'I mean, no offence, but I'm not sure any of the guys I dated could remember their Facebook password, let alone navigate their way past a multinational tech company's cyber security.'

'Well okay, so what if *they* didn't manipulate the app then,' said Lyons.

I laughed. 'I told you, none of those guys should be up there with Ryan Gosling or Ryan Reynolds. Or *any* of the Ryans to be honest with you. There's definitely something wrong with their rankings.'

'No, I mean, what if someone else did it,' Lyons continued. 'What if someone manipulated their rankings without them knowing?'

'But why?'

'To get them in your eyeline,' he said. 'Maybe someone is using the app to connect you to these particular men. Maybe whoever is doing this is trying to send you a message.'

'Well, I wish they'd just call and tell me then,' I said. 'I'm not great at picking up subtext.'

'Yeah, I can see that,' he said, almost under his breath.

'So now what?' I said. 'We've hit a dead end.'

'In most homicide cases, the perpetrator is known to the victim. So who would know all these men *and* you?'

'I can't think of anyone I know who gives off a psychopath vibe,' I said.

'Psychopaths don't give off a vibe, Gwen. They seem

perfectly rational. They don't run around waving a bloody Stanley knife in broad daylight. They're smarter than that. You said you thought Parker was trying to frame you, so let me ask you again, are you *sure* you never pissed anyone off?'

'Oh, Aubrey,' I said, turning round and leaning backwards on the dock railings. 'I've pissed off a *lot* of people.'

He looked at me blankly.

'But no one who I think might be capable of murder, okay?' I said. 'I think you're just going to have to come up with a new theory, detective.'

He thought for a moment.

'Okay, so maybe Parker isn't someone you've pissed off, maybe it's the opposite – someone who likes you too much. Why did you ask Jamal about Charlie Edwards? That's your employee at the van, right?'

I gritted my teeth. 'I should tell you something.'

'Go on,' Lyons said.

'You remember Colin Parker, the guy whose office I burst into and accused of being a serial killer?'

'Yes, Parker stole his photos for his Connector profile.'

'Well, he's friends with Charlie on Facebook,' I said.

Lyons puffed out his cheeks. 'And you didn't think to tell me this earlier?'

'Because it's got to be a coincidence. I can tell you for a fact Charlie isn't Parker, that guy is all about drinking matcha tea and listening to Ethiopian jazz, murdering people is really not his vibe.'

Lyons leant against the railings, deep in thought as I kicked at some moss on the pier with my trainer.

'Your napkin. There was another name on it, wasn't there? You tore it off,' Lyons said. 'Was it Charlie?'

'No,' I said firmly. 'There is no other name, Aubrey. I told you. And Charlie is just a friend. He is not a killer. He's not Parker. And I have never been on a date with him, okay?'

'You told Charlie every detail of your dates, so he had plenty of information if he wanted to track them down,' he said. 'And I noticed he disappeared pretty quick when you told him I was with the police, so I did a background check.'

'You did a background check on him?' I said, surprised.

'We've done a background check on all your friends, Gwen. We need to tick all the boxes. It's part of the job.'

'Part of the job you've been doing for all of ten minutes,' I huffed, folding my arms.

'Do you have feelings for Charlie?' he asked.

'Feelings? No, Grandad. Are you going to ask if he's courting me next?'

'You know what I mean.'

'No, I don't see him that way. He's more like a little brother,' I said.

'Gwen, he's only three years younger than you, right?'

I flinched. He really had done his research. 'Well look, I suppose it's possible he has a teeny tiny crush on me. I'm his boss, he probably looks up to me, right? Plus we're trapped in a van together all day, so it's either flirt with me or stare out at the sea for eight hours.'

'So he *does* flirt with you?'

'Okay, yes, maybe sometimes, but it's more just mucking about, you know? I'm not even 100 per cent sure he's straight, come to think of it.'

'Don't you think Charlie could be a "teeny tiny" bit jealous when you go on all these dates?'

'Jealous enough to murder three people? No. I just don't

see it. Charlie wouldn't hurt a fly. In fact, I'm pretty sure he thinks he's going to get reincarnated as a fly.'

'He used to work in coding, you know that, right?'

'Yeah,' I replied. 'But he gave all that up, to come and work with—'

'With you,' Lyons said. 'You never wondered why a guy earning upwards of seventy thousand a year gave it all up to serve coffee in an ice cream van?'

'Um, no, because working with me in an ice cream van is way cool,' I said.

'Charlie was sacked from his coding job,' Lyons said.

My eyes widened. 'What? He never told me that. He said he'd had enough of working for The Man. What did he do?'

'It seems he signed a non-disclosure agreement with the firm, so we don't know exactly,' Lyons said. 'But NDAs are never about anything good.'

We stood in silence again for a moment, the wind whipping around our legs. The water rippled beneath us, reflecting a mix of red, blue and white light from the city above it. I shivered.

Lyons beeped his keys towards his car. 'I need to speak to Charlie, right now,' he said, marching off towards his Fiesta.

I ran after him.

'Wait, you don't really think he could have anything to do with this, do you?' I said. 'He's a total pacifist – he even likes seagulls. And we just checked, he doesn't have a Connector profile.'

Lyons didn't look back. 'He doesn't have one under his own name,' he said. 'But that doesn't mean he doesn't have one.'

'He's not Parker!' I cried. 'What about Seb? He's the next person on the napkin – we need to find him.'

'Yes. And I think there's a chance your friend Charlie might know where he is,' Lyons said. 'Where is Charlie right now?'

I looked at my watch. It was almost six.

'He'll be at the van, probably wondering where the hell I am. But listen, I'm telling you, he's got nothing to do with—'

'I'll drop you at the station on the way,' Lyons said, holding the car door open.

I tilted my head at him.

'Oh, come on, I think we're past these games now, Aubrey,' I said, climbing in the passenger side. 'I'm coming with you.'

TWENTY-NINE

By the time we arrived at Cuppacino, the sun had almost disappeared behind the horizon, and the few straggling dog walkers were heading home. We parked up on the Royal Parade and walked down to the pitch.

I thumped my fist twice on the side of the van.

'Charlie!' I shouted, peering through the van window. 'Get out here.'

Charlie had his head resting on the bags of coffee beans, baseball cap pulled over his eyes. I looked over apologetically at Lyons.

'Charlie!' I yelled again. 'We have a visitor.'

He sat up quickly, pulled his cap off, and slid open the window and stuck his head out.

'Bring your date to work day, is it?' Charlie said, aiming a raised eyebrow at Lyons. 'Where have you been all afternoon?'

'Believe me, you do *not* want to know. Charlie, this is *Detective* Lyons. Remember? The officer investigating those murders I told you about,' I said, before mouthing 'BE COOL' at him behind Lyons's back.

'I am cool,' he said out loud, before catching himself. 'Oh

sorry, right. Got you. Is everything alright? Do you want a coffee?'

He straightened his apron and attempted a winning smile.

'Relax, he just wants to ask you a few questions, Charlie,' I said.

'Actually, I'll have one of your Mr Whippys there, please,' Lyons said, his eyes scanning the chalkboard menu that hung behind Charlie.

'Do you have time for that?' I looked at Lyons like he was mad.

'I can take it from here, Gwen. Why don't you go and wait in the car?' Lyons said to me before turning to Charlie. 'Extra strawberry syrup, please.'

'Um sure, okay,' Charlie said, squeezing the bottle of sauce over the dripping ice cream cone.

As I instinctively started clearing away the empty cups from the tables, Lyons gave me a sharp look.

'Car, now, please, Ms Turner,' Lyons said firmly and turned back towards Charlie.

I sloped off towards the battered Ford Fiesta, trying to earwig as Lyons began his questioning, asking Charlie how long he'd worked there and how long he'd known me. But just as I was pulling open the passenger door, I heard him say, 'What's your relationship with Gwen like?'

I looked round to see Lyons leaning over the counter. Instead of stepping inside the car, I closed the door softly, and doubled back before he could see me. I snuck round to the other side of the van and pressed my body close against it.

'My relationship with Gwen is great, thanks,' I heard Charlie say. 'She's cool. We're good mates, we go down the pub. I'd consider her a friend. A good friend.'

'Perhaps more than friends?' Lyons said.

'What? No way, man. She's my boss.'

'So you're not attracted to her?'

I felt my cheeks blush.

'No!' he said, a bit too loudly for my liking.

'Robert Hamilton. Frederick Scott. Joshua Little. Dev Desai. Do you know these men?' Lyons asked him.

'Only because Gwen was mooning over their photos on Connector. Those are the guys she went on dates with, right?' Charlie said. 'She told me she'd been into the station to speak to you about it. Did she use me as her alibi or something? I can vouch for the fact that she was at work every day last week.'

'And what about *your* whereabouts last week?'

'What do you mean?' Charlie spluttered. 'You don't think…'

'I'd simply like to know where you were on the following dates,' Lyons said, pulling out his notepad.

'What the fuck? Why would I hurt anyone? I've never even met these people,' Charlie cried.

'Because maybe you didn't like the competition? Or maybe you thought these guys didn't treat your friend very well?'

'Excuse me?' Charlie laughed. 'You think I did this because I fancy Gwen?'

'Oh, so you *are* attracted to Gwen then?'

'Even if I was,' Charlie continued, 'I'm not sure the best way to win her over would be to go around murdering her exes.'

I clenched my fists and resisted thumping the back of the van. 'Not. My. Exes,' I mouthed.

'How do you know Colin Parker?' Lyons asked Charlie.

'Who?' he replied.

'You're Facebook friends with a Colin Parker. Do you know him or not?'

'I haven't been on Facebook for years,' Charlie said. 'It's not really my scene. Maybe I worked with him once or something. Why is this important?'

'We think more lives are in danger, and we need to know the truth,' Lyons said sternly. 'It's imperative we locate Sebastian Hunt.'

'Why would I know where he is?'

'Do you know his whereabouts or not?' Lyons asked again.

'Exactly what are you accusing me of here, detective?' Charlie spat.

'Let me spell it out for you, Charles. Three people have been murdered, and you not only knew who they were, you had a motive.'

'Is that what you're calling a motive now?' Charlie said, his voice getting louder. 'A non-existent crush on my boss?'

'Do you have romantic feelings for her or not?' Lyons asked.

'I really don't have to answer your questions, do I?' I could tell Charlie was getting majorly pissed off now. The only person I'd ever heard him get this annoyed with before was the customer who said our almond butter cookies tasted like pasteurised dog turds.

'You will if I ask you to come down to the station to make a full statement,' Lyons said. 'Why don't you just show me your phone, and we can put this to bed right now.'

'No,' Charlie replied. 'Why do you want to see my phone?'

'Do you have Connector on there?' Lyons asked.

'I don't.'

'Prove it,' Lyons demanded.

That was it, I'd had enough. As mildly amusing as this cock battle had been, it wasn't getting us anywhere. I took a deep breath and walked round to the front of the van.

'Just show him, Charlie,' I said. 'I know you don't have it on there.'

'Gwen!' Lyons snapped. 'How long have you been there? I said wait in the car.'

'You did say that, yes,' I said. 'And yet, somehow, here I am. Now, Charlie, just show the nice detective your phone and we can all move on from this colossal waste of time.'

Charlie sighed, pulled his phone out, entered his passcode and showed the screen to Lyons.

'Look,' he said, swiping across the screen so we could see all the apps on there. 'Deliveroo, Citymapper, even fucking Daily Horoscope.'

Lyons peered at the phone screen as Charlie cycled through his apps.

'Happy now?' Charlie asked, stuffing his phone back in his apron pocket. 'Jesus, man, I don't give a shit about any of those guys Gwen dated. I just wanted her to find someone she actually liked and maybe even manage a second date. But none of these clowns sounded like they were worth her time. In fact, sounds like some of them deserved what they got.'

'Charlie!' I cried, genuinely shocked. This definitely wasn't like him. *None of this was like him.*

'I have to say, Mr Edwards, you're not exactly talking like a man who didn't murder anyone,' Lyons said.

Charlie pulled off his apron and threw it behind him. 'Go to hell,' he said.

With that, he pushed open the van door and stomped off

towards town. As he reached the street, he turned his head back towards us.

'Oh, Gwen, by the way, I'm taking tomorrow off. Call it a "mental health day",' he called back as he disappeared into the milling pedestrians.

I stared at Lyons.

'Guess I hit a raw nerve,' he shrugged.

'Nice one, Luther. I'm still going to have to pay him, you know. And you didn't even touch your ice cream.'

Lyons carefully picked up the Mr Whippy with a napkin and dropped it into the bin by the van.

'You gonna go arrest him then?' I asked.

'No,' Lyons sighed.

'Good,' I said as I climbed into the van.

I filled the espresso machine with fresh beans and pressed the button. My body was demanding dopamine and crisps, and I was not going to deny it any longer. As the machine whirred into life, I grabbed a packet of some sort of artisan cracked pepper potato chips and began eating them.

'Honestly, I think you're barking up the wrong tree,' I told Lyons, pouring out two espressos into tiny cardboard cups. 'The guy barely has the energy to push a broom round the cafe, let alone stab someone.'

I leant out the window and held out a shot of coffee.

'We'll see about that,' he said, ignoring the espresso, picking up Charlie's apron and taking his phone from the pocket.

'Shit,' I said. 'Charlie, you idiot.'

Lyons began scrolling through the apps on Charlie's phone.

'How'd you get in?' I asked. 'What about the code?'

'Simple, when he drew a pattern to unlock the phone, he

left a greasy mark on the screen,' Lyons said. 'Good job he had sticky fingers.'

'The Mr Whippy,' I said, as it dawned on me. 'So they did teach you something in Detective School after all.'

'In chess, we call that a gambit,' he said. 'Now let's see what he was hiding on here.'

'You won't find anything. I told you, the guy's harmless.'

'Seems to me that pretty much every unattached person in this town *is* on Connector. Made me wonder why he isn't,' he said, scrolling through Charlie's phone.

'You're single, and you're not on it,' I offered. 'Should I be suspicious of you?'

Lyons looked up from the phone screen and met my eyes. 'Charlie has got a motive. He knows how to code, he's had access to your phone and knows every detail about your dating life. I think I have grounds for suspicion, don't you?'

He went back to tapping away on Charlie's phone.

'So?' I asked, watching his face scan the screen. 'Anything on there?'

'I'm not sure if you should see this,' he mumbled, engrossed in whatever he was looking at.

'Um, I've seen a dead body in a crazy golf course, I think I can take it,' I said.

Despite my bravado, I took a deep breath and quickly downed my espresso in preparation. I grimaced as the warm, bitter liquid hit my throat. *Gross.*

Lyons slid the phone across the counter to me. I picked it up. And my jaw dropped.

THIRTY

I looked at the phone in disbelief. There were countless messages from different people on Charlie's WhatsApp, and they were all saying the same thing.

'What is all this?' I said. 'They're talking about transferring Bitcoin to him, in exchange for… for what?'

'Keep scrolling,' Lyons replied.

'It's all about Connector profiles. But Charlie always made out like he wasn't interested in any of this stuff,' I said. 'He said these apps were for screenoholic wankers.'

'From the looks of that lot, he's *very interested* in this stuff,' Lyons said, watching me as I read through a few of the message threads. They were mostly from men, all arranging payment for Charlie to boost their Connector profiles.

I felt like someone had punched me hard in the stomach. He'd lied to me this whole time. He'd been doing this under my nose while I was blathering on about my stupid dates. I took a breath, picked up Lyons's shot of espresso and downed it.

'Alright, so what,' I said, wincing and wiping my mouth. 'He's running a side business, but this doesn't prove he's murdering anyone.'

'It proves he's not been telling either of us the truth. It's not just a side business, he's blackmailing these men.'

'What?'

'His phone number, Gwen, it matches the unknown number we found on Rob, Freddie and Josh's phones. And I'll bet you it's on Dev's too. He's threatening to name and shame them online unless they pay him thousands. And look at this,' Lyons said.

Reaching over the counter, Lyons scrolled through the WhatsApp chats on Charlie's phone until he reached the most recent message, sent just twenty minutes ago.

Charlie: Time's up. I need the money now.

Seb: Come to The Eye, I can give you cash.

'The Eye?' I said. 'Charlie must be meeting Seb at the Eastbourne Eye.'

A monstrous tourist trap built from white steel and bad ideas, about two miles up the seafront, the Eastbourne Eye Ferris wheel was almost exclusively for out-of-towners or terrible first dates.

'I need to get to him before Charlie does,' Lyons said.

'So what are we waiting for? Let's go!'

'Not this time,' Lyons said. 'You're staying here. I'll get someone from the station to come and pick you up.'

'I'm going to be 100 per cent safer with you than sat by myself in an ice cream van on a deserted beach waiting to get stabbed. What happened to watching out for me?'

For a second, Lyons looked like he was about to acquiesce, but then pursed his lips and shook his head.

'I *am* watching out for you, Gwen. And this could be very dangerous. Stay in the van and lock the door,' he said firmly, pocketing Charlie's phone. 'Understand?'

He got in his car and slammed the door.

And with that, I found myself standing alone, surrounded by crusts and crumbs, damp coffee grounds and a feeling of immense uselessness. Slumped over the counter, I watched Lyons drive off in the direction Charlie went. Then I sat down on my favourite crisp box, defeated, and thought about Seb.

THIRTY-ONE

I turn away from the mirror.

'No, no, no you don't,' Sarah says, placing a hand on each of my shoulders and turning me slowly back round. 'This is it, Gwen, this is definitely the one.'

I take a deep breath and squint at the flamingo-pink vision in front of me. Yep, no shit she thinks this is the one. She was going to drift down the aisle like an elegant swan, while I'd be waddling in front of her dressed as a giant prawn.

'You look amazing,' Sarah coos over my shoulder. 'How much do you love it?'

'Um, about exactly as much as the first time I tried it on four months ago,' I say.

I feel like I've spent the last twenty-two weekends in this bridal shop, endlessly trying on slight variations of the same dress. Sarah snakes her arms around my waist and perches her chin on my shoulder.

'I know it's totally not your thing,' she says. 'But thank you for pretending.'

I let the word hang in the air for a moment. Pretending.

That was something I was going to have to get really good at. I wriggle out of her embrace and face her.

'Look, are you absolutely, positively, definitely sure about Richard?'

'Not this again,' she sighs. 'I honestly do not know what you have against the guy.'

'Nothing!' I squeal. 'It just sometimes seems like you're more interested in the idea of getting married than the man you're marrying, that's all.'

I always thought that Sarah had an overly romanticised view of marriage. Her parents had the sort of relationship you only see in Richard Curtis movies – dedicated, loving and solid as a rock. She'd grown up in a gorgeous (and massive) cottage in Haywards Heath, surrounded by idyllic countryside, and while she didn't technically own a pony, I was pretty sure she hung out with one on a regular basis. It was classic British romcom territory, so no wonder she always dreamt of a bumbling English fop to sweep her off her feet. Maybe it was these high standards that had kept her single for years, but it was more likely that every guy she'd dated before Richard had treated her like shit. Nevertheless, she'd held out for her knight in shining armour, and remarkably, he had arrived. Or so she thought, anyway.

'I love Richard,' she says. 'I know he's a little boring, but I like that about him. I had quite enough bad boys, thank you very much. Richard is gentle. Sensible. Harmless. Reminds me of your dad a bit, you know?'

I flinched, but I knew she meant well. Sarah had idolised my dad almost as much as I did.

She'd been with me the day it happened. We'd just won the netball quarters and we were about twelve shots down at

Flares when I got the phone call. Sarah put me straight in a cab and went with me to the hospital. I'll never forget seeing Mum dry sobbing in the car park when we arrived. I was too late, and nothing would ever be the same again.

'It's just that…' I try to explain. 'I just want you to be happy, you know that, right?'

'Gwen,' she says. 'I hear you. But no more of this talk, okay? You can make me happy by getting along with Richard and supporting my decisions. You're maid of honour, after all.'

'Yeah, okay,' I mumble. '"Here if you need", right?'

'That's better,' she smiles. 'Now, are we going to try on just one more, just in case?'

'No,' I say. 'This is the one, remember? Besides, I've got a date in about forty-five minutes.'

'Another date?' she sighs. 'I keep telling you, you don't have to bring someone to the wedding. In fact, I'd prefer it if you didn't. The day is supposed to be all about me, remember? Not you trying to make Noah jealous.'

'There's no chance of that in this dress,' I say.

'Hey, remember what we said about supporting my decisions!' Sarah squeals.

'I should really get going. We all good here, bestie?' I smile at her, winningly.

'Yeah, okay, we're good,' Sarah says after a moment. 'I'll see you back at home later. Go meet Mr Completely and Utterly Wrong, and don't say I didn't warn you.'

'Might take this off first,' I say, grabbing my things and heading to the changing rooms. 'Not sure that Mr Blobby is the best look for a first date. Love you.'

'Hey, wait a minute, what do you mean Mr Blobby?' Sarah says, her voice rising.

But I was already gone.

As I walk down the promenade to meet Sebastian, it occurs to me that I don't have a clue what he actually looks like. It's not that I thought he'd used old photos, or Facetuned his profile to Kardashian levels of flawlessness, it's more that the pictures left only the vaguest sense of what his real face looked like. A slightly out of focus shot of him at a rugby match, a group shot at a wedding taken from a distance and one of him with sunglasses and a baseball cap on some sort of boat. I mean, sunglasses and a hat on a dating profile pic? That's just ridiculous. But from the little of what I could make out, I thought there was at least a 60 per cent chance of him being really handsome, and that was a bet I was willing to take.

His profile listed his profession as 'actor / screenwriter', and he messaged like he was born in about 1840 – calling me Gwendolyn and referring to me as a woman, not a girl. So I'm sort of looking forward to being courted by what I like to imagine is a young Hugh Grant type.

That's why I said yes when he suggested a spin on the Eastbourne Eye. Sure, me and Charlie had spent many hours mocking the tourists who sat on the painfully slow wheel as it creaked round, offering them an aerial view of the town's rapidly deteriorating architecture. But secretly, I've always liked the idea of being in one of the little glass pods, cut off from the world, even if it was just for twenty minutes.

When I arrive, I am pleased to see my gamble seems to have paid off. Seb is wearing a crisp blue shirt, opened maybe one button too far. He has a light, unseasonable tan and blond wavy hair. The smooth skin on his face looks like he'd never had to shave in his life. He steps aside to let me climb into our pod first, and we begin to slowly climb into the air. He smells a bit like my mum's posh hand wash. I think about saying that to Seb just to watch his face.

'This is great.' I smile, gazing at the sea that I'd looked at a million times. But to be fair, it does look amazing from up here. I can almost see my van, Alfredo, all the way down the beach. 'Have you been on The Eye before?'

'I actually come here quite a bit,' he said. 'Not on dates, I hasten to add! I come here to practise my lines. Rehearse. Just be. *It's so peaceful in these capsules, you know?* No *one can disturb me. I call it my safe space.'*

'Yeah,' I say. 'I know what you mean.'

'I'm glad you like it. I wanted to make our first date special,' he purrs, before joining me at the glass. 'So, what would be your idea of a perfect second date?'

He puts a hard emphasis on the word second, and aims his pearly white beam directly at me.

'Laser Quest, definitely Laser Quest,' I say.

'Not the theatre then?' he smiles.

'I'm more of a pizza and beer type of girl, if I'm honest,' I say. Shit, I am really bad at flirting when I actually fancy someone.

'Dinner it is then...' He grins. 'I'll make a reservation for next week.'

'Uh, well maybe let's see how tonight goes first,' I laugh.

'Well, let's see if this helps to convince you,' he says, opening his small bag and pulling out a bottle of champagne.

'Oh wow, nice,' I smile. 'I thought actors were supposed to be skint!'

'Ah, well,' he says. 'It helps when you have a very generous father. He's been so supportive. Well, with his money anyway.'

Seb looks away for a moment, his smile vanishing as he

busies himself with the foil wrapper on the bottle. He then pops the cork expertly, and pours the champagne into the two plastic flutes also secreted in his manbag. I take a sip just as the pod jolts forward a little, and cough when the bubbles hit the back of my throat.

'Keep going,' Seb says. 'It's an acquired taste.'

'Just like me,' I say, biting my lip and trying to continue my terrible attempt at flirting.

'So how has dating been going for you so far?' he asks.

'Um, well, I'm still single,' I shrug. 'So I guess not great.'

'You just haven't met the right person yet,' he smiles.

'Ha, yeah ain't that the truth,' I say, rolling my eyes.

'Been on a few bad dates, hmm?'

'Well, first there was this guy Rob. Seemed nice enough, but he started pretending we were being filmed for a reality TV show. Every time he knocked his wine glass over, or said something stupid, he gestured to the corner of the bar and said, "Graham, make sure you edit that bit out!".'

'Sounds thoroughly toxic,' Seb says, nodding.

'The next guy, Freddie, when there was a lull in the conversation, he started leaning towards me and counting down out loud, like he was a spaceship getting ready to blast off. He was actually counting down to kiss me.'

'Hopefully that was to make 100 per cent sure that you fully consented,' Seb says.

'Oh yeah,' I say. 'I had at least three seconds to change my mind before "launch".'

'Any more?' Seb asks.

'Well, then there was Josh,' I say. 'I ended up assaulting him with a golf club. Don't ask.'

'I'm sure he deserved it,' Seb smiles.

'And last but not least, Dev, who ghosted me.'

'Men!' Seb rolls his eyes dramatically. 'Please allow me to apologise on their behalf.'

'Well, at least they turned up for a date.' I shrug. 'Most men on Connector just want me to send them nudes, to be honest.'

'And do you comply?' he asks, arching an eyebrow.

'Hardly ever,' I say. 'But mostly because I can never get a good angle.'

'For me, seeing a woman naked isn't seeing her without any clothes on. It's seeing her hopes and dreams and fears, does that make sense? If someone sent me a nude, I'd probably just crop it so it only had her face in.'

'Wow, that's so, um, progressive?' I offer.

'I guess what I'm saying is, the quality I look for in a woman is her personality,' he says.

'Well, that's good because I've got loads of them,' I smile.

He looks confused.

'My mother brought me up to respect women, whatever their… ah, issues might be. She always said I was her little Prince Charming and James Bond all rolled into one.'

'Your mum sounds great,' I say.

'She is,' he says, his gleaming smile turning downwards as he looks away towards the sea. 'She's not been well recently. Starting to forget things. I promised her she could walk me down the aisle this year! If that's okay with you, that is?'

He flashes his bright white teeth at me again, his brief moment of introspection gone.

'Um, well, like I said, let's see how this date goes first, shall we?' I blush and look out the window.

'Ah, I see. You've been hurt before, haven't you?' he says, pointing at me with his index finger.

'Excuse me?'

'You put a brave face on, but your eyes betray you. I'm very good at reading people,' he says.

'Give over,' I laugh.

'It's alright, you don't have to talk about it. But trust me, you'll feel better if you do.'

I can feel my blood slowly simmering, but I mentally reduce the heat and carry on.

'I'm okay, thanks, Seb,' I tell him, sipping more champagne.

'All I ask is that you shouldn't judge us all by our worst examples. I promise you, there are some good men left out there,' he continues. 'I've been hurt too, you know. But I try not to close myself off because of it. Maybe I could show you how?'

'Are you sure you want to? Maybe I'm a psychopath. I used to squash spiders on the reg. Don't worry, these days I scoop them up and chuck them outside. Is that worse, do you think? Being chucked out at a terrifying height onto concrete? How would you prefer to go? Squished by a giant fist or catapulted to your doom out of a window?'

I'm babbling, but I just really want to change the subject.

'Gwen, is this about spiders or is this about you? I think this hot mess manic pixie dream girl thing is just a bit of an act, isn't it? What are you hiding under there?'

'Sorry, I thought this was a date, not a psychotherapy session,' I say.

'No need to be so defensive,' he smiles. 'Relax, I told you, this is a safe space.'

That's the second time in a week I've been accused of being defensive, and suddenly the glass bubble seems very small indeed. I turn to look out the window again, just as our pod reaches the crest of its orbit. I pretend to gaze at the water below, as if it's changed at all during the last eight minutes, and take the opportunity to pull out my phone and text Sarah.

Gwen: Pros: he brought champagne. Cons: incredibly full of himself.

Sarah: Well, that probably means he's a really good kisser.

Gwen: How would you know? ;-)

Sarah: I wasn't a virgin before I met Richard, you know? I have had some experience dealing with players, and trust me, the arseholes are always the best kissers.

Gwen: Well I'm not ready to officially assign him arsehole status just yet.

Sarah: You're going to stick it out for a few glasses of free fizz?

Gwen: Well I'm literally stuck in a glass cage, so yeah, I kinda have to.

Sarah: Isn't there an emergency brake in those things? Can't you press the alarm button or something?

Gwen: Gotta go. He's saying something. I better give him my undivided attention.

I turn around to see Seb talking to someone on his phone.

He holds up a finger to indicate – what? He'd be one minute, or I should shush? I wait while he finishes his conversation. Eventually he puts the phone down and smiles at me.

'Sorry about that,' he says. 'Now, where were we? You were opening up about your previous relationship?'

'Was I?'

'Trust me, Gwen, I'm a good listener. I know women get talked over a lot. It happens in my improv class all the time. But I always let my "supporting actresses" have their say before I decide how the scene is going to go.'

'Wow, they should give you a certificate or something,' I say.

Seb laughs again. 'I know, I know,' he says. 'I don't mean to patronise. I'm just saying, I'm an ally. I'm one of the good ones.'

'Pleased to hear it,' I say.

'I love women,' he says. 'And by love, I actually mean respect. I'm honestly really pissed that my latest screenplay doesn't pass the Bechdel test. Granted, it's an arbitrary bar to judge by, and my work has some feminist themes in it that are hopefully a little more deep-rooted than that, but I do worry about it.'

I'm tempted to start clapping my hands very, very slowly.

'I mean, the characters are all women, of course, which was really refreshing to write. They're all fighting over the same man, a rather dashing chap named Jeb. It really helped me understand the female struggle. One of the characters –Trish, wonderfully coarse sense of humour, real salt-of-the-earth type – she waits tables at the local cafe, menial work, like yours. I'd love a sensitivity read if you have time?' he says.

I go over to the door of the pod, but we're still only

three-quarters of the way round. Stepping out now would be a fifty-foot drop. It's either die or read this guy's screenplay. Tough choice.

'Um, yeah, maybe,' I mumble.

'Ah, yes, I see what you're getting at. You think it's not my place, as a man, to tell these women's stories. You're quite right, we've heard enough male voices now. Time to let the ladies have a go. Now, normally I'd totally agree, but I really think this might be my best work, so maybe we could make an exception for little old me?' he says, arching an eyebrow. 'Like I said, we're not all monsters, you know. Now, I'm very sorry if you've been treated badly by a man in the past, but that doesn't mean that...'

'I didn't say I'd been treated badly,' I interrupt.

'Really?' he says.

'Really,' I say.

He places a hand on my shoulder and squeezes. 'Tell me, what happened, Gwen? Who hurt you?'

I close my eyes and take a deep breath. There's no escape.

'It was my fault, not his, if you must know,' I say quietly. 'It was me. I fucked up, okay. And I'd do anything to change that. But it's too late.'

I push my hair behind my ears and take another breath.

'Anyway,' I say, forcing a smile. 'Let's not tell our sad stories. Not while there's still champagne left.'

Seb strokes my arm and pushes out his bottom lip, making an exaggerated sad face.

'You know, my therapist says that physical massage can be a really effective way to heal psychological wounds. If you need someone to work out your issues on, I'd happily consent.'

'No, thank you.'

'Or I could give your neck a little rub right now. Ease out that tension. Of course, the real tension is right here.' Seb points at my chest.

'My breasts?'

'Your heart.' He reaches towards me with both hands, wriggling his fingers.

I step back.

'I said, let's talk about something else.'

'Of course, but before we do, can I just say—' he begins.

'You know, for someone who is such a good listener,' I snap, 'you sure do have a lot to say.'

'She says, as she interrupts me in the middle of a sentence for the third time tonight.' He smiles.

'You're the one who took a phone call in the middle of a date,' I sigh.

There's an awkward silence before he speaks again.

'That was my mum,' he says. 'I call her at the care home at the same time every evening, routine is really important for her.'

I feel a pang of guilt ripple through me. 'Oh right, sorry, Seb,' I say. 'Can we go back to talking about spiders now?'

'I don't have a lot to say about that,' he says quietly.

We spend the rest of the time pretending to see something incredibly fascinating in the endless grey swathes of ocean beneath us.

When I look over at him, he's got his phone out again. I catch a glimpse of the screen only to see he's got bloody Connector *open. Great, now he's swiping in the middle of our date. Probably lining up his next 'supporting actress'. This is next-level negging. I squint, trying to make out the name on the profile he's looking at. Starts with a P. Then an A, followed by an R...*

Suddenly, before I can see the rest, the wheel jolts to a stop, and Seb looks up. Seeing me staring at him, he quickly stuffs the phone back in his pocket and forces a thin smile.

'Terra firma,' he says.

An attendant pulls open the door of the pod and I feel the presence of some much-needed fresh air. When Seb tries to take my hand to help me out, I decline.

'Well, it was really nice meeting you,' he says as we walk across the grass that surrounds the Eye. 'But I must bid you farewell. Things to do, people to meet.'

'Like another date?' I mutter under my breath.

His face flushes, but he pretends not to hear me.

'I hope you had a pleasant evening, Gwendolyn.'

And with that, he pecks me on the cheek and disappears towards town. As I trudge home across the beach, my phone beeps.

Seb: I need to be honest because the last thing I want to do is lead you on. You're too fragile to be messed around. Regrettably, I didn't feel a connection on our date. I hope you don't mind, but I wanted to offer some advice for the future: if you continue to keep your guard up, you'll likely discover that it's very difficult to find the happiness you're looking for. But I'd be happy to email over my screenplay if you'd still like to read it. Stay safe.

Five minutes later, another message arrives.

Seb: Send nudes?

As the last of the light fades, I sink my thumb onto the 'block' button and kick a pebble as far into the receding waves as I can.

THIRTY-TWO

My thoughts were interrupted by a beep from my phone. I looked down to see a Connector message.

> Parker: not sure the Eye is going to be a safe space much longer

I stared at the message, my brain struggling to compute what I was reading.

Safe space. That was what Seb had called the Eye…

I tried to ignore my thumping heart as I attempted to figure out what the hell that could mean. Then something hit me. I squeezed my eyes tight and tried to picture the name on the profile that Seb was looking at on our date.

Wait.

It was Parker. The name on the profile was Parker. It didn't seem relevant at the time, but now it all made sense. He wasn't swiping through women's profiles, it was his own.

'Fuck,' I said out loud.

Charlie wasn't Parker. Seb was Parker.

I'd told Seb everything about Rob, Freddie, Josh and

Dev. He knew who I'd dated and how they'd treated me. He'd killed them, and now Charlie was next. And, if Lyons got there before him, he was going to run straight into a knife.

I had to warn them. I looked at the clock on the dashboard – ten to seven – I didn't have much time. The Eye was all the way down the seafront. There was no way I'd catch them up on foot. Jumping into the driving seat of the van, I scrambled through the many, many useless keys on my key ring until, finally, I found the one.

'Alright, Alfredo,' I said, jamming it in and starting the engine. 'This is your big moment. Let's do this.'

Poor old Al hadn't been driven since Noah and I parked him up on the seafront three months ago. Praying there was enough petrol left in the tank to get me to the other side of town, I pulled off the handbrake and whammed my foot on the accelerator. Al spluttered into life, sending the paper cups and cutlery shaking off the counter behind me. I ignored them, spun the wheel and pulled onto the Royal Parade towards the town centre. In the distance I could just make out Charlie, but I couldn't see Lyons's Fiesta anywhere. I hit redial on his phone number, jabbed the 'speaker' button and chucked my phone on the passenger seat.

'Come on, come on, pick up,' I muttered as it rang endlessly.

When it eventually connected to his voicemail, I yelled into the receiver. 'It's not Charlie, it's Seb,' I cried. 'Parker is Seb! Ah fuck it, you're never going to listen to this, are you.'

I kicked the accelerator. Up ahead, I saw Charlie turning into Colbert Street. I sped up and followed him, but as I turned left, my heart fell. The road was jammed with traffic. I desperately scanned the dashboard for the horn, before remembering there wasn't one. My eyes fell on the box of special controls for the ice cream van. I jabbed the button marked 'music' and tinkling melodies began to pour out of the speaker system on the roof.

As I whacked the volume dial up to ten, the insanely annoying music reached an almost unbearable level. I wound down the window and stuck my head out.

'Get out of my way,' I screamed at the cars. 'It's an emergency!'

Miraculously, the cars in front of me started to pull over onto the pavement. I hit the accelerator again and charged through the gap in the middle. I could see Charlie ahead. Hearing the music, he turned around to see the van motoring up the street towards him.

I saw his jaw drop. He broke into a run.

'Wait,' I yelled out of the window. 'It's Seb! Seb is Parker! He's going to kill you!'

He didn't seem to be able to hear me over the damn tinkling music blaring from the speakers. The road was clear here, so I slammed my foot down until the speedometer was kissing forty.

'Bloody hell, Al,' I said. 'Help me out here, will you?'

The chassis scraped across the tarmac as Al just about made it over the hill. Charlie was reaching the end of the street now, and I saw him heading towards the steps to the Promenade, the blinding sun silhouetting him as he disappeared over the horizon.

I couldn't follow, but I could cut him off by driving over Wishtower Slopes. I spun the wheel again and the van trundled over the pavement and onto the grass. I sped past a distressed-looking mother clutching the hands of two small children. Their eyes suddenly lit up as they heard the damn ice cream music.

'Sorry!' I yelled out the window as their little faces fell. 'Can't stop!'

The mother mouthed an unrepeatable word at me as I whizzed past them. I'd lost sight of Charlie, but I could see the huge steel spokes of the wheel come into view ahead of me. The van bumped up and down as I sped through the park. The grass, which had been so vibrantly green in the summer, was now sparse and yellow, and patches of muddy snow still remained in the shadow of The Eye. I could feel Al's wheels slipping as I struggled to steer him through the locals walking their dogs or strolling around the park. In the centre of the park, the Eye dominated the skyline, slowly revolving as the few tourists who'd braved the cold climbed on and off.

I peered out through the windscreen, but I couldn't see Charlie or Lyons among the groups of people milling around, waiting to buy a ticket.

'Come on, come on!' I shouted at Al as he spluttered towards them.

I scanned the glass pods. Straining my eyes, I could just about make out two male figures standing in one of the lower pods. One of them seemed to be wearing a baseball cap, but the other I couldn't see well enough to recognise. They must have just got in, as the wheel was only just beginning to turn.

As I approached, I could see the pod slowly rise. There was no way I could reach them in time. There was only one option. Jamming my foot down, I whacked the music back up, deafening the small crowd in front of the Eye, who scattered as I sped towards it.

'Out of the way!' I screamed, as the van gained pace down the slope towards the seafront.

People started yelling as they ran out of my path, leaving the van headed directly for the Eye. I could see the horrified faces of the onlookers on the promenade as they realised what was about to happen.

I closed my eyes, and with a guttural crunch, the van crashed into the bottom of the wheel, jamming itself between the giant spokes. I jerked forward, my seat belt straining as my phone flew off the passenger seat and the boxes in the back clattered to the floor, scattering Flakes everywhere. With a horrible screeching noise, the giant wheel lurched to a halt.

I jumped out of the van. Thin smoke seeped out from the crumpled bonnet while a single spark flickered pathetically from the cracked left headlight. To my relief, the tinkling music slowed and gradually faded, like a wind-up toy slowly running out of power.

Onlookers started shouting as the passengers in the top pods began to bang on the glass of their now-stationary metal prisons. Ignoring them, I jumped up onto the bonnet and reached for the door of Charlie's pod. As I swung it open, I saw Charlie pressed against the back window, his hands up and face contorted in horror. Lyons was standing motionless, staring at something on the floor of the pod.

I must have screamed when I realised what it was, because Charlie looked up at me, seemingly only just noticing I was there.

'I... I didn't...' he stuttered.

'Don't move!' Lyons shouted. But nobody was moving, least of all the dead body on the floor.

Seb's dead body.

THIRTY-THREE

Two hours later, I was sitting in an empty waiting room in Eastbourne police station.

I sat there and stared at the wall, which was a particularly bland shade of oatmeal. I put my hands through my hair and scratched behind both ears simultaneously. It felt like I'd been waiting there for an eternity.

When I listened to *Danger Land*, I'd always imagine how I'd react if I was a witness to a murder, what I'd say to the police and how my evidence would be integral to solving the mystery. But now, sitting in a cold, beige police station, I knew the reality was actually fucking horrible.

I hadn't solved a thing. I was too late, and now Seb was dead, like the others. He'd never go on another date, never finish that stupid screenplay. Never see his mum again. And it was my fault. Parker had been right in front of me the whole time, but my head had been stuck too deep in the sand to see it.

I got out my phone and googled Sebastian Hunt, found his Instagram feed and scrolled through the photos. Some of them I'd seen when I'd stalked him before our date, but once

I'd scrolled past the posed shots and the relentless sunsets, I found pictures of him laughing with his mates around a table in Pizza Express. A bit of deeper digging led me to his Facebook profile, which had not been updated for years, but showed some very sweet childhood photos. Him and his (I assume) brother gleefully stuffing birthday cake into their mouths and an awkward but adorable public school photo. Seb must've been about eleven, and his hair had been tightly combed back across his head, probably an attempt by his mother to make him look smart that had resulted in him looking a little like a mini mafioso gangster. I thought about his mum in the nursing home, waiting for her evening phone call that never came. That was on me.

Lyons had told me to stay put in the waiting room, but I couldn't just sit there and look at the wall any longer. I got up and poked my head out of the door. It was nearly midnight, and the station was deserted.

Somewhere halfway up the strip-lighted corridor, I found myself face to face with my reflection in the station's sole vending machine. The person that stared back at me, partially obscured by a Toffee Crisp, looked tired and confused. It was only marginally better than the view of that beige wall.

I stared at my puffy, panda-eyed face, wiped my eyes with the sleeve of my hoodie and fished around in my pockets for change. Of course, there was nothing there but empty gum wrappers, so I leant against the wall and listened to the buzzing of the strip lights.

A week ago, my biggest problem was sourcing a job lot of hilarious novelty straws for a hen do. And now here I was, on the brink of unravelling in an empty corridor, weeping for men I'd barely known, temporary acquaintances, fodder for anecdotes at best. But my life would be intertwined with theirs – forever.

Eventually, Lyons appeared with a cup of tea. He handed it to me. As a goodwill gesture, it didn't quite meet the mark, but I took it anyway.

'We've arrested Charlie. He's with his lawyer,' he said.

'And? It was him? He killed Seb? He's really Parker?'

'Yes. We found a knife in the pod – it's with forensics now. If only I'd got there sooner, but I must have been just minutes too late.' Lyons looked at his shoes.

I turned back to my reflection in the vending machine, unable to formulate any words worth saying.

'Come on,' Lyons said, holding out his hand. 'My office is a lot comfier than the corridor, and I'm sure I've got something stronger than tea in there somewhere. I'll show you what we know so far.'

I kept my eyes trained on the chocolate bar.

'Okay,' I said. 'But first, have you got any change?'

Five minutes later, I was sitting on a swivel chair, stuffing the last of a Toffee Crisp in my mouth and watching as Lyons pointed to a map of Eastbourne, stuck to a pinboard. Freddie, Rob, Josh, Dev and Seb's names were pinned to the map, alongside various photos and Post-it notes.

'I think that thing was two years out of date,' Lyons said, looking at the chocolate smeared around my mouth.

I wiped my face with my sleeve.

'This is your office?' I said, spinning the chair and looking around. 'I thought you were just a rookie?'

The office was, in truth, only *slightly* comfier than the

corridor. There were a couple of desks in each corner, and a battered-looking old leather sofa pushed against the back wall.

'Uh, well, normally this is Forrester's office, we took it over as a sort of nerve centre. I sit over there, but look, I want to show you something,' said Lyons, pointing to the pinboard. It was full of scribbled words and arrows, and in the middle, surrounded by several red circles, was Charlie's name.

I let the swivel chair gradually come to a stop and chucked the chocolate wrapper in the bin.

'Okay, so, looks like your friend Charlie has been running a nice little business boosting profiles on Connector,' Lyons explained. 'Basically, he's a hacker, linked to several 4chan accounts. Men, and it is almost *all* men, are paying him a hundred dollars in cryptocurrency to push their profile to the top of the rankings. Reckons he can guarantee they'll get seen by one hundred times more women. We know Charlie was fired from his old job, and was in some serious debt.'

'He used to work with Richard,' I said. 'But I never heard about any of this.' I thought for a moment. 'What does all this app stuff have to do with the murders?'

Lyons went over to his desk. 'Look at this,' he said, spinning the monitor of his computer round so I could see. 'Our cyber team tracked down a list of all Charlie's customers. These are all the profiles he boosted – there must be thirty odd names here,' he went on. 'And the five names on your napkin? All there.'

I stuffed my hand in my pocket and felt for the napkin. It was still there. I crumpled it in my hand and squeezed it hard. It seemed to pulse in my fist, like a telltale heart.

'Seems like one hundred dollars a pop wasn't enough to

pay off his debts. Charlie was blackmailing them, along with half his customers,' Lyons continued. 'And not just about manipulating the app. Charlie's code gave him access to all their Connector data. Seems like the five men on your napkin were in the habit of sending women some pretty horrible stuff.'

'Like what?'

'Unsolicited nudes, demands for pictures in return, threats to share the images if they didn't agree to more dates, abuse, even death threats. More than enough to get them cancelled, fired from their jobs, or even end up in court if the women pressed charges.'

I felt sick. 'Okay, so they were scum. But why would Charlie kill them?' I asked. 'Wouldn't that be a really shitty business decision?'

'From the messages, it looks like the five men on your napkin had enough of paying up, and threatened to go to the police.'

'Wait, if Charlie was trying to cover this up,' I said, 'then why taunt me as Parker on the app? It doesn't make sense.'

'I'm sorry, Gwen. He was setting you up to take the fall. Don't you see? He was making sure you were seen at all the crime scenes. And look, here, on his list of customers,' Lyons said.

I leant closer to the screen. There was Parker's name.

'You think it's the same one?' I said.

'How many Parkers can there be in Eastbourne?' said Lyons. 'It's got to be him. We can see the Parker profile was boosted, but there's no record of any monetary transaction between Charlie and Parker, no messages to arrange payments, nothing.'

'So they're the same person? Charlie really is Parker? But he didn't have the app on his phone.'

'Not this phone, no. But I'm willing to bet Charlie has many different phones. And it's likely he deleted the Parker profile when he realised I was closing in on him.'

'I don't believe it,' I said quietly. 'He was always so…'

'So nice?' Lyons said. 'Yeah, well, it's the nice guys you have to watch out for. In my experience, there's no such thing.'

I nodded my head slowly. 'But what about Seb? He was looking at Parker's Connector profile, I saw it on his phone on our date.'

Lyons paused to consider this. 'We think Charlie was probably using the Parker profile as proof of concept, you know, showing clients that his coding worked.'

I couldn't believe Charlie – my friend Charlie – would do this. Had his whole 'stoner dude' vibe been just a big act? All those days in the van we'd spent laughing about my terrible dates. I'd told him every last detail about all of them. Had I given him the ammunition to kill them? My eyes seemed to pulse, as if they were preparing to hold back the tsunami of tears that was fast approaching. I pinched the top of my nose, which didn't really help, but it did shield my face from Lyons.

'It's okay, Gwen. It's over. We did it,' he said.

Somehow, that didn't make me feel any better. I thought once we found Parker, stopped him, things would go back to normal. But right now, I couldn't imagine ever feeling normal again.

'I guess you'll get your promotion then. Back off to London. Congratulations,' I mumbled. 'What will happen to Charlie?'

'We have him in custody, and we can charge him with the

blackmail while we wait for forensics to match him with any of the evidence from the murder scenes.'

I put my head in my hands.

'Anything else?' I asked.

'Well, the damage to the Eye wasn't too serious, they should have it up and running for summer season.'

'So my only employee is a serial killer, my dates are all dead and now I'm going to get sued by the council. Any more good news?' I said.

'Your van is a write-off, I'm afraid,' Lyons added.

I didn't care. I'd stopped listening and was staring at the pinboard. Those names crudely written in blue marker pen were people, people I knew, or *had known* for a couple of hours at least. Whatever they'd done, they hadn't deserved this. Charlie, who I thought was my friend, had betrayed me. Worse, Lyons was saying he really was a cold-blooded murderer.

'This is all my fault,' I said quietly. I could feel my eyes welling up again, and I rubbed them fiercely in another futile attempt to stop the inevitable.

'It's not, Gwen, it's really not. You didn't pick up a knife, you didn't hurt anyone. I know this is horrible but you can't blame yourself.'

'You don't get it, do you?' I snapped.

Lyons came over and wrapped his arm around me. 'I get it, I do,' he said. 'You act like you don't care, you make jokes, but I know how terrifying this is.'

I nestled my head into his chest. It felt like that space was moulded to fit my skull, like an old armchair that retains the shape of its owner after years of familiarisation with their buttocks. I must have started to cry a little, because Lyons rubbed my back and repeated the words 'It's okay' like a mantra, just the way Noah used to do. For a moment, I wished he was here, that it was his arm around my shoulder, that I was wiping my eyes on his sleeve. I wanted him to tell me this was all a bad dream, and then tell me off for smudging his shirt with mascara. Then we'd curl up on his sofa, eating bad pizza and watching even worse TV.

I wanted so much to be back there and not here, I almost convinced myself that the police station was the fantasy, and Noah and his TV and his pizza and his arms were real. And maybe, if I never opened my eyes again, I could be there forever.

I wanted everything else to disappear. I wanted to never leave his arms again.

And shit, I really, really wanted another Toffee Crisp.

I opened my eyes, and reality came slowly into focus. I was still there in the cold, sparse police station office. I pushed Lyons's arms off of me.

'Don't,' I said. 'Just don't. Sorry, but you don't know me. You don't know anything about me.'

'Hey, hey, it's okay,' Lyons said gently.

'Yeah, you keep saying that. I know it's okay. I don't need you to tell me it's okay.'

Lyons stepped back. 'We have police counsellors you can talk to, Gwen,' he said.

I didn't want to speak to a counsellor. I just wanted to feel something different, to turn off my brain and not think about any of this.

'All I need is to get drunk and have a bath,' I said.

I slapped my forehead, remembering we had absolutely no alcohol in the flat. Sarah used to love being in charge of all the shopping, but since she was moving out, the organisational house duties had been left to me. And, you know, with all the murders and stuff, it just hadn't really been top of my list of priorities.

'What time is it?' I asked.

'Past midnight, sorry,' Lyons said.

'Damn,' I sighed. 'You said you had something stronger to drink? I'm betting DCI Forrester must have a sneaky bottle of Famous Grouse stashed under his desk.'

Lyons scratched the back of his head. 'Yeah, I'm pretty sure there's something back here that might help,' he said.

After rummaging in the bottom drawer of the filing cabinet for a minute, he emerged triumphantly with a half-empty bottle of Malibu.

'Finally, a Detective Lyons I can get on board with,' I said, taking the bottle from him and swigging it. 'Where'd you get this?'

'Confiscated item,' he said.

'Busted a teenage beach party?' I said, wiping my mouth, half disgusted and half delighted by the sickly tang of coconut. It tasted like a sunscreen milkshake.

I thrust the bottle towards Lyons. He shook his head, but I kept holding it there until he took it. He grabbed a large mug off one of the desks and poured some Malibu in.

'Yours?' I said. I noticed someone had taken a Sharpie to the 'No.1 Dad' slogan on the mug, scribbling a big fat zero next to the '1'.

'I think Forrester's wife bought it for him,' Lyons said. 'He's up in Lewes with the team. We're the only ones here.'

'Forrester really thought I was the killer, didn't he?' I asked.

'You know I really can't discuss that with you, Gwen,' he

said, but I saw his eyes flick down as he looked away from me.

'I knew it!' I cried. 'I knew he had it in for me from day one.'

Lyons said nothing. He sat down on the sofa, closed his eyes and put the mug to his lips. The more liquid he poured in his mouth, the more life seemed to drain out of him. When the mug was empty, he slumped back against the cushions. He looked older in the harsh office lighting. Still handsome, but in a crinkled sort of way, like a tired lion.

'Let's talk about something else,' he said.

I span around on the chair again, surveying the office. Lyons's desk was covered in receipts, business cards and Post-it notes. Nestled among them was a set of four passport-sized photos. The only sort of photo anyone bothered actually printing out these days. It was black and white, and it showed a woman with her hair pulled back tightly, looking seriously at the camera. She had sharp, beautiful features, thin delicate eyebrows and eyes that hurt a bit to look into.

'You never told me what happened with your wife,' I said.

'You really want to hear about that?'

'Yes, come on. Christ, anything that isn't, you know,' I waved my hands towards the whiteboard, 'that stuff.'

I sat down next to him on the sofa. 'Tell you what, let's play Truth or Drink,' I said.

'Isn't it called Truth or Dare?' Lyons asked.

'Nope, it's definitely Truth or Drink. Definitely. I ask you a question, you can either answer it truthfully, or drink. Question one, is she dead?'

'Gwen!' he cried. 'No.'

'Okay, divorced?'

Lyons took a big gulp from the mug.

'Oh right,' I said. 'I'm sorry. Was it recent?'

'Just over a year ago now.' He looked up at the ceiling and exhaled. 'Me and Olivia had been together pretty much since college. Got married too young. It seemed like the thing everybody did, you know? Move in, get married, have kids. Except we didn't quite get to that last bit. It felt like we were going through the motions. Eventually we were just treading water. I wasn't earning much in teacher training, and she was all about moving up, you know? I was the one letting the side down.'

'So you just gave up?'

'We didn't go to marriage counselling, or anything like that, if that's what you mean. But we did try. Well, I tried. Last year, she came home and told me she'd met someone else – her boss at the dental surgery where she worked. I wasn't surprised, and to be honest it was kind of a relief. That's when I quit my job and joined the Detective Programme. Coming back here was probably for the best, a fresh start.'

'And then what? You solve this case, get a promotion to the Met and return to London as a hero? A decorated homicide cop? Don't tell me you still want to impress her, Aubrey?'

He took another drink.

'Oh God, you do, don't you?' I cried. 'Even though she cheated on you? Don't you hate her?'

'I don't really see it like that. She wanted something more than I could give her. Someone she could build a future with, not a teacher who was never going to do better than Deputy Head in a grubby South London comprehensive. One of us needed to pull the trigger, and she did it. Hurt like hell, but it was sort of brave, really.'

'Bullshit,' I said. 'How can it be brave to cheat on someone?'

'No, the brave bit was owning up. That counted for a lot.'

I closed my eyes and took another swig of Malibu.

'My parents, they got divorced, you know?' he went on. 'It was awful for me and Grace. I never thought that would happen to me, but at least it happened before we had kids.'

'Yeah, I think I remember. Your sister was devastated. She missed about three weeks of school. We must have only been about thirteen.'

'That's right, and I was about to go to university. But after Dad left, I couldn't just up and leave as well. So I stuck around for a couple of years.'

'No wonder you grew up fast,' I said.

'I had to,' he said. 'And I think that's what Olivia liked about me. At first, anyway. I was responsible, practical, all that stuff.'

'So you're just fine with it?' I said. 'The divorce, the cheating?'

'For a long time I wasn't, but yeah, I think I am now. We're both in a better place,' he said.

'Well, she definitely is,' I said. 'She's shacked up with some dentist and you're drinking fricking Malibu out of a novelty mug with a strange woman at midnight.'

Lyons let out a low chuckle. 'For what it's worth, I don't think you're a strange woman, Gwen.'

'Good,' I said. 'Because I am very, *very* normal.'

'But you're right,' he said. 'Perhaps this isn't how I should be spending my weekends. Maybe it is time I got back out there.'

'Well, you know what I always say, Hakuna Matata.'

'What?'

'My motto. It's something I learnt from my time in Africa,' I said. 'It means "no worries", you gotta put your past behind you and move on.'

'Wait, you've been to Africa?'

'Oh come on, Aubrey,' I laughed. 'You really should know *The Lion King*. That's totally your era.'

He smiled and shook his head. 'I keep telling you, I am only five years older than you, Gwen. I am not old!'

'Right, you're not old.' I smiled. 'Just sensible.'

Lyons frowned. 'Is that really your motto?' he asked. 'No worries? Put your past behind you?'

'I thought it was,' I said. 'I wanted to "get back out there" too, but the harder I try to meet somebody new, the more I realise that anyone new isn't him, you know?'

'Noah?'

'Yeah. It's funny, out of all the men I've met since we broke up, you're the only one who didn't turn out to be a complete jerk.'

'Uh, thanks, I guess,' Lyons smiled.

He leant back into the sofa, his shoulder brushing against mine.

'Okay, my turn,' he said, passing me the bottle of Malibu.

'Go for it,' I said.

'What was the name you tore off the napkin?' Lyons asked. 'I know there was another name there, Gwen.'

The words pricked at my skin. I didn't answer. Instead, I lifted the Malibu bottle to my lips, closed my eyes and took a large swig. It wasn't until I felt Lyons's hand on my shoulder that I put the bottle down. When I opened my eyes, he was looking at me very seriously.

'Hey. It's over. We got him,' he said, so close now our noses were almost touching. 'It's okay. You can tell me. No one else is in danger.'

I opened my mouth to say something. I rolled the truth around in my mind for a moment before letting it slip down to my throat and sit on the tip of my tongue, just begging to be let out. But I couldn't say it. I couldn't say it out loud. Not after what Lyons had just told me.

'In which case,' I said eventually, 'it doesn't matter. Anyway, I drank! You know the rules, that means I don't have to answer.'

'But all the same, we should probably check on whoever it is, just to tie up any loose ends,' Lyons said.

'Loose ends,' I said. 'You're right, we don't want any of those.'

I leant in closer towards him and titled my head slightly. His eyes met mine and I could smell sweet coconut on his breath.

'You know, it wasn't just my mates who fancied you at school,' I said softly.

'Gwen, I—' he started.

But before he could finish, I kissed him.

'What are you doing?' he said, without any urgency in his voice. 'We shouldn't…'

'Shouldn't we?' I asked, kissing him again.

He placed his hand on my waist and kissed me back, hard. I ran my hands under his jacket, and pulled him closer. Suddenly my fingers reached leather where I expected cotton.

'Wait, are you even allowed to have one of these?' I asked, pulling back his jacket to see the holster strapped around his ribcage.

He removed his jacket and reached his right hand round to the chunky yellow Taser.

'They're not standard issue, no. But when there's a potential serial killer at large, we can get authorisation. Here, you just unclip this,' he flicked the clasp and took the Taser out, 'which allows you to withdraw the weapon quickly, and...'

'Is that supposed to impress me?' I asked.

'No, it's supposed to disable any approaching assailant. This is the X2 Double Shot, you know, top of the range. Fires a back-up shot if you miss the first time. Anyway, I was just making sure the safety catch was on. We don't want this discharging at—'

I placed my finger on his lips. 'Aubrey Lyons, I swear you are the worst flirt of all time,' I said, replacing my finger with my lips. 'Just shut up for a minute, will you?'

'Okay, how about this,' Lyons said, making an attempt at raising one eyebrow. 'How *you* doing?'

'What the hell was that?' I said.

His cheeks flushed slightly. 'Flirting. You know, "How you doing?", like Joey from *Friends*. Uh, the nineties references... I thought—'

'Okay. That's enough,' I smiled, pushing him back on the sofa and kissing him again.

His stubble rubbed against my face, but his lips were surprisingly soft, and the combination only made me kiss him harder. Strands of my hair slipped down between our lips as we kissed, and I had to pause to pull them away. I grabbed at his shirt, pulling it hard enough to rip off two buttons.

'Woah,' he laughed, looking down at his exposed chest. 'Don't hurt me, Gwen.'

'You're the one with the handcuffs,' I said, straddling him

and gently unbuttoning the remaining, unbusted, buttons. 'Now those *are* standard issue, right?'

''Fraid not,' he said, smiling. 'I think you watch too many American police shows.'

'I mainly watch baking shows, actually,' I said, running my hand over his now bare chest.

'Now you're teasing me?' He smiled. 'I can't keep up.'

'You're not meant to,' I said, and pulled off his belt with a flourish.

I looked down at his face, my shadow dividing it, one half in darkness and one in light. He laughed, and I couldn't tell if he was excited or slightly terrified.

'Gwen, we shouldn't...' he started. 'The rest of the team will be here in the morning...'

'Shhh, don't pick now to get all chatty again, Aubrey,' I said gently, pulling off my top and leaning down over him, kissing him reassuringly.

His hands rose up my body until they were tangled in my hair, and he abandoned any hesitation. I felt his hand move slowly up from my waist to my breast, and maybe it was the neat Malibu or perhaps the stress of being stalked by a serial killer, but something broke inside me and when it did, it was like an avalanche.

Afterwards, we lay there on the scratchy sofa, half-naked and covered only by Lyons's jacket. I rested my head on his chest and listened to the thump of his heart slowly come down.

'You take me to all the best places,' I said, surveying the shabby office, now strewn with discarded clothes and spilt Malibu.

'Well, when this is all over,' Lyons said, 'maybe we could go on like, a proper date?'

'What, like, somewhere that doesn't have a map of crime scenes pinned to the wall?' I said.

'Yeah,' he said. 'Somewhere like that.'

'As a rule of thumb, though, maybe don't bring a deadly weapon on the first date.' I tipped my head towards the holster lying on the carpet.

'To be fair, it's not actually deadly. It will send about 1000 volts through you, though.'

'Oh, you don't need a Taser to do that, Aubrey,' I said, leaning in to kiss him again.

So maybe it wasn't exactly electricity, but there was definitely a little fluttering of some description going on in my stomach. For the first time in ages, I felt the heavy cloud that had been over my head begin to shift.

'I'm serious, Gwen,' Lyons said, breaking off the kiss and looking me in the eye. 'We'd make a good team, don't you think?'

I opened my mouth to say something, but then paused. I thought about Olivia, his wife, and what she'd done to him. He didn't deserve someone like me, and I didn't deserve someone like him. Mentally, I grabbed those butterflies in my stomach and squished them, hard.

'I dunno,' I said quietly. 'You're a nice guy. And I'm… I'm not exactly who you think I am.'

Lyons looked down at me. 'What exactly did happen with you and your ex?' Lyons asked.

'Hey, no fair, we're not playing Truth or Drink any more,' I said.

'I know, I know,' he said, shifting his weight so he was

looking directly into my eyes. 'But I'm interested. Why did you break up? You seem like a pretty good catch.'

'It was my decision,' I said firmly. 'I decided it wasn't working.'

'Just like that?'

'Yep,' I said. 'Just like that. Not everything needs deducing, Aubrey.'

He narrowed his eyes at me, like he didn't believe me for a second. I couldn't tell him that Noah might have every reason in the world to hate my guts, that none of this was his fault. That it was me who had torn our world apart.

'I see,' he said.

I closed my eyes and turned onto my back. It was a moment before I spoke again.

'You were right, what you said. I know people think I'm immature, that I make a joke out of everything, and maybe that's true. But really, it's just an act, or at least it is sometimes. I'd just got a promotion at work. Noah and I were in love. Things were finally good. Settled. Then came Noah's crazy idea to travel round the country in that dumb ice cream van. On paper, that should have been perfect for me. At least, it was perfect for the Gwen he knew. Or thought he knew. The one who's impulsive and silly. But I knew if we did that, if we just ran off, ran away from all our problems, then I was giving up on what I really wanted.'

'Marriage? Kids?' Lyons asked.

'Ha, steady on. Maybe one day.' I smiled. 'No, I mean my career, my own place, you know? I'd been running away from responsibilities, from real life, ever since my dad died. It was time to grow up, so even though I loved Noah, I couldn't go through with it.'

I closed my eyes for a second.

'I still love him, I think.'

'So what really happened?' Lyons asked.

I gave him the abridged version.

THIRTY-FOUR

'I'm sorry, Noah. I can't do this any more,' I say.

And just like that, the last three and a half years were over, in less time than it takes to drink half a pint of beer. This person, who had set up my mum's Wi-Fi router, attended both my sisters' weddings (even the one I barely spoke to), and knew how I'd secretly buried my first cat (Binky) in the playground sandpit aged seven, was gone.

This man, who'd seen me naked more than any other human, save my aforementioned dear mother, would never wake up next to me again.

And while I couldn't have predicted it would end here, sat on a damp wooden bench outside a pub on a drizzly Friday evening, I'd always known that one day, I'd be doing this. But, hey, at least that meant I'd had plenty of time to think of some really cool comebacks.

'I'm sorry,' I say again.

Yes, this was the carefully curated speech I'd spent the last two weeks rehearsing as I lay looking at the ceiling at 2 a.m. every morning. Saying it out loud now, it sounded just as trite as it had in the darkness then. But it was either that or continue to stare dumbly into my beer, trying to decide if this really was worse than the time I decided to debut my groundbreaking interpretive dance routine to 'Hips Don't Lie' during school assembly.

'Yeah, you said that. But I don't understand – what happened? Talk to me.'

Noah sips his orange juice and lemonade. In all our years together, he's never managed to look quite as handsome as he somehow does in that moment. The bastard.

'I just don't feel the same way any more,' I say. 'And I can't fake it.'

He must have seen my shoulders trembling, because he reaches across the table and places his hand on my arm.

'You gonna be okay, Gwen?'

'It's fine. I'll be fine. Everything is fine,' I say, brushing off his hand and reaching for my drink.

There was no point in trying to pretend that this was a blip, a bump in the road or just a goddamn dumb decision. Because everything had changed, and we both knew it.

The first time I saw Noah Coulter, he was laughing. Laughing his bloody head off. I had no idea about what, and come to think of it, I still don't. He was standing in the queue at The Truck Stop, at the University of Sussex cafe, with a group of the usual acolytes goading him on. I was six people back, clutching a lukewarm jacket potato and a packet of pickled onion Monster Munch. I think every single person in that queue had the same thing on their tray. J-Po & Cheese held the dubious honour of simultaneously being the cheapest – and yet most filling – item on the menu.

Back then, I had pixie-short hair and thought wearing capri pants was a bold fashion statement. But Noah was beautiful,

I thought. Okay, maybe beautiful is the wrong word. I'm trying to sound romantic here. He was fit. Cropped brown hair, with a semi wave, a seemingly permanent light tan (and these were the days before you could get a decent self-tan on the shelves of Boots). Yes, okay, he was slightly on the short side, but I was never one of those women who was obsessed with a boy's height. I could tell just by looking at him that he was popular, confident and probably as unobtainable as good vegan sausages.

Turned out I was wrong about all three of those things.

The next time I saw him was at our hall's Christmas party. The social society had put on a cheap and cheerful Christmas dinner, just before we broke up for the holidays. When I'd pulled my cracker with Sarah, who was sitting next to me, the contents had, of course, gone flying everywhere. And while I'd safely secured the paper crown, I was desperate to find my number one favourite thing about Christmas: the cracker joke.

'Nooo! Where did it go?' I screamed drunkenly, scanning the table. 'It's gone!'

Several people around us began looking on the floor, assuming I'd dropped something of actual value. And one of them happened to be Noah Coulter – who I would later find out lived for the drama of seeing a lost cracker joke escalate into an international incident, among other things. As I scrabbled around on the floor, I saw a foot dragging a small square of paper towards a denim-clad leg. He bent down, picked up the joke and strode over to where I knelt on the floor. Placing it on the table, he announced sexily, 'Is this what you're looking for?'

I got up and straightened the flimsy bright yellow crown on my head.

'A gift for my princess,' he said.

'Fuck off, I'm the queen!' I said.

'These things are always terrible,' he smiled. 'Why are you so desperate for it?'

'I like jokes,' I said. 'It's part of my brand.'

He sat down in the chair next to me, unfolded the piece of paper, and cleared his throat theatrically.

'Where's the best place to hide a book?' he read out loud.

'Why would anybody want to hide a book?' I asked.

'That is incorrect,' he said, in the manner of a bad quiz show host. 'The correct answer is... a library.'

'I don't get it.'

'Well, it's not going to stand out there, is it?' he said. 'Among all the other books.'

'That,' I announced, 'is a shit joke.'

'Shall we get you another?'

I grabbed a spare cracker from the table and held out one end to him. He took it and we both pulled. With a pathetic little snap, the cracker burst open, spilling its cargo of plastic goodies onto the table.

'Did you feel that?' I asked.

'The earth moved for me,' he smiled.

We never read the joke from that cracker, because we were too busy snogging each other's faces off.

That set the precedent for the next year. Noah was the one with all the solutions, I was the one with the problems. I was dramatic and he was practical. It was the kind of booze-powered, lust-driven relationship you could only have at university. But deep down, I think we liked the theatrics, almost like we were subconsciously re-enacting the exciting adult relationships we'd seen on TV. After every fight I would punish him by going out and coming back in the early hours of the morning. It was destined to burn out fast, but we actually kept it up for over the summer break and well into our second year.

And then everything collapsed in a single moment. I lost Dad, and I lost myself. Dad was the person I could always rely on to look after me – whatever dumb shit I pulled – and without him, I spiralled. And Noah, well, he tried his best. It wasn't that he didn't care, he just didn't – couldn't – understand. I was so angry at the world, I just wanted to shut everything off and hide away. His manic pixie dream girl had curled into a pangolin of grief, and I couldn't blame him for slowly backing off. I'd finally become a problem he couldn't solve. We were already outgrowing each other anyway (or maybe he had just outgrown me), so we agreed to call it a day.

Sure, there were times I missed him, and I spent a few evenings mooning over his Instagram, searching for any clue that he might be missing me too. But eventually, for my own good, I blocked him. Wasting tears over a boy seemed pointless. Everything seemed pointless back then. It was Sarah's idea to move to Eastbourne together after we graduated. It was just a few miles down the coast, close to Mum. That run-down two-bed flat was our little seaside refuge, and Sar nursed me through the storm, drip-feeding me cheese toasties and cheap wine until I began to feel close to normal.

I didn't see Noah again, until maybe five years later, at something that should have no longer existed. A speed dating event. It was an outdated notion even then, as dating apps had long since proved themselves God's gift to single people (and not-so-single people). But there was a novelty to actually speaking to someone face to face, and as no one spoke to each other at bars any more, it seemed like at least something different to do on a Wednesday night.

My hair was longer, dyed and re-dyed so many times I wasn't 100 per cent sure what colour it was to begin with, and my capri pants had long since been ceremonially destroyed. By then, I'd had my fill of cheap one-night stands with cheap boys who faded away faster than the nightclub stamps on the back of my hand. And none of them ever seemed to live up to him, my first love.

Myself and Sarah turned up to the venue in Meads and immediately surveyed the other attendees before the event started. And that's when I spotted Noah. Among the nervous people on their own, who were obviously taking it very seriously, and the groups of lads and girls who were clearly there for a laugh before getting tanked at a terrible nightclub round the corner, there he was.

I'd never actually unblocked him from social media, and thus had no idea what happened to him. He now had a light stubble that made him look, not older exactly, but more like an adult. And his old combat trousers and faded AC/DC T-shirt had been replaced by obviously expensive jeans, a spotless white v-neck and a bomber jacket. He was drinking something colourful from a straw and scanning the room while his friends chatted. Our joint scans met and, recognising what we were both doing, he laughed that dumb laugh of his. I smiled back and shrugged. And in that moment I immediately knew I was going home with him. It was like seeing land again after being lost at sea for so long.

When he finally got to my table (an excruciating number sixteen out of twenty), I'll admit it: I was quite drunk.

'Seen anyone you like?' he laughed.

A sticker with his name on was stuck over his chest.

'Maybe, Noah,' I said, peering at the sticker in an exaggerated fashion. 'Maybe.'

When the organiser – an energetic Australian improbably named Chico – blew the whistle that signified it was time for the male daters to shuffle around the room, we hadn't stopped talking. A week later we met again at a restaurant that claimed to serve Italian tapas, and we picked up right where we left off all those years ago.

Noah was now a graphic designer for a software company, lived just outside of town and didn't understand how risotto could be tapas. The fact that we had dated before gave us a safety net that I'd never had with previous boyfriends. With them, I always felt a little terrified, like they'd suddenly realise who I really was and dump me. But with Noah, I could just about pretend I was the old Gwen, and everything was like it used to be, before Dad died.

Whenever things felt a little rocky, our shared history was an anchor that steadied the ship. He stopped me from getting distracted, righted my course whenever I wobbled. Our trusted in-jokes and rituals – like ordering half the menu at Five Guys, then taking it home and eating it off plates with knives and forks, stopped us from drifting apart.

I was living with Sarah, but, mostly at his insistence, I was always at his. It seemed sort of effortless, like the natural order of things. We were very happy there, playing make-believe at setting up house. I helped him choose cushions and some cheap art prints, the only things he could change without the landlord's permission. It felt grown up, cooking for each other in the evenings and spending weekends going shopping, drinking with friends and watching bad TV. We had no responsibility beyond choosing the next takeaway or Netflix series.

But it couldn't last forever. His mum got ill. Cancer, of course. She was doing okay, responding to treatment. But it scared him, I think. And one day, messing around, he suggested chucking in our jobs and trying to go to every festival in the country. That turned into searching eBay for second-hand ice cream vans, and all of sudden, it was happening.

When he announced we'd won the auction, an auction I didn't even know he'd bid in, and we were now the proud owners of an ice cream van, we'd had a huge row about it. The future I'd seen solidifying in front of me was melting away, and in its place was a rickety old mobile cafe daubed with a crude painting of Mickey Mouse eating a 99 with a Flake. It felt like he was pulling up the anchor and leaving us adrift.

'I thought we were still talking about it,' I said.

'You're still talking about it,' he told me. 'If I left it to you, we'd be talking about it forever. So I made the decision for both of us. You can hand in your notice tomorrow.'

I told him I couldn't do it. He told me he couldn't do it without me. Defeated, I went home and tried to block everything out with reality TV and multiple bottles of cheap rosé. But deep down, I knew it was a stalemate and there was only one way out.

And so, more or less, that's how I ended up here, sitting outside a shitty pub telling him that it was better to end things now, rather than in thirty years when we were bitter and broke and resented the hell out of each other.

'Remember this?' he says, pulling out a scrap of paper from his wallet. He flattened it out on the table. The badly printed

ink had faded, but it was the cracker joke, from the night we met. He'd kept it all this time.

'It's still a shit joke,' I say, trying to force a smile.

'It always was,' he says, sticking it back in his wallet. 'But I liked it.'

We spend a few more seconds staring at each other in silence before I pour the last of my beer down my throat, stand up and leave. On the short walk back to my flat, as I weave past the discarded Christmas trees on the pavement, I repeat my mantra of 'It'll be fine' to myself. It was still early, and the sun and the moon were sharing an increasingly reddening sky. I tell myself that the rest of my Friday night – and maybe my life – is free to enjoy as a newly independent, single woman, one with no need for the trappings of relationships and suburban mundanity.

Of course, within five minutes of getting through my front door, I've installed the only dating app I could stand and eaten two packets of Quavers. Call it a pity party if you want, but if you'd been there, you'd know it was actually a really cool party where I got to flirt with hot guys and eat loads of crisps while still wearing pyjamas. Besides, everyone knows the only thing that can salve a break-up is the attention of strangers.

And yes, okay, Quavers.

'And that was that,' I said. 'He hadn't quit his job yet, and I had, so it made sense for me to keep the van. I'd paid for most of it, after all. He told me to sell it, but that van was the last piece of Noah I had, and I just couldn't face letting go of it. And part of me wanted to prove I could do it on my own. But I failed at that too, didn't I?'

I looked up at Lyons. His eyes were closed, and I could tell by the gentle rise and fall of his chest that he'd dozed off. Sure, he looked pretty goofy with his mouth hanging open, but it was true, I'd not met anyone like him since Noah – someone who wasn't a massive racist, or lying about his age or cheating on his wife. I reached to the floor for my discarded jeans and I pulled out the napkin with the names on it.

'Guess we don't need this any more,' I said quietly.

I reached over for a pen from the desk beside us and crossed off Seb's name. With one hand, I screwed up the napkin and tossed it into the wastepaper bin, where it spun around the rim for a second before falling in.

Then I pulled Lyons's jacket up over us, let the waves of exhaustion wash over me, and fell asleep.

The next thing I knew, I was being awoken by Lyons's phone ringing incessantly and ominously. I poked him a couple of times in the chest, but when he failed to wake up, I unwrapped my limbs from under his body. I ran my hands over the sofa trying to locate the phone, but by the time I'd fished it out from between the cushions, where it was nestled next to one of my socks, it had stopped ringing.

The screen lit up at my touch, showing the time, 7.22 a.m., and a missed call alert from 'Forrester'. But sitting underneath that was a message notification.

'You have a new Connector match!' it said.

THIRTY-FIVE

What. The. Actual. Fuck.

Instinctively, I swiped on the alert, but instead of showing me the match, the phone demanded a passcode. Why the hell was Lyons getting Connector messages when he didn't even know what a dating app was until about three days ago?

'Hey,' I shouted at Lyons's sleeping face. 'You got a message.'

It took a few more pokes, but eventually his eyes opened.

'Morning,' he smiled sleepily.

'I said, you've got a message.'

'Is it Forrester?' he mumbled, sitting up and rubbing his eyes.

'Nope,' I replied.

I held his phone up very, very close to his face.

'It's from the new Mrs Lyons,' I said.

He looked at me, rubbed his eyes, and took the phone, peering at the screen like he was trying to read the bottom row on an eye test.

'Oh, right,' he said, the smile disappearing from his face.

'I thought you didn't believe in dating apps?' I said. 'In fact, I could've *sworn* that you told me you'd never used one.'

Lyons stood up, put the phone on the desk and started pulling on his clothes.

'I thought,' he said defensively, 'that as I was investigating a multiple homicide case where the killer used this app, it might be wise to actually download it.'

I stared at him. 'Right, sounds completely believable,' I said, in a tone that made it incredibly clear that I definitely did not believe him *at all*.

'You were always talking about the app, so I thought I'd see what all the fuss was about,' he said, fishing around the sofa for his belt.

'I'm always talking about it because I'm being fucking stalked on it!' I snapped.

'Why are you getting upset?' he asked, pulling on his jacket.

Wow, this was about to be a full house at 'my least favourite questions of all time' bingo.

'I'm not upset,' I said, in my best not-upset voice. 'I just want to know why you lied about it.'

'It's not like that. I didn't lie about it, I just didn't tell you about it,' he said. 'There's a difference.'

'Sounds like something one of your suspects would say.'

'You're being dramatic,' Lyons said.

'Well, last time I checked, this was a pretty dramatic situation,' I replied.

He carried on getting dressed without saying anything.

'I knew it,' I said under my breath. 'You're no different to all the others. Boy, did I make a huge mistake last night.'

'Gwen, don't be—'

'I'm just wondering what else you haven't told me about,' I said, glancing at the pinboard on the wall.

'Don't be absurd, I…'

I folded my arms and looked at him patiently.

'You've been through a lot the past couple of days,' he said. 'So I'll let that go. I've told you far more than I should have about this investigation already. Believe me, we've got our man. It's okay, it's over.'

'Fine,' I said. 'Aren't you going to have a look then? At your new love connection?'

'Later.' He picked up the phone and stuck it in his jeans pocket. 'I have to go. This might be over for you, but I still have work to do. I need to go and meet Forrester in Lewes.'

'Great. And what am I meant to do?'

'Sorry,' he said. 'You should wait here. When the team gets in, they'll want to speak to you about Charlie.'

I opened my mouth to say something.

'I mean it, Gwen,' he interrupted. 'Wait here. They'll look after you.'

He stepped towards me, seemingly unsure whether to hug me, kiss me on the cheek or shake my hand.

Suddenly, I grabbed his arm.

'What's that on your sleeve?'

'What?'

'That mark. What is that? It looks like blood.'

He raised his arm to his face and examined the stain.

'It must be Dev's,' he said. 'He was bleeding everywhere.'

I thought for a second.

'You weren't wearing your jacket at the bowling alley,' I said. 'Which, come to think of it, was kinda weird. It's been minus two out there for weeks.'

'Well, it must be from the Eye then, when I checked Seb's pulse.'

'What happened to the hoodie, the one Parker dropped outside the alley?' I asked.

Lyons looked confused. 'Forensics have it. It's evidence. I told you, we'll try and match it to Charlie.'

'You got to the bowling alley pretty quick, didn't you?' I said. 'Right after Parker escaped.'

'I'm not sure what you're implying—'

'How tall are you?' I asked.

'About six foot, what's that got to do with—'

'Bullshit,' I snapped.

Lyons's expression tightened as his bewilderment gave way to anger. I suddenly felt like I'd gone too far.

'What are you saying, Gwen? You think I'm Parker? Is that what you're saying?'

I don't think I'd ever heard him raise his voice before.

'No, I—' I stuttered. 'That's not what I meant, Aubrey.'

'Well, why are you bringing it up then? I haven't heard you giving a running commentary on all the other stains on my jacket.'

I hung my head. Suddenly I felt more confused than ever. 'Look, I'm tired and I'm scared and I want to go home,' I said. 'I don't know what I'm thinking any more.'

'I'm probably the only person you can trust right now, Gwen.'

'Well, don't start yelling at me then. I can't stand it when guys start getting aggressive because they know they're in the wrong and can't admit it.'

'And I can't stand it when people start accusing me of murdering people, okay? "Parker" is currently sitting in custody waiting for his lawyer. So just slow down a minute, will you?'

'I'm not accusing you—' I started.

'I have to go. I'll call you,' he said, and then quickly added, 'I mean, about Charlie. You'll probably want to know the next steps.'

'Can't wait,' I said, petulantly kicking the empty Malibu bottle that had been thrown on the floor during the previous evening's activities.

'And Gwen,' he added, 'um, you should probably put on some clothes, you know, just in case anyone walks in here.'

It was all I could do not to throw the Malibu bottle at his head. But I figured that might be a bad look when you were half-naked in a police station at nearly half past seven in the morning. I watched Lyons walk out of the office, leaving me standing there in a bra and jeans.

I shut the door behind him and surveyed the debris of sofa cushions and ankle socks scattered across the office. As I went round tidying up, I noticed a pile of paperwork on what must have been Forrester's desk. Recognising the name typed across the top sheet, I pulled it out. It looked like a search warrant for Jamal's boat.

'Forrester, you git,' I thought, folding it up and sticking it in my bra. If Jamal got into trouble for helping me, I'd never forgive myself.

I slumped down on the swivel chair and pulled my socks on. As I spun myself round, I ran my tongue over my teeth and cursed the lack of a toothbrush. My brain seemed to spin faster than the chair. Could Aubrey really be lying to me? He'd acted like dating apps were a complete mystery to him, which was clearly untrue. If he really was Parker, then *maybe* he could have got through the bowling alley window, dumped the hoodie and run back to the bathroom in time to find me with Dev. He didn't seem the murdering type, but then again, neither had Charlie. When the chair came to a natural stop, I found myself staring at my reflection in the black mirror of Lyons's computer monitor. I idly jabbed 'Enter' on the keyboard. The screen lit up and asked for a password.

'What else are you hiding from me, detective?' I murmured.

I thought for a second and tapped in 'aubrey1'. The screen jolted and asked me to try again.

'Okay, fine, if you insist,' I told the computer.

I remembered what Jamal had said about passwords — most people chose something personal to them. Now, the password *I* always used was 'b1nky', with a number one instead of an 'I'. Binky, because that poor old fluffball was a total legend and I loved him to bits. And '1' because no hacker would ever crack that code. But what would a man like Aubrey Lyons choose as a password? A man who appeared to have so little joy in his life?

I typed in 'gamb1t'. The screen shook again.

I span the chair round again, scanning the office for clues. My eyes settled on the black-and-white passport photos next to Lyons's computer. I turned back to the keyboard.

'olivia', I typed. The screen jolted again.

'Okay, one more try,' I said to myself.

'ol1v1a'.

Suddenly the dark screen was replaced with a bright stock photo of a palm tree bending over a picturesque beach.

'Told you I was a good detective,' I muttered under my breath.

I opened Google and pulled up the search history. Among the searches for '*Tesco opening times*', '*Dragon*', '*Netflix shark movie*' and '*Gwen Turner*', one phrase made my chest contract.

'*Colin Parker images*'

I took a sharp intake of breath. I clicked on it and the screen filled with very familiar pictures: a sexy zombie, Colin laughing in the pub with his mates, all the same images from Parker's Connector profile.

What the hell are you doing, Aubrey Lyons?

My stomach churned like a bad wedding DJ was attempting to remix my insides. Lyons had been there at the bowling alley when Dev was attacked. And there again at the wheel when Seb was murdered. He had Connector on his phone, despite saying he'd never used a dating app in his life. And now I'd found out he'd had Parker's profile photos in his search history. But he couldn't really *be* Parker – could he?

Shaking, I shut down the browser and found the email icon on his desktop. There were twenty-two unread emails, but one stood out. I clicked on the email from Dragon Ltd.

FAO Detective Lyons,
We received your official request for the data pertaining to the Connector account 394518Z for user 'Parker'.
The information connected to the account is as follows:
NAME: Parker Smith
EMAIL: PrinceCharming007@rajakov.net
DATE CREATED: 29th December
LAST LOGGED ON: 00:37 February 13th

I squinted at the date in the bottom left corner of the screen. February 13th. That was today. Parker had logged in *today*. My heart started to beat faster. Charlie had been in custody all night. Lyons had taken his phone. *He couldn't have logged on to Connector.*

I rushed over to the office door and went to open it, before realising I was still in my bra. Pulling on my top and hoodie, I popped my head out into the station. Staff were beginning to arrive, sipping on takeaway coffees and switching on computers. But Lyons was nowhere to be seen.

I grabbed my phone and went to dial his number but then stopped. I couldn't remember seeing him use his mobile last night, but he could have easily sent a message while I was asleep.

Charlie had betrayed me. Lyons had lied to me. Noah had disappeared. I didn't know who to trust any more. Besides, I realised, tomorrow was Valentine's Day. Sarah and Richard were getting married. Me and the rest of the guests were meant to be meeting at the pier at 9 a.m., ready to be ferried over to Eastleigh Island. Sarah would already be there with their parents.

Parents. I thought again about Seb's mum in the nursing home as they tried to explain to her that her son wasn't coming to visit any more. My mind drifted to Rob's ex and her message on the tribute website. And Dev's wife, getting a knock on the door from a solemn-looking police officer.

I felt a horrible pang of guilt jab at my insides. Well, either it was guilt, or the fact that I'd had nothing but a Toffee Crisp and Malibu for dinner last night.

There was still the name I'd torn off the napkin. If Charlie wasn't Parker, then that person was still in danger. And I couldn't let anything happen to him.

I had to reach him before Parker did — but how?

On *Danger Land,* they always looked for a pattern.

Something the killer always did, some clue – deliberate or otherwise – that led the police to them. And if Parker was trying to frame me, he'd leave clues that pointed to me. I sat back down on the swivel chair and looked at the map of Eastbourne. A pin was pushed in at each of the locations where the bodies had been discovered.

Rob was found in Sovereign Park.

Freddie was found in a large bin in an alley behind South Street.

Josh at the crazy golf course.

Dev was at the bowling alley.

And Seb had the indignity of being murdered at the Eastbourne Eye.

I don't know if I expected them to form a pentagram or spell out 'Gwen' or something, but I was getting desperate. I got up and found the wine bar that me and Rob went to on the map. It was directly opposite Sovereign Park. Then I looked for Toppo's, the Italian me and Freddie ate at. It was on South Street. I'd found Josh's body at the Jolly Jungle, and Dev at the mall. And of course, me and Seb went on the Eye. This was no coincidence, I realised. There was a pattern.

Parker was luring the victims back to where I went on the dates.

I still didn't have a clue who Parker was, but at least I could work out where he'd strike next. There was only one date left, so I knew exactly where I had to go.

THIRTY-SIX

Sarah marches into the flat and slams the door behind her.

'It's over,' she barks.

'What?' I ask, momentarily distracted from my cosy rosé and Married at First Sight *marathon. Noah's just told me I have to quit my job, and all I want to do is bury myself under sofa cushions and empty crisp packets.*

'The engagement, the wedding, everything. Richard says it's all happening too fast. I threw the ring at him,' Sarah says.

Her face is red with fury.

'You did what?' I gasp.

She collapses on the sofa next to me and reaches for the bottle of wine on the table.

'Okay, okay, stay calm,' I tell her, reaching for the remote and turning off the TV. 'What did he say exactly?'

'It's too expensive, we should wait until next year after he gets his bonus, blah blah blah bullshit,' she growls.

I remove the bottle from her grasp, fill up my glass and hand it to her. She takes slow gulps until her breathing starts to return to normal.

'So he's not actually calling it off?' I say. 'Maybe he just needs a bit more time to get used to the idea?'

I see Sarah's nostrils flare as she puts the empty glass down and immediately refills it.

'Used to the idea?' Sarah scoffs. 'Is the idea of marrying me so fucking terrifying?'

'Right now? A little bit, yes,' I say. 'Take a breath. He's not breaking up with you, he's just asking for time.'

'You're giving me advice on relationships? That's rich,' she snorts.

'Well, I'm just saying—' I begin.

'Oh I get it, you just don't want me to move out, do you? And this is your chance to keep me here. You've never liked Richard, and now you've sensed blood. Is that right?'

'No, that's not right!' I say, my voice cracking a little. 'It's just that you've always been so careful with guys. Why such a rush now?'

'Because Richard and I are perfect for each other,' she says, like it's an indisputable fact. 'Whether he realises it or not.'

'Can you really be that sure? You've barely dated since uni.'

Sarah's eyes narrow. 'How would you know? You've always been too wrapped up in Noah to take any notice of my life.'

Sarah had dated a few guys before she met Richard, but despite her overly healthy interest in my love life, she never wanted to spill the tea on what went down with them. Sometimes I worried something really bad might have happened, but maybe it was just that none of them could meet her impossibly high standards.

'What does that mean?'

'Oh come on, Gwen, you're like a lovesick teenager around Noah,' she says.

'I am not!'

'Yeah you are,' Sarah says. 'You idolise the guy, always have. It's pathetic.'

'Where's this come from?' I say, starting to feel my blood boil.

'You're terrified to stand on your own two feet. You wrap yourself up in Noah like he's your safety blanket. You could do so much better, and deep down you know it.'

'That's bullshit,' I snap. 'I've known Noah for years, you've known Richard for about ten minutes. So I'm not sure you're in a great position to lecture me here.'

'You're not happy, you're sinking. You're about to throw your life away to follow that guy around the country like a devoted poodle. Talk about co-dependent.'

'Hey, hang on a second,' I say, trying to gain control of the situation, which seems to have turned on me. 'Maybe this van idea is dumb, but I need some direction. I lost my way, you know, after...'

'After your dad died? You can say it out loud, Gwen. It happened.'

Her words sting me, like a thousand tiny daggers.

'I know it happened,' I say, my voice turning as cold as the Arctic.

'This isn't what your dad would have wanted for you,' she says. 'He'd be so disappointed.'

My body goes stiff, like someone just stuck me with a cattle prod. 'Tell me you are not going there,' I say quietly. 'You are not telling me what my dad would think.'

Sarah's face blushes red, just for a second, before she gathers herself. 'Noah can't replace your dad, Gwen, and it'll be me who has to pick up the pieces when it all goes south, just like last time,' she says. 'But here you are, siding against me.'

'I'm not siding against you, Sar, I—'

With that, she downs her wine, gets up and stomps upstairs, leaving me wondering what just happened.

Later, when I get off my shift at Delicioso, I text Richard, asking him to meet me in The Brown Derby. I feel terrible about my fight with Sarah, and I'm hoping maybe if I could fix things between her and Richard, I could make it right.

After he's finished recounting the non-events of his latest trip up a random Welsh hill, I try to steer the conversation around to Sarah. It's slightly awkward, as it's never just the two of us. Normally I have either Sarah or Noah to help soak up some of the hiking anecdotes. (Note: I am using the word anecdote very generously here.)

'So what happened with Sarah?' I ask him, playing dumb. 'You didn't bring her back any Kendal Mint Cake?'

'We had a stupid row about the wedding,' Richard says. 'I think it's all over.'

'Let me guess, you want teal place settings, and she wants turquoise.'

Richard sighs. I can tell he's already a bit drunk, which was unusual for him on a work night. He explains that he'd asked Sarah if she would consider postponing the wedding until they were a little more financially secure. She had reacted in classic Sarah fashion by taking off her engagement ring and chucking it in the front garden.

I'd intended to tell him to give himself a slap and beg her for forgiveness, but the more we talk, the more I feel a bit sorry for him. I realise I've never really spoken to him properly before, always preferring to join Sarah in teasing him or tuning out when he starts talking about his many, many manly hobbies. But, and maybe this was the bottle of Merlot I'd bought 'for the table' (aka me), I was beginning to see a whole new side to him.

'We've only been together a year,' he says. 'We don't even live together. Sometimes I think she's more in love with the idea of a big church wedding than she is with me. She told me I'm on my final strike. Says I better not embarrass her any further.'

I try to make him feel better by telling him how I am shitting myself about giving in my notice at work and plunging all my savings into this crazy idea of Noah's.

'Things are going really well at work. I just got a promotion. And now it's like he just wants to up sticks,' I say. 'Sometimes I wish something crazy would happen, you know? Something that took all this out of my hands, so I didn't have to make this decision any more.'

'What, like, you get kidnapped?' he asks.

'No, I mean a huge distraction. An act of God. I dunno, an alien invasion.'

'Or a nuclear bomb?' Richard laughs.

'Ha, yeah, something like that. Or a natural disaster. Anything that could get me out of this.'

'I know what you mean,' he says. 'If a volcano erupted in Eastbourne tomorrow, then surely the wedding would get cancelled.'

'Well, Sarah losing her temper is a little like a volcano erupting,' I offer.

Richard suppresses a smile.

'Noah was always my anchor, you know?' I go on. 'But ever since his mum got ill, he's discovered this whole new "live each day like it's your last" attitude. How am I meant

to tell him that I haven't, though? After the year he's had, he needs something to look forward to.'

'What about what you need?' Richard asks.

I look down at my phone, where there's a message from Noah asking: 'Did you do it? What did your boss say?' I don't reply, and stick my phone in my bag.

'It doesn't matter what I need,' I tell Richard. 'I'm just going to have to do it. And it'll be fun, I guess.'

'You didn't come this far only to come this far,' he says, which takes my sozzled brain a moment to realise is rather poetic. He might resemble a more preppy Bear Grylls, but he was actually capable of being quite sweet.

'Well, that's what we say when we reach base camp at Nevis,' he adds.

'Base camp,' I smile. 'That's so lame.'

'Hey!' he laughs. 'That's also where I proposed to Sarah, you know?'

'What, halfway up Ben Nevis?'

'No, halfway up Roseberry Hill, behind the church on Eastleigh Island. I insisted that she went on a hike with me, and that was as far as she got before complaining her hamstrings were sore.'

'Classic Sarah,' I say.

'I said, "That's okay, this is base camp. I have a protein bar in my pocket." And pulled the ring out. The rest is history.'

'And now you're getting married there,' I say.

'Well, maybe not any more,' he says, looking down into the murky brown depths of his IPA.

After a few more pints for him, and a tequila chaser for me, we walk home together. We pass Richard's place before mine, and he asks if I want to come inside for a nightcap. And, in a spectacularly brilliant moment of masterly decision-making, I say yes.

'Sarah's got my key,' he says, lifting the flower pot outside the front door and picking up the spare. 'Our little secret.'

'What?' I ask, the tequila suddenly clouding my brain.

'The spare key,' he says, waving it at me. 'Don't tell anyone about my secret hiding place!'

Inside his very neat flat, he fixes us some drinks that we really don't need, and starts drunkenly showing me his walking gear. I can't stop laughing at him as he models various body warmers, ankle supports and waterproof trousers. At one point, I find myself collapsed on the floor after successfully pulling a stubborn hiking boot off his left foot. The next thing I know, Richard has joined me on the rug, and offers to help me remove my Converse in return. My head is woozy, and it feels like my thumping heartbeat is the only part of my body in control. Before I know it, we start pulling off more of each other's clothes, until suddenly, we're kissing. And then more than kissing. Everything is a blur. Then, in what seems like seconds, it's over. It's done, and I can't take it back.

Afterwards, I walk straight home in a daze. Thank God, Sarah's in bed when I get in. I throw up twice and fall asleep.

The next morning, I go outside, find the ring lying in the dirt, rinse it off and give it back to Sarah when she gets up. I apologise for our row, and tell her she was right, Richard is a prick and she shouldn't wait for him to make his mind up. She tells me she has to, he's the only good man out there, and that she's invested so much in this relationship that she has to make it work, whatever. She says she isn't about to give up on it because he'd had a few pre-wedding jitters. I feel like throwing up again.

And that was that. For the next few days, Noah keeps asking me if something's wrong. I brush him off and suggest we get the tequila out. Every time he brings up the van, or the future, I change the subject. Every time I feel the urge to tell him, I push it down. The following Saturday, we're due to spend the weekend at his mum's. I can't face it, and fake a stomach ache.

As I watch Noah leave, I feel empty. I'm heartbroken, and it's all my fault. And it's me who is wielding that power to bring everything down. With just a few words, I could destroy everything. Or I could keep schtum and keep this secret forever. It was a responsibility I didn't know how to bear.

The wedding is back on, and Richard repeatedly texts me, but I can't bear to even look at them, and I delete his number off my phone. By the time Noah comes home the following day. I still don't know what to do. I'd spent the weekend at his flat, in a daze of pyjamas and Quavers, wondering if I could even find the words to tell him. But when he walks in the door, he says something that takes away every bit of agency I have left.

'It's Mum,' he says. 'The cancer's gone, she's in remission.'

He was so happy, so excited – there was no way on earth I could destroy that. I always said we were best friends, and I couldn't figure out why I would do this to my best friend. It was just sex, I told myself. It didn't mean anything. It didn't change anything. But sex was never just sex. I convinced myself of fantastic things – that I could move past it, that the van was a new start for the both of us, I even gave in my notice at work – but deep down I always knew the real truth. Even if he never found out, it could never be the same as it was before. No matter how hard I tried to push what I'd done beneath the surface, I'd always know it was there. I'd created a fault line that would slowly crack through our whole relationship.

For the next few weeks, Noah's mum got steadily stronger, and we carried on a pretence of domesticity for a while, but I couldn't get excited about our new life together. I slowly began to get more and more distant, avoiding time alone together, cancelling plans and stopping sleeping with him altogether, until he couldn't help but stop loving me. Well, that was the plan anyway.

Because we didn't officially live together, there was no long, complicated drawn-out break-up. No passive aggressive texts. No bad back from sleeping on the couch. When I walked away from that pub on that drizzly winter night, years of shared history just disappeared like melted snow. I must have missed it, somewhere in the small print of the relationship, where they said this was possible.

The break-up gave me a sort of superpower. Suddenly I could download dating apps, armed with a magical immunity to any hurt or rejection, because the only person who I cared liked me was Noah Coulter. It didn't matter if any of these app guys ignored me or doted on me, because they weren't him. And for a while that distracted me from the pain a little. I locked all the memories of Noah away, and left them there to biodegrade naturally, like stale sandwiches rejected by seagulls.

It wasn't until weeks later, just after my date with Seb, when we'd all taken the ferry to Eastleigh Island for the wedding recce, that it happened. I'm sitting on a pew in the back of the church swiping through Connector as Richard and Sarah argue about the order of service for the seventy-third time that afternoon.

I can't say I was uber-shocked when I saw the profile pop up on my phone. He'd used a fake name of course, and his profile photo was deliberately obscured, but it was Richard alright. When I flick through the rest of his photos, I recognise them all from his Instagram. That evening, I swipe right, so I can send him a message on Connector.

Gwen: Richard, wtf, I know this is you. What we did that night was stupid, but we were smashed. Now you're on a dating app? You're getting married next week ffs.

'Meet me, base camp,' he types back.

I sneak out of my hotel room and walk up Roseberry Hill. Halfway up, I find Richard, encased in his cagoule and beanie hat, almost in tears. He starts telling me how he'd downloaded Connector for work, as his company was building a rival app.

'I was just interested in the algorithms, how the code worked, you know? But then I got kind of addicted,' he says. 'I'm just chatting to girls. I don't meet anyone. I love Sarah, I really do, but everything's about the wedding and I can't bear it. This helps me cope. After we get married, I'll stop.'

'Bullshit,' I say.

He looks at me angrily. 'Fine,' he snaps. 'You want the truth? After, you know, what happened with me and you, I went to pieces. I can't stop thinking about it. You won't talk to me, so I chat to girls on Connector. It's a distraction, I guess. But I'll never do anything, it's just flirting.'

Classic. So this is all my fault.

'Tell Sarah. Cancel the wedding, Richard,' I say.

'I can't,' he says. 'It would break her heart.'

'So will marrying her if you don't love her,' I say. 'You're clearly not ready for this wedding.'

'I have to be,' he says. 'Everything's paid for, she's moving in with me. It's too late, Gwen. And I do love her, I swear I do. This is just a wobble. The marriage will be a new start. Anything that happened before doesn't matter.'

'I'm not sure I can just pretend none of this happened,' I say, looking straight at him and leaving no doubt what I'm referring to.

'You have to,' he pleads. 'Because I am, and I will be for the rest of my life. You can't tell her, Gwen. Stick your head in the sand and forget it ever happened. Please, promise me you'll never tell her. Our little secret, right?'

I look out over the hills at the church.

'I can't promise you that, Richard,' I say. 'This isn't right. Sarah needs to know.'

He's quiet for a moment.

'If you tell her about this, then you know what other secrets will come out,' he says eventually. 'What do you think Noah would say?'

'That doesn't matter any more,' I say.

Then he puts a hand on my shoulder and turns me round to look directly at him.

'It will destroy Sarah, you know. What you did will utterly destroy her. You wouldn't want that to happen, would you?'

I stare at him, and it takes all my strength not to shove him off the hill.

'You bastard,' I mutter.

He doesn't reply, instead he looks down at his feet. I grab his phone out of his cagoule pocket and hand it to him.

'Alright, you win,' I say. 'But you need to stop being a dick and delete the app. Now. And you have to swear to me that you'll never, ever, do anything like this again.'

'Okay,' he says, and I watch as he presses his thumb hard on the app icon until he's given the option to delete it.

I turn away, leaving him alone on the hill, clutching his phone. Back to the hotel, I cry until I don't think I can cry any more. And then, well, then people started dying, and all that seemed a little less important.

THIRTY-SEVEN

So, if you want the actual list of the worst things I ever did in my life, well, here we go:

3. That stupid Shakira dance routine I did in assembly.
2. Punching Kelly Sanchez when she copped off with Darren at the sixth-form ball (and, yes, technically it was more of a punch than a slap).
1. Sleeping with my best friend's fiancé.

Okay, yes, one of those is a bit worse than the others. Alright, alright, fine – a lot worse. See, told you I wasn't perfect.

After a minute of hammering on his door, I expected a sleepy-faced Richard to appear. But there was no answer. Of course, this would've been easier if I hadn't deleted his number. Cold, snot-like blobs of sleet had begun to fall, and I shivered on the doorstep.

I tipped the flower pot on the step over with my foot, and was pleased to see the front door key was lying under it. I let myself in and went up the hall stairs to his flat. A half memory, forced out of my brain, of climbing those steps began to creep back in.

I pushed open the door into the lounge and looked around. Nothing seemed out of place. There were a couple of suitcases, packed and ready for the honeymoon, sitting by the door. I instinctively grabbed an umbrella for protection from the coat stand, and slowly stepped inside.

'Hello?' I shouted, inwardly wondering exactly how I would defeat Parker with an old H&M umbrella that looked barely big enough to keep the rain off me, let alone double as a deadly weapon.

I poked my head around the empty lounge, brandishing the umbrella like a sword. When I realised no one was there, I looked for any signs of a struggle. I'd only been to Richard's flat that one time before, and I'd blotted that memory out as much as I could. It was unremarkably suburban, tidied within an inch of its life, with modern furniture mixed with just-on-the-right-side of mawkish family photos and art prints. Cushions had been carefully placed on the ends of each sofa and ornaments had been neatly arranged across pointless shelves, leaving no trace of any personality at all. The place was a vision of domesticity, as if it had been built to dispel any notion that their marriage would be anything less than perfect. But I could see the cracks.

I went up the stairs, pushing open the bathroom door with the umbrella. *Empty.* I moved on to the bedroom, stepping inside gingerly.

'Richard?' I called out.

There was no reply. If Parker was following the pattern, he should be here. Richard was the final name on the list, the one I'd torn off. Our 'date' was here, at his flat. That was where it had happened. Something was wrong, I could feel it.

I glanced around the bedroom, it was neat and tidy, with no signs of a scuffle. Maybe – hopefully – Richard and Sarah were at the venue already. But that's when I saw something on the bed. I leant closer and tugged at the duvet.

My hand went straight to my mouth to stifle a scream. The sheets were red with thick, wet blood.

'No,' I croaked, staggering away from the bed. 'No, no, no, no, no.'

My arm went out instinctively behind me, steadying myself on the bedroom wall. Suddenly it occurred to me that whoever did this could still be in the flat. I gathered myself and scanned the room, looking for anywhere someone could be hiding. I saw there was a trail of blood leading to the window, and sighed with relief. Whoever had been here was gone, I hoped. I turned back onto the landing and sat on the top step of the stairs. I put my head in my hands and waited for my heartbeat to calm the fuck down.

Just then I noticed something on the carpet, what looked like a scrap of paper. I leant over and picked it up. Barely the size of a cloakroom ticket, it was folded down the middle, with a battered crease that looked like it had been opened and closed many times. I took it in the palm of my hand and slowly pushed it open with my finger.

It was a cracker joke.

'Where's the best place to hide a book?' it read.

THIRTY-EIGHT

What the hell was that doing here? I hadn't seen that joke since me and Noah broke up. It couldn't be here, it just couldn't. Unless…

Suddenly, there was a noise from downstairs. Quickly, I shut the bedroom door and ran down, only to see Lyons and Forrester stepping into the lounge.

'Gwendolyn Turner. Why am I not surprised?' Forrester said. 'I trust you have a very good explanation for being here.'

'This is my friend's flat,' I stuttered. 'What are *you* doing here?'

'We had an anonymous call at the station,' Lyons said. 'Telling us to come to this address. The door was open.'

'And here you are,' Forrester said.

'The call said they'd heard screams from the bedroom,' Lyons continued. 'Have you been up there, Gwen?'

Forrester didn't wait for me to answer. He pushed his way past, went upstairs and opened the bedroom door.

'Wait, don't—' I stammered. But it was too late. I watched his back stiffen as he took in the scene in front of him.

'Lyons, don't let her leave,' he said eventually.

'You don't think…' I said. 'You can't think I had anything to do with this.'

'I think we just need to go down to the station and figure this all out,' Lyons said.

'No, you don't get it, do you,' I said. 'The killer is still out there. Think about it, who do you think made that anonymous call? It's Parker. You're wasting time. He's not finished – people are still in danger.'

'Who, exactly, is still in danger, Ms Turner?' Forrester said, shutting the bedroom door. He walked down the stairs towards me, slowly and carefully, as if making calculations in his head with every step. 'Whose blood is that in the bedroom?'

'There's still someone on the—' I reached into my back pocket for the napkin, but it was empty.

'Are you looking for this?' Forrester said, holding up a crumpled Cuppacino napkin. 'I found this in the wastepaper bin in my office. I believe this is from your mobile cafe, correct?'

He pointed at Al Pacino's gurning face on the napkin logo. It had never seemed more unfunny than at that moment. I nodded meekly.

'Am I to take it that you wrote this list of victims, Ms Turner?' He enunciated the word 'victims' with a relish that made my stomach turn.

'Yes, but—'

'And did you cross off each of these names?' he continued.

'I know this looks bad,' I said. 'But Aubrey can vouch for me, I was trying to help, I—'

Forrester wasn't listening. He was already on the phone to the station, firing off instructions. It was clear that within minutes, this place was going to be drenched in police tape and forensic teams, and I was going to be back in that ugly, cold interrogation room – or worse, a jail cell.

'Check the kitchen, will you? Do a sweep.' Forrester put his hand over the receiver and motioned to Lyons to search the flat.

I slumped against the living-room wall as Lyons started poking about in Richard's spotless kitchen, and Forrester barked the orders that would surely seal my fate. There was no way out. My despair was briefly interrupted by the familiar buzz of my phone in my pocket, and I fished it out with a grim sense of inevitability.

Parker: Sorry, Gwen. It's been fun, but I don't think this is going to work out in the long run. I'm looking for something a little less… complicated. So I guess we're just not a good match after all. I wish you the best of luck out there!

The words winded me, like someone had swung a baseball bat into my stomach. Parker was setting me up, and there was absolutely nothing I could do about it. Before I could even take a breath, Forrester had turned his fire in my direction.

'Ms Turner, put that phone down now.'

He'd ended his call and was walking towards me, his face as red as his moustache.

Just then, I heard the noise of keys in the front door, and we both turned to see Sarah pushing her way in, arms full of shopping bags. For a second, I was filled with relief, until it hit me – somehow I was going to have to explain why her fiancé's flat was about to be full of police officers.

'Who the hell are you?' she stammered at the sight of Forrester. 'Gwen? What's going on? Who are these people?'

'I'm Detective Chief Inspector Forrester,' he told her, flipping out his ID. 'Is this your residence?'

'Yes,' she said. 'Well, it's my fiancé's. What are you doing here? Is something wrong? Gwen, is this something to do with that Rob guy?'

'You're Sarah?' Lyons had emerged from the kitchen and was surveying the scene in front of him with his trademark bemusement. Before she had a chance to answer, he turned to me. 'Gwen? This is Sarah?'

I managed a nod.

'Where is your fiancé right now?' Forrester asked her.

'He probably left for the wedding venue already. St Mary's, on Eastleigh Island,' Sarah said. 'What's going on? Gwen, what are you doing here? We're supposed to be at the church in a couple of hours to set everything up.'

'I can explain,' I said, my heart pounding. 'Just, just give me a second, okay?'

I scanned the room, desperately looking for anyone who might listen to sense.

'You can explain at the station,' Forrester said. 'Right now.'

'You're arresting me?' I asked.

'No,' Lyons said. 'We just need to find out exactly what happened here.'

'Actually,' Forrester said, holding up a hand to silence his colleague. 'Gwen Turner, I am arresting you on suspicion of murder. You do not have to say anything, but it may harm your defence if you do not mention, when questioned, something which you later rely on in court. Anything you do say may be given in evidence…'

Adrenaline shot through me like a lightning bolt. This couldn't be happening. I could feel my whole body start to shake.

'Gwen, what the fuck?' Sarah gasped.

'Okay, okay, wait, just wait,' I stuttered. 'This isn't how it looks.'

'Don't worry, Gwen, you're not going anywhere, you haven't done anything. We'll get you a lawyer or something,' Sarah said. 'And you two can get the fuck out of my house, please. This is my best friend, she's not a murderer.'

Forrester folded his arms and looked at Lyons.

'Exactly how much more leniency are you going to show your little girlfriend here?'

'Excuse me?' I growled. 'What's that supposed to mean?'

'Let me handle this, Gwen,' Lyons said, turning to Forrester. 'I've got this, Pete. She's coming with us, just give her a minute, will you?'

Lyons looked back at me. 'You don't need to do this. I figured it out. I know who the last name on the list is.'

'What is he talking about? What list?' Sarah shouted, her hand on her forehead like she was about to faint. 'Will somebody please tell me what the hell is going on here?'

'I think I know why we're here, Gwen,' Lyons went on. 'It fits the pattern, doesn't it?'

My legs buckled. I couldn't let him say it. Not in front of Sarah.

'What does he mean, Gwen?' Sarah barked.

I looked to Sarah, then to Lyons, then to Forrester.

'I... I... I...' I stuttered.

If I went with them to the station, that was it. Parker had won. But there was no escape – Lyons was standing firmly in front of the door. I closed my eyes for a second and took a deep breath. I had to do something, and fast.

I needed a distraction.

When I opened my eyes, I wasn't shaking any more.

'Wait,' I said. I slipped my arms around Lyons's waist. I lifted myself on tiptoes so our lips were level.

'Gwen,' he hissed. 'What are you doing?'

I had no idea what I was doing, I just needed to stop him talking – right now. With that, I kissed him. As I did, I slid my hand under his jacket and my hand hit something cold, something metallic…

The Taser.

Quickly, I unclipped the holster, just the way Lyons had shown me back at the station, and slipped the Taser out.

Lyons stepped back, surprised by the kiss, and looked at me like I was truly insane.

'Gwen!' Sarah shouted. 'What are you doing? What the hell is going on?'

'This is a crime scene, Detective Lyons!' Forrester barked angrily.

I held the Taser up, my arm shaking, and waved it towards Lyons and Forrester.

'Gwen, don't be stupid,' Lyons cried.

'Don't come any closer,' I said, my finger resting on the trigger. 'I'm leaving.'

Lyons stood back, and, still holding out the Taser, I stepped very slowly backwards out of the door. Once I was on the stairwell, I slid the Taser into my hoodie pocket and ran like my life depended on it.

My heart felt like it was going to explode as I headed into the estate next to Hampden Park, and, after clambering over three fences, I sat in a kid's playhouse for half an hour. By the time I poked my head out, the sun had gone down and the streets were almost empty. The air blowing in from the sea was freezing, and I pulled my hood over my head. I doubled back and jumped on the back of the number fifty-four bus, hopping off when we got near Old Town. From there I made my way to the Pentangle offices.

I was praying that no one would want to steal a twelve-year-old Raleigh with only one brake working, and I was right. My bike was still where I'd left it – wet with melted snow and freezing to the touch, but very much unstolen. I zipped up my hoodie and got on the saddle. It began pouring with icy rain. My hood was useless against the storm. Cold air and sleet rushed past my face as I sped through the dark streets (of course I had no lights, have you met me?). I cycled behind a solitary Ocado van, feeling the heat from the exhaust on my legs. It was the first time I'd felt warm in hours. I couldn't go home, that's the first place they'd look, and Alfredo was probably in a scrapyard by now. So I went to the one safe place I could think of.

Noah was the only one who could help me, the only one I could trust. He'd hate me when I told him the truth, but I knew I had to. It was the only way to save Richard – *if he was still alive*. If I confessed, and told him everything, then this would be over. If only I could figure out why the cracker joke was at Richard's flat? Noah had carried that stupid thing in his wallet ever since that night we first met, so did that mean he'd been there? Had Parker lured him there to hurt him?

Unless… What if Noah had somehow found out about me and Richard…?

What if… No. I stopped myself from thinking it. There was *no way.*

I let my tired legs pedal me to Noah's on autopilot. When I arrived, I looked up at the closed curtains and dark windows, took a deep breath and pushed the buzzer.

No answer.

I got on my knees, cupped my hands around my mouth and yelled his name through the letterbox. Then I tried peering through into his hallway. I couldn't see anything that looked like it could be a dead body – just a pile of junk mail on the mat. It looked like he hadn't been at home for a while. At the bottom of the heap, I could make out the corner of a stiff cream-coloured envelope that looked familiar. I thanked the Lord for my child-size hands as I stuck my arm through the letterbox and pulled it out. It was already torn open, so I tugged out the card inside.

'To Noah, we'd love the pleasure of your company at our wedding,' it read, in a script font that looked like my nan's handwriting. 'Love Sarah & Richard. P.S. sorry for the late invite, hope you can make it x'

My heart flipped. It didn't make sense. Sarah had told me she wasn't going to invite Noah. *She promised me he wouldn't be there.*

Sitting on the doorstep, I dropped the invite and put my head in my hands. The street was quiet, save for the odd car trundling past at 20 mph. I pulled the cracker joke out of my pocket and turned it over in my hands. It was funny — well not funny haha, it was still an objectively terrible joke — but funny how it kind of summed up my life. Always hiding in plain sight. Like a leaf in a forest, or a playing card in a deck, I'd tried to hide my heartbreak among a hundred bad dates.

I let the joke go, and it fluttered towards my feet, dancing in the wind for a second before eventually settling on top of the wedding invite, right next to Richard's name.

Then it hit me.

The best place to hide something was among its own kind.

I'd been so stupid. No, not stupid, I'd known all along, deep down. I just didn't want to see it. Sarah was right, I'd been an ostrich, burying the truth for far too long. And it was time to take my head out of the sand.

Quickly, I got out my phone, shiny unicorn case and all, loaded up Connector and began typing.

Gwen: I know who you are, Parker, and I'm coming.

Parker: I'm waiting. Base Camp. Don't bring your plus one.

I knew where I had to go, there was only one place left. And to get there, I was going to need a boat.

THIRTY-NINE

As I jumped on my bike, all of a sudden I saw two bright lights behind me. I looked back to see the dark shape of a car before the headlights blinded me. I turned sharply into a side road. The lights followed me.

The sleet was coming down even harder now, landing on my face like freezing splatters of dog slobber. The cotton of my hoodie was losing its battle against the weather, and its heavy, cold dampness was pressing onto my face. I could feel my wet jeans catching in the chain as I rocketed through the city streets. A Deliveroo driver's horn blared as I swerved in front of traffic and hopped onto the pavement to avoid the red lights. I kept my eyes on the road and pedalled harder. But the car behind me carried on through the lights. I looked back and saw a hand reach out of the driver's window and place a flashing siren on top of the roof.

Shit.

I felt the front tyre of my bike slip on the sleet. Suddenly I was on the pavement, my face scraping hard across the kerb. Red-hot pain shot through my cold skin. The driver of the car jumped out. In the darkness, I couldn't quite make out the features. As the figure stepped into the gaze of the street light, their face came into focus.

'Where the hell were you going?' he said.

I went to stand up, wobbled, and tried to steady myself on the lamp post. My hand went to my face, it felt sticky. I looked at my fingers, red with blood. I was bleeding from where I hit my head.

With my last ounce of energy, I curled my hands into fists and turned to face the figure. If I was going down, I was going down fighting.

'It can't be you,' I choked. 'You're not Parker. You can't be.'

'I think you better come with me,' Lyons said softly, reaching out a hand to help me up.

'Okay,' I said quietly, not taking my eyes off my hands. 'But why are you on your own? I thought they'd have a search party out for me.'

He paused, and, in that moment, I grabbed onto his arm, hauling myself off the cold pavement. As I did so, I scooped up a fistful of sleet and gravel with my other hand and threw it into his face. As he recoiled, I ran, as fast as I could, in the opposite direction.

'Gwen, wait!' he shouted after me, wiping his eyes.

I didn't look back. Instead I raced in the direction of the docks, my mind spinning as I darted down the Grand Parade. Parker had been luring the victims back to where I'd had the dates. But my final Connector date hadn't been at Richard's flat.

I'd gone to the wrong place.

When I reached the docks, I ran along the pier until I saw the battered starboard of *The Nautilus*, and I hammered on the hull. When no one opened up, I fished the search warrant

I'd taken from the police station out of my bra, and slipped it under the door.

Seconds later, a bleary-eyed Jamal poked his head out of a porthole.

'Gwen?' he croaked. 'Jeez, it's the middle of the night. What the hell do you want?'

'I need your boat,' I panted.

'Why? To go where?' he asked.

I looked back down the pier into the gloomy darkness. There was no sign of Lyons. I'd lost him.

'Eastleigh Island,' I said, turning back to Jamal. 'I have a wedding to attend.'

FORTY

I stood on the deck as *The Nautilus* chugged across the Channel. A low mist was covering the sea, giving the impression that if you stepped off the boat, you'd just keep falling forever.

Spits of seawater splashed up into my face as I leant over the edge and looked into the darkness, straining to see the black mass on the horizon that was Eastleigh Island. Inside the boat, Jamal sat at the helm, surrounded by several empty cans of Red Bull. He'd been a little unsure about helping me at first, but when I told him how I'd taken the search warrant from Forrester's office, he figured he owed me one.

'Can't this thing go any faster?' I shouted to him through the Perspex window of the cabin.

He shrugged back at me and mouthed 'What?' Shaking my head, I went inside and Jamal swivelled round to greet me.

'How long now?' I asked.

'Twenty minutes,' he said. 'Sorry, water's choppy and she's a bit rusty. I've never taken her this far out before.'

I leant against one of the servers and chewed my gum

loudly. Rocco was curled up on the desk, warming himself against a softly humming hard drive.

'Where's your detective friend?' Jamal asked.

'Um, okay, Jamal, full disclosure, I'm kinda like, on the run right now,' I said. 'The police think I'm Parker.'

'But you're not, right?' Jamal said slowly. 'Parker is on this island, and now you're going to confront him? Am I getting this right?'

'Listen,' I said. 'You ever hear that old riddle? Where's the best place to hide a book?'

'What, we're doing riddles now?' he said. 'No, I don't know it.'

'A library,' I said.

'Right, the book would get lost among all the others,' he said. 'I get it.'

'So where's the best place to hide a murder?'

'What?'

'We were looking for a reason someone would want to kill *all* of these guys,' I explained. 'But what if someone only had a reason to kill *one* of them? And just made it look like they had a grudge on every dickhead who'd taken me on a terrible date?'

'I get it,' he nodded slowly. 'You've been wasting your time chasing a serial killer, trying to figure out a pattern. But really there is no pattern, he's just trying to cover up the one murder he has a real motive for.'

'Right,' I said. 'Hiding the book in the library.'

'But why your exes? Sorry. Not exes. Just guys who…'

'Who I dated. *Once*,' I said. 'To throw suspicion on me.'

'Who would want to frame you for murder?'

'Someone who'd lost everything,' I said. 'Because of me.'

We were interrupted by the jagged white cliffs of the island slowly coming into view. As Jamal slowed the boat and guided it up to a decrepit wooden pier, I leant over to the fruit bowl and picked the final banana out.

'One more thing. You know the guys' profiles we showed you before? Is there any way of cross-referencing who they matched with on Connector?'

'You mean, can we see if they matched with any of the same people?' Jamal asked.

I nodded, slowly peeling the banana. Somehow Parker had managed to get Rob, Freddie, Josh, Dev and Seb back to the locations of our dates. And there was only so far you could get dragging someone along the street with a knife to their throat before you got arrested. So I figured they had to have gone willingly.

'Alright, watch the helm for a sec,' Jamal said, reaching for his laptop. 'Well, with this many profiles, it would be unusual to get a lot of crossover. But let's have a look.'

Jamal tapped away for a couple of minutes.

'Oh, so there's only two. You, of course, and…'

He screwed up his face and took another sip from his can of energy drink.

'Weird,' Jamal said. 'This profile is called Parker, too.'

'Another Parker?' I asked. 'Can I see?'

He hit enter and a profile flashed up on the screen. Deep down, I knew what was coming, but when I saw the photos, my stomach still turned. The name said Parker, but the face was one I knew very, very well.

FORTY-ONE

I hopped off the boat and, grabbing hold of the mooring rope, tugged it towards the pier. As I tied it to a seaweed-covered post, I took a moment to catch my breath. In the darkness, I could make out the winding hill path that led up to the tiny collection of houses that constituted the island's only residents. Jamal came out of the cabin and stood on the deck.

'You sure about this?' he asked, wiping the sleet off his glasses.

'It's two in the morning and I'm about to break into a really spooky-looking old church to confront a murderer,' I said. 'What could go wrong?'

Jamal looked towards the church, which sat ominously at the top of the hill, and shivered.

'Should I come with you?'

'No,' I said. 'Stay here with Rocco. I'm going to need a lift back. Hopefully.'

I left him and made my way up the path until I reached the refurbished eighteenth-century building that Sarah and Richard had chosen for their wedding venue. I pushed on the big wooden doors.

Locked.

Taking my hoodie off, I wrapped it around my fist and, gritting my teeth, slammed it into the small glass pane beside the door again, and again, until it shattered. Then I carefully reached inside and unlocked the door. Shaking the loose glass off the hoodie, I pulled it back on and slowly peered inside.

I steadied myself. This was it, the moment I walked through this door I was going to come face to face with Parker. This person, who I thought would always be there for me, protecting me, was just the opposite. A killer. We'd cried on each other's shoulders, shared losses and victories together. I never dreamt they'd be capable of hurting anyone, but I'd forgotten: there was nothing more dangerous than a wounded animal.

The draughty hall was barely any warmer inside than it was out, and it had that peculiar, musty smell that every old church in the country seemed to have by law. The only light was the strains of moonlight breaking through the broken glass behind me. In other circumstances, it might have been quite beautiful. Every step I took seemed to reverberate through the building, breaking the eerie silence, but I forced myself to keep going. I couldn't hide from what I'd done any longer.

As my eyes adjusted to the darkness, I saw the brightly coloured bunting and decorations that were spread across the walls, like they were mocking me. Past the pews, I could just about make out a person.

I squinted, not quite believing what I was seeing. Slowly, their features came into focus, and when they did, it felt like someone had punched me hard in the stomach.

It was Noah.

FORTY-TWO

As I took a step towards him, I realised something was very wrong.

He was sitting on a wooden chair at the end of the aisle, his head slumped against his chest, eyes closed, and his arms and legs were fastened to the chair with cable ties.

I began to run down the aisle towards him.

'That's far enough,' came a voice from behind him.

I froze in my tracks and watched as the figure emerged from behind the altar.

Sarah.

'So it is you,' I said. 'You're Parker.'

'No shit, Sherlock,' she replied. 'I'm not sure a guy would have had the organisational skills to do this.'

Part of me was sort of relieved she wasn't in her wedding dress. I mean, I knew she had a taste for the dramatic, but that might have been a step too far. I could feel my whole body shaking, but I took a deep breath and tried to steady myself.

'Well, this isn't how I imagined the big day,' I said. 'But big round of applause for you for conducting a successful killing spree.'

'It was actually a lot easier than arranging an entire wedding on my own,' she replied.

For the first time I noticed she had a large knife in her right hand, and she began tapping it on the back of Noah's chair.

'If you've hurt him, I'll—'

'Relax, he'll wake up in a minute,' Sarah said. 'It was actually pretty easy to lure him here on the pretence of helping out with the wedding, especially as he was so keen to see you again. Richard took a little more… uh, persuading. You saw the blood at our flat, didn't you?'

She cocked her head to her left, and I followed her gaze to see Richard, in nothing but boxer shorts, tied to another chair, a gag around his mouth. When he saw me, he started grunting and struggling, almost manically. I could see the sweat visibly dripping down his forehead.

'Richard, be quiet,' Sarah barked at him.

He stopped almost immediately, and hung his head, utterly defeated.

I felt sick.

'How? Why?' I asked, this time unable to hide the tremble of fear in my voice.

'It's simple. I made a Connector profile that I knew you'd go for. A totally basic loser. Exactly the wrong type of guy. I went through Charlie's Facebook friends until I found some poor himbo that looked just your type, and used his old photos. Then all I had to do was put "Parker" right at the top of the app rankings.'

'You hacked Connector? But I thought Charlie—'

'Charlie and Richard worked out how to hack Connector months ago, back when they worked together. They'd been running that sordid little side business together for nearly a year, helping all those horrible men boost their profiles. I found it all on Richard's laptop. Didn't take me long to work out how to use the code – I'd been listening to Richard drone on about bloody Java for months.'

'And you used it to put Parker to the top of the Connector rankings, so you knew he'd show up on my app,' I said. 'Then, at the hen do, you...'

'Swiped right, just to make sure. And true to form, you couldn't resist yet another loser, could you, Gwen? From there, it was so easy to send you running all over town, just at the right time to get caught with the bodies.'

'But how... how did you kill all those people?'

'I made my own Connector profile, with my own photos, I called her Parker too. Used the code to make her the number one female profile on the app, so it wasn't long before all your little lover boys matched with me. You'd shared every bloody boring detail of those dates with me, even sent me screengrabs of their profiles. It wasn't hard to find them. Then I either waited for them to ask me out, which of course they usually did, or I'd suggest a date.'

'Back to the same places, the places I went with them?'

'Yep, thanks to all those location pins you sent me, I knew exactly where to go. All it took was a little prompting. As you know, these aren't exactly the most imaginative guys in the world we're talking about. Then I got them drunk, listened to all their bullshit, and when it came to closing time, I dragged them somewhere quiet with the promise of making all their dreams come true. It was so easy. I can sort of see why you liked it so much. I wiped any trace of me from their phones, and walked out, just as easily as I walked in.'

'So when I saw Seb looking at Parker's profile on his phone, that was you, that was your profile,' I said, as my brain slowly ingested what she was saying.

'Ah, yes, good old Seb,' Sarah smiled. 'You should've seen some of the unsolicited filth he sent me before our date. We had a wonderful time on the Eye, well, for a little while. After I killed him, I sent a message from his phone to Charlie, sending him running straight into the scene of the crime.'

'But… But Seb didn't hurt anyone. None of these guys did. They didn't deserve to die.'

'Didn't they? Are you sure, Gwen?' Sarah's tone sharpened to a hiss. 'They were paying to get to the top of that gross app, trying to screw every woman in Eastbourne. Threatening them with revenge porn, hounding them endlessly for sex. Sending unsolicited dick pics, cheating on their wives, lying about their ages, all in a futile attempt to get laid. Are you seriously telling me anyone's going to miss them?'

My stomach curdled. My best friend had done all this, killed those men, because of me. Whatever terrible things they had done, Sarah was wrong, their loved ones would miss them.

'That stupid app, it's supposed to help people find true love? All it's caused is pain. Look at this piece of shit here, for example.' She motioned to Richard beside her. 'You know how many absolute arseholes I had to go out with until I found this charmer? I must have dated every single guy on Connector, each of them worse than the last. So many stupid dates with so many stupid guys. And then finally, just as I was about to give up, I matched with Richard. My knight in shining armour. Sure, he only had marginally more personality than a chunk of his Kendal Mint Cake, but at least he wasn't a liar, or a cheat or a misogynist pig. Compared to the others, he was an oasis in the middle of a desert of shit. And you took him, Gwen. You destroyed my happy ending, so now I'm going to destroy your life.'

'You never told me you were on Connector,' I stuttered. 'You always said you hated dating apps.'

'I do hate them,' she said. 'Even after I got screwed around at uni, I was still naive enough to think there might actually be some good guys out there. But Connector soon proved me wrong. It was the same toxic cesspool of incels and fuckboys as before, only now they had an app to make it even easier for them to abuse us. But after this, no one will ever use Connector again, and the world will be a much better place without it.'

'And what about me?' I asked.

'Oh, don't worry, I'll leave you alive, but no man is ever going to touch you again. When the police find you here, with the dead body of your ex, they'll have no doubt who "Parker" really is. The papers will call you the Black Widow.'

'That is quite a cool nickname, to be fair,' I said, hoping she couldn't hear the sound of my heart pounding on my ribcage.

'So funny,' Sarah sneered. 'You think you can distract me with your dumb jokes? Well, it won't work, I know what you're doing, Gwen. It's time you stop hiding behind your so-called sense of humour. It's not going to help you in prison.'

'Yeah, but without my sparkling sense of humour, what have I got?' I asked, taking another step towards her. If I could just keep her talking, maybe I could get close enough to take the knife off her.

'Good question,' she said. 'Maybe that's why you always had a problem facing reality. Because the truth is – like I told you – without Noah, you're just a lost, heartbroken little girl with a shitty ice cream van.'

'Now, that is not such a cool nickname,' I said, keeping

my eyes fixed on the knife. 'So all this is about… revenge? Because of what happened with me and Richard? How did you even find out?'

'Richard came in very drunk one night after I'd gone to bed. He fell asleep immediately after climbing in next to me, and I decided to have a look at his phone. Of course I knew the passcode – I've watched him type it in a thousand times. So I reached behind his head, and very, very slowly retrieved it from his bedside table. He had the app, the fucking Connector app. And who had he matched with? You, Gwen. You. Yes, that's right, I read the messages. I know all about your little meet up at "base camp".'

The bastard. He never deleted it.

'But the question is, who *doesn't* know?' Sarah went over and nestled the knife against Noah's Adam's apple. 'He still loves you, you know. Kept that little cracker joke all this time, even after you dumped him. Isn't that sweet?'

'How did you get it?'

'Wasn't hard to fish out of his wallet during our little post-break-up debrief. Poor thing really needed a shoulder to cry on. He just could not understand why you broke his heart,' Sarah smiled. 'But don't worry, I left out the juiciest details. I thought those would be so much better coming from you. So why don't you tell your poor little boyfriend here exactly what's going on?'

She bent down to rip Noah's gag off, gently slapping his face until his eyelids fluttered open.

'Gwen, what the fuck?' he mumbled, his eyes widening in panic as he took in the scene around him. 'What is this?'

'Noah, I…' I looked at the floor, unsure how I could even put it into words.

Sarah put the knife to his throat and motioned for me to continue.

'Noah, I cheated on you,' I said. 'I slept with Richard. I'm sorry.'

'What?' Noah choked.

'Sarah found out, and now, well, now we're here. This is all my fault. You have to believe me when I say that. I just made a stupid, drunken mistake.'

There was a brief silence, and for the first time I felt how cold it was in the empty church.

'You should've told me,' he murmured. 'I thought you'd… I thought you'd just fallen out of love with me.'

I didn't say anything for a second.

'Deep down, I think maybe I had. For so long, you were everything I wanted, but it was just what I *thought* I wanted. I didn't know how to tell you, and so I did this terrible thing.'

He went silent again for a moment and I noticed his fists were clenched so tightly all the blood had run out of them.

'Those dates Sarah is talking about, they were my punishment,' I went on. 'I thought those awful guys were all I deserved. I wasn't trying to replace you, I was trying to get over you. It was a distraction from all the hurt I'd caused.'

'It was what?' he asked.

'A distraction,' I said.

He mouthed the word back at me – 'distraction' – then looked downwards at his arm. I followed his eyeline to see the part of the chair his legs were tied to was loose.

Rotten.

FORTY-THREE

I gave Noah the tiniest of nods and looked back at Sarah. She still had the knife to his throat. How the hell was I going to distract her long enough to let Noah make his move?

'Sarah, please, let them go,' I said, concentrating on sounding reasonable. 'I admitted everything – that's what you wanted, right? No one else has to die. What's the endgame here? You have seventy-five wedding guests arriving in about six hours. You're going to run? For the rest of your life? Think about it. What happens when I tell the police what you've done?'

'You really think they'll believe you? What proof do you have, Gwen? They'll find you here with two more bodies – two more to add to your string of dead dates, all covered with your DNA. They couldn't keep their hands off you, could they?'

She was right. Between the groping, unwanted kisses, manhandling, snogging and attempted massages, my prints would be all over them.

'You'll take the blame for all this, while I, the heartbroken victim, will run away to Canada to grieve for my poor fiancé, murdered on the eve of his wedding,' Sarah continued. 'That sound like an endgame to you?'

'Canada? This isn't *The Shawshank Redemption*, Sarah, you're a fucking project manager from Sussex, not Andy Dufresne.'

I saw her fingers grip tightly around the knife.

'Okay, okay, sorry,' I said quickly. 'It's a really great plan. I just have one small addition to make it better: let us all go.'

'I'll tell you what, I have an even better idea,' Sarah said, a thin smile spreading across her face. 'Since you seem to struggle to make good choices, why don't we do a little swiping. I'll let you choose which one of your lovers here is going to die first. Your poor little ex here, or your paramour Richard.'

'Sarah, I'm not doing this.'

She jabbed the tip of the knife very gently into Noah's Adam's apple.

'Why not? It is Valentine's Day, after all. Come on, who do you want to pick? The steady, reliable ex-boyfriend? Handsome. Witty. A great cat-dad. Little bit on the short side, but apart from that, he seems pretty perfect, right? Not sure why anyone wouldn't want to choose him? Right? Right, Gwen? You'd have to be mad to throw this one away.'

I didn't say anything.

'Okay, not sure? Well, what about the lovely Richard here?' She went over to him and pulled his gag off. 'Washboard abs, *absolutely* terrific calves, thirty years old, a boring job in IT with a big fat salary. Some first-grade camping anecdotes. And oh yeah, completely terrified of commitment. You two should get on like a house on fire. Oh, I forgot, you already did. We all know which way you'd swipe on this one, huh?'

She pressed the tip of the knife against Richard's temple. His eyes were closed, and he was trying to keep as still as possible. A single bead of sweat dropped off his eyebrow and splashed onto the blade.

'Please…' he mumbled.

'Right. Or. Left?' Sarah said, very slowly and deliberately.

'I told you, Sarah, I am not…'

I saw her fingers tighten around the handle again and looked over to Noah. If he could break free now, while her attention was on Richard, maybe he'd have a chance to grab the knife.

'Not so fun now, is it?' Sarah said. 'When there's something actually at stake? It's pretty easy just to swipe yes or no on a screen, but when your actions actually mean something, it's not so fun, is it?'

Anger boiled up inside me. 'Fuck you,' I spat.

'Well, that would give you the hat-trick, wouldn't it? I'm the only person here you haven't fucked yet.'

Quick as a flash, she moved back over to Noah, and held the knife so close to his throat I could see the skin pinch. *Damn it.*

'Make your choice,' she said.

I tried to speak but nothing came out. She pressed the knife slowly into the flesh of his neck.

'Wait, stop, stop it,' I eventually managed to splutter. 'Richard. Kill Richard.'

'Ah, I should've known you'd never let any harm come to your precious Noah,' Sarah said, pulling the knife away. 'Alright, looks like it's darling Richard's turn first.'

As she turned towards Richard, I gave Noah another nod. It was now or never, and I had one more ace up my sleeve, or in my pocket to be precise.

I pulled the Taser out.

'Not so fast,' I said, pointing it at Sarah. 'Remember this?'

She flinched, and in that moment, Noah swung his legs and broke free of the chair. Everything happened in a blur. Noah lurched into Sarah, knocking her backwards. She steadied herself on the altar and made a sweep at him with the knife. But with his arms still fastened together, all Noah could do was shoulder-barge into her.

My finger hovered over the Taser trigger, but before I could fire, Sarah sidestepped Noah's attack, and he crashed head first into the altar. In a split second, Sarah quickly grabbed him from behind, holding the knife up against his throat, shielding herself with his body.

'Well, looks like Noah will have to go first after all,' she panted. 'Process of elimination, huh?'

I steadied the Taser, gripping it with both hands. But there was no way I could hit her with Noah in the way.

'Shoot her!' Richard shouted.

'Have you ever fired one of those before?' Sarah sneered.

'No, but I'm very good at Laser Tag,' I said.

That wasn't true, I was absolutely terrible at Laser Tag. And had no idea if a) I even knew how to work a Taser or b) had the guts to use it. I kept the Taser trained on Sarah, but my wobbling arms betrayed the fact that, no, I hadn't held a weapon before. I held it as steady as I could, and tried to remember what the cops said on TV.

'Don't move,' I growled.

'Seriously?' Sarah said. 'Don't move? That's what you're going with?'

'Yep, seriously. You've just murdered half of Eastbourne's

least eligible men, you think I won't stick you with a Taser? This thing fires from ten feet away.'

'You're bluffing,' Sarah said, forcing the knife against Noah's neck. 'You can't even score a hoop from inside the goal circle. There's no way you can make that shot.'

I wavered, my finger releasing the trigger. My legs felt like they were about to give way and my hands were shaking. Sarah was right. With Noah in front of her, there was no way I could hit her.

'One step closer, and I'll slit his throat,' she said.

'Don't do it, Sarah,' I said.

'Why not? After what you did to me, you deserve this.'

'But he doesn't,' I pleaded. 'Noah's not some random stranger, he's your friend. If you hurt him, you'll never be able to live with yourself. Believe me, I know what it's like trying to live with a terrible mistake.'

'Oh, Gwen,' Sarah said. 'Sleeping with Richard wasn't your mistake. You betrayed me way before that. From the moment Noah came back into your life, you idolised him, just like you did before. And you always, *always* chose him over our friendship, even when he was stopping you from making the most of your life. And then when you finally woke up and dumped him, you just sought out attention from a bunch of worthless men, instead of reaching out to me. Your best friend.'

'I couldn't,' I said. 'Not after what I did to you.'

'Bullshit, Gwen. I watched you cry over what you did to Noah, but where were the tears for me? "Here if you need"? What a joke. And you know what's really funny? It was always me who said that to you. You never once said it back. You know why? Because you were never there for me. So now you're going to suffer, on your own, like I had to.'

'Those tears,' I said. 'They weren't for Noah. I see that now – it was guilt. I couldn't ever be happy after what I did to you.'

'So guilty that you were prepared to just let me blindly walk into this poisoned marriage?' Sarah went on. 'To this man who couldn't keep his pants on for more than ten minutes?'

'I thought, I thought…' I stuttered. 'I thought by not telling you, I was protecting you.'

'You were protecting yourself. And look where that got you,' Sarah said.

I lowered the Taser and walked slowly towards her.

'You're right,' I said quietly. 'I should have told you.'

'So drop the Taser,' Sarah said. 'It's over.'

I took another step closer.

'I said *drop it*,' Sarah barked.

I stopped just in front of them and held the Taser above my head. Slowly, I leant in towards Noah's face, close enough that our lips were almost touching. I rested my forehead on his, and closed my eyes.

'I'm sorry,' I said to him.

Then, with one swift movement, I swung my arm down, jabbed the Taser hard under Noah's ribcage and pulled the trigger. There was a loud crackle and a flash of blue electricity as the shock made my arm recoil. Noah's eyes rolled back in his head as it slumped to his chest, and he fell to the ground.

'*Now* I can make the shot,' I said, pointing the Taser directly at Sarah's forehead. 'Drop the knife.'

She let it go, and it clattered onto the stone tiles of the church. I kicked the knife, sending it skidding on the floor across towards Richard.

'What… what are you doing?' Sarah said, her voice cracking.

'I'm letting you go,' I said.

FORTY-FOUR

So, remember that list of the bad things I've done? Well, full disclosure, there's a brand new entry, straight in at number one, and it's a doozy.

I'd realised something. I could list a million stupid choices I've made (and really, who hasn't screwed up at some point in their life?). But it wasn't my mistakes that had led me here, pointing a Taser at my best friend's head – it was believing that if I buried them deep enough, everything would be fine. It was time I started owning my choices, before they could own me.

So yes, I was about to let a serial killer walk away, scot-free. Don't @ me.

Sarah was standing in front of me, her mouth hanging open as she waited for my next move.

'Here's my choice,' I said. 'I'm swiping right on you, Sar. Like I should've done from the beginning. This was never about Noah, or any of these men, it's about me and you. So, go. Run. And when the police get here, I'll tell them you got away. Richard will back me up. That okay with you, Dickie?'

Richard nodded meekly. I turned back to Sarah, who looked at me like I was the insane one.

'If you go now, you can make it to the airport before anyone starts looking for you.'

She hesitated. 'They'll catch up with me eventually.'

'Yeah, they will,' I said. 'You won't get away with this, Sarah. One day, you'll have to pay for what you did. But I'm giving you a head start. A chance to say goodbye to your family. And it's either that, or stay here and fight me to the death, and, well, like we established, I'm the one with the Taser.'

She stood there, staring at me, dumbfounded.

'Why?' she asked. 'Why are you doing this?'

I hesitated. It was a good question. I thought about breaking up with Noah, about losing Dad, how in my worst moments, when everything seemed to be falling apart, it was Sarah who had looked out for me. So maybe yes, this would end up being the worst thing I ever did, but the truth was, I owed her.

'Here if you need, remember?' I said.

She gave an almost imperceptible nod of her head.

'Let's call this evens,' she said after a moment. And with that, she took one last look at me, glanced down at her snivelling fiancé and walked past me and out the door.

Just like that, it was all over. I slumped down next to Noah, lifted his head up and rested it on my arm. He dribbled on my sleeve.

'Good boy,' I said.

I lay against the pew, exhausted until, eventually, I heard the sound of police sirens echoing off the stained-glass windows.

EPILOGUE

'Almost perfect,' I shouted into the kitchen, taking a sip of the freshly brewed tea.

'Almost?' the reply came from deep in the fridge. 'Too much milk?'

'Not the tea, this,' I said, motioning to the room.

It was a Sunday afternoon. The TV was on in the background, gently playing out some American cookery show where a homely woman was baking gigantic cinnamon buns in the biggest oven I had ever seen in my life. I was still in my pyjamas. As I watched her drizzle horizontal lines of icing over them in one smooth motion, a hand placed a plate of hot, buttered toast onto the coffee table. I reached for the biggest slice.

'I'll take this one, on account of all my post-traumatic stress,' I said, taking a huge bite.

'So what's missing?' Aubrey lowered himself next to me on the sofa. 'Jam? You had sod all in the fridge.'

I ignored the question. I hadn't told Aubrey exactly how it went down in the church, but I'd let him take credit for solving the whole thing, and saving Noah and Richard, so that had bought me some brownie points.

It had been two weeks, and the police were closing in on Sarah. They knew she'd flown to Vancouver from Gatwick, but so far she'd managed to avoid detection. I'd been assured the Canadian Security Intelligence Service had their very best people on it, and it was only a matter of time before she was caught. When that happened, I knew I'd have to answer a lot more questions. But for now, the sun was shining. It was spring at last.

Charlie had been given a suspended sentence. Richard sold his story to the *Mail Online*. I got my old job back. Amazingly, thanks to Noah's foresight to get highest liability, the insurance paid out on the van, and I hadn't needed to get a new flatmate just yet.

Holding the toast between my teeth, I opened up my phone. There was Connector, sitting unopened, unloved and unneeded. I hadn't had the strength to even think about it. Every time I accidentally saw the app on my screen, I quickly put my phone away and did something else.

I took a deep breath and pressed on the Connector logo with my thumb. Shielding the screen from Lyons's eyes, I set the distance to the lowest possible setting and waited as it searched for any available profiles. The app's little thinking wheel whirred round on the screen. After about ten long, long seconds, a message popped up: 'No profiles found. Why not try widening your search?'

'So, how's it going on Connector then?' I asked. 'Any matches?'

Aubrey ran a hand through his hair.

'It's embarrassing, but I downloaded it because I thought maybe, just maybe, I was feeling ready to meet someone again. You know, after Olivia, things were hard. People are weird about dating coppers, you know.'

'Let me get this straight. A murder-spree spurred on by a dating app hit you right in the feels? You feeling okay, Aubrey?' I asked.

'It wasn't because of the case,' he said.

'So, you met someone already?' I asked, holding up my phone to show him the screen. 'That was quick.'

He looked away, and I swear his cheeks blushed a little.

'I thought maybe I had, yeah,' he said.

I stared at him, wide-eyed.

'You mean me?' I coughed. 'Because of that night at the station? Oh Aubrey, don't get too hasty. I'd drunk half a bottle of Malibu, seen two dead bodies and just crashed twelve thousand pounds' worth of ice cream van. I'm not sure I'd start looking for an engagement ring just yet.'

He looked a little crestfallen.

'What about Olivia?' I said. 'I thought you were going back to London to sweep her off her feet?'

'You know, I used to think I was still in love with her,' he said. 'Maybe I always will be, a little bit. But I don't think anything I do will change the fact that she wasn't in love with me. So I have to let it go. Move on. But that doesn't mean I have to turn off my emotions, or that I can't ever love anyone else ever again. I just have to learn how to do it differently. And I thought maybe I had.'

He looked across at me with a hopeful smile.

'So, just to 100 per cent clarify, you're not a catfishing bloodthirsty psychopath?' I asked.

'No,' Aubrey said. 'That would really be a setback in my career as a homicide detective.'

'Hmmm, okay, but why should I believe anything you say?' I smiled.

He thought for a moment. 'Gwen, remember in Year Ten when you did that Shakira dance routine?'

'Yeah,' I said. 'But what has that got to do with—'

'It was bloody awful,' he said. 'See, I wouldn't lie to you.'

'Huh, well, you know, I never wanted to admit it, but you're right. Maybe it was a little under rehearsed. Okay, fine, I believe you. You're far too boring to be a serial killer anyway,' I grinned.

'So, remember we talked about going somewhere, somewhere that isn't a dingy police station?'

'Or a decrepit fishing boat?' I said.

'What about a nice trip on the Eastbourne Eye?'

'Too soon, Aubrey,' I said. 'Too soon.'

'Alright, what about that pub you like, The Brown Derby?'

I thought about it for a second. I could feel the butterflies in my stomach again, and this time, I didn't feel the urge to stamp on them.

'Are you asking me out on a date?' I asked.

'You're a better detective than I am,' he smiled. 'You work it out.'

I'd always thought of Noah as an anchor, holding me safely in place. I realised now, yeah, he was an anchor alright – he was never letting me sail away. But now, I really was ready to move on. Sure, I was definitely going to make a million more bad choices in my life, but from now on, I was going to start taking responsibility for them,

I looked down at my phone. My thumb hovered over the

Connector logo, two little linking chains, one pink, one blue. I pressed it, and held my thumb there until a little message popped up on the phone screen that asked: 'Delete app?'

Aubrey peered over my shoulder. 'Finally doing it, huh?' he said.

I took another bite of toast and put the slice back on the plate.

'Well, what do you reckon?' I smiled.

Acknowledgements

Thank you for reading this book, I hope you liked it.

I'd like to thank my mum for reading to me every night, and my dad for doing the voices.

And Danielle, the final piece of the puzzle. Te amo (and thank you for not running for the hills on Date One when I told you I was writing a book about psychopathic serial killers on dating apps).

I'd also like to say thanks to:

James Wills, for making this all happen.

Helena Maybery and everyone at Watson, Little.

My brilliant editor Peyton Stableford and Jo, Polly and everyone at Head of Zeus.

Elliot Stubbs, Laura Bassett and Amber Harwood, you're the best (at spotting grammatical errors and plot holes).

Vicki Laycock and Lucy Rainer for their vast murder mystery expertise, constant cheerleading and invaluable insight on everything from out-of-season peaches to J-Pos.

Rosie Mullender, for excellent advice, empathy and (allegedly) listening to all the voice notes.

Jack Barnes, for being patient while I attempted to smile for the photos.

Alex Buckland, Laura Gerrard, James Melia, Sue Gibbs, Amy Rowland, Peter Knight, Hayley Steed, Mark Stay, Nicola Skinner, Lisa Cutts, Samm Taylor, Jane Common, Helen Wright, Ben Chilton, Ewan Chilton, Jimmy Barnes, Kirby (RIP total legend), Bucky, The Sherlocks, The Crumpets/Croissants, The Dudes, Kaftans and the Chums.

Thanks to everyone who shared their own terrible dating stories, and to the many excellent dating influencers, like Beam Me Up Softboi and Tiny Moron, for inspo and horrifyingly toxic screengrabs. The *My Name Is... Lucy* podcast was a great source of info on app algorithms and human dating behaviour.

And to everyone I went on a date with circa 2012 to 2020, you're in there somewhere.

About the Author

L.M. CHILTON is a journalist with fifteen years' experience working on TV shows such as *This Morning*, *Loose Women* and *The One Show*, as well as writing columns for *Cosmopolitan*, *Glamour*, *Metro* and *The Mirror*. He lives in London, thinking of twists for murder mysteries while practising the banjo, much to the annoyance of his neighbours. *Don't Swipe Right* is his debut novel.

The Illustrated AutoCAD Quick Reference

Release 13 for DOS

Third Edition

Ralph Grabowski

Delmar Publishers

years

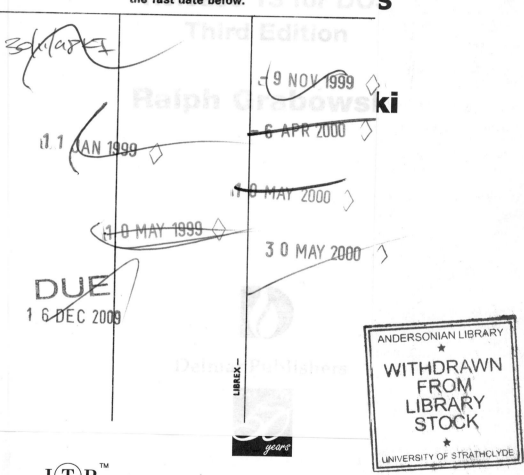

I(T)P™ An International Thomson Publishing Company

Albany • Bonn • Boston • Cincinnati • Detroit • London • Madrid
Melbourne • Mexico City • New York • Pacific Grove • Paris • San Francisco
Singapore • Tokyo • Toronto • Washington

NOTICE TO THE READER

Publisher does not warrant or guarantee any of the products described herein or perform any independent analysis in connection with any of the product information contained herein. Publisher does not assume, and expressly disclaims, any obligation to obtain and include information other than that provided to it by the manufacturer.

The reader is expressly warned to consider and adopt all safety precautions that might be indicated by the activities herein and to avoid all potential hazards. By following the instructions contained herein, the reader willingly assumes all risks in connection with such instructions.

The publisher makes no representation or warranties of any kind, including but not limited to, the warranties of fitness for particular purpose or merchantability, nor are any such representations implied with respect to the material set forth herein, and the publisher takes no responsibility with respect to such material. The publisher shall not be liable for any special, consequential, or exemplary damages resulting, in whole or part, from the readers' use of, or reliance upon, this material.

Cover Design: **Michael Speke**
Book Design: **Ralph H Grabowski** (*CompuServe 72700,3205*)

DELMAR STAFF

Publisher: **Michael McDermott**
Acquisitions Editor: **Mary Beth Ray** (*CompuServe 73234,3664*)
Project Developmental Editor: **Jenna Daniels** (*CompuServe 76433,1677*)
Production Coordinator: **Andrew Crouth** (*CompuServe 74507,250*)
Art and Design Coordinator: **Lisa Bower**
Publishing Assistant: **Karianne Simone** (*CompuServe 76433,1702*)

Printed in the United States of America

1 2 3 4 5 6 7 8 9 10 XXX 01 00 99 98 97 96 95

Library of Congress Cataloging-in-Publication Data

Grabowski, Ralph.
The illustrated AutoCAD quick reference: for DOS Release 13/ Ralph Grabowski. - 3rd ed.
p. cm.
Includes index.
ISBN 0-8273-6645-0 (perfect)
1. Computer graphics. 2. AutoCAD (Computer file) I. Title.
T385.G69243 1995
620'.0042'02855369-dc20 94-43746
CIP